Fresh Water

The Adventures of John Grey
Book Four

Frederick A. Read

A *Guaranteed* Book

First Published in 2009 by
Guaranteed Books

an imprint of Pendragon Press, Po Box 12, Maesteg
Mid Glamorgan, South Wales, CF34 0XG, UK

ISBN 978 1 906864 01 9

Typeset in *Book Antiqua* and *Garamond* by Christopher Teague

Printed and Bound in Wales by
Print Evolution
www.print-evolution.com

www.guaranteedbooks.net

Chapters

Foreword

This book is about a ship that had seen better days, but set sail on a very long voyage around the rim of the North Atlantic.

It was a voyage to nowhere, as the captain was forced to tramp his ship around getting as much cargo as possible to warrant the expenses incurred to keep her afloat.

In the meantime, John Grey was able to enjoy his voyage and rise up the promotion ladder to his ultimate goal, that of being a 'Chief Engineer'.

But it was the long arm of the dead Captain von Meir that put paid to the voyage, with his war time legacy of indiscriminate mine laying along the major shipping lanes the ship was to sail through.

When they finally managed to get ashore, they found themselves on the most dreaded stretch of coast-line the world possessed, where nobody survived to tell the tale.

But obviously John Grey and his friends had other ideas about that, and for the series to continue.

Author's Note

By the time you have read this novel and progress through the series, you will have gathered that the author is a 'Non-PC' (Politically Correct) person, who will not apologise for any words, phrases, or expressions used within that might upset some of you.

The words and language used can be found in the English language, and have been used long before the self-righteous Politically Correct Brigade came along.

Chapter I
Sky Scrapers

The S.S. *Inverlaggan* sailed out into Liverpool Bay to leave the hustle and bustle of its famous docks behind and settle down to its scheduled first leg of a very long swim around the entire expanse of the Atlantic Ocean.

John was still able to see the last of the harbour lights twinkling in the murky distance, as he climbed up the steep ladder of the companionway onto the bridge to make his customary deck rounds report to the captain.

"All deck and auxiliary machines satisfactory and handed over to the 1st mate, captain." he announced cheerfully.

"Hmm!" the captain replied slowly, as he was preoccupied with scanning the horizon through his binoculars.

"We have a new set of watertight doors for'ard that still respond too sluggishly for my liking, a dodgy ventilation system and steering tackle. Lets hope for your sake 3rd, that nothing goes wrong with the latter, else we'll end up in the East Indies instead of the West. Its just as well I still use a sextant for my navigation." he muttered, before dismissing John.

John made his way through the bridge and out onto the boat deck where the wireless office was situated, sometimes referred to as 'the Shack'. He peered through the small window in the steel door and saw his good friend Bruce Larter with another person whom he judged to be his junior but fellow Radio Officer.

When he opened the door, a gust of wind blew inside and scattered papers all over the floor, for which John immediately apologised as the other person glowered at him.

"What Ho Bruce! Glad you're aboard!" he greeted happily as this was the first face he had recognised since coming on board.

"John! Glad you made it. You were supposed to join us at Belfast, what happened?" Larter greeted with equal pleasure.

"It's a long story, starting with some time with Helena in Antwerp, and ending with our old friend Cresswell in Belfast." John started.

"That is one story you must tell me, but in the meantime I'm glad you came. But before I start, meet Radio Officer, Peter Southgate." Larter said swiftly, making the brief introductions.

"We've got a dodgy emergency generator that needs your attention a.s.a.p. John. The power circuit to this shack is also shaky and I have been forced to use the jenny more than once since leaving Southampton.

For you to know, I've checked the power circuit this end, so it must be a dry joint somewhere between here and the motor room. That's where the jenny has the advantage, as its' leads are visible all the way from the motor to my circuit board." Larter stated.

"I'll come back shortly once I've reported to the chief, and had my supper. Will that do?" John offered.

"Try to make it sooner than later, as I've a feeling the next few days will be hell and literally high water, if my old friend on the 'Mid point' weather ship is anything to go by. Anyway see you then!" Larter said with a smile, as John nodded before leaving the office.

"How do you know the 3rd Bruce?" Southgate asked politely.

"He and I go back a few voyages now, as we always seem to be on the same ship contract. He and another old friend, Chief Bosun Sinclair!" Larter replied with a knowing smile and pleasure in his voice.

"I've heard he's a thorn in the side of the Board of Governors, and has got into many a scrape. But apparently a very fine engineer for all that!" Southgate responded.

"Yes! We've had our fair share of trouble with management, but at least we've proved our worth to the company for them to retain our services, unlike your last company, Peter. The Grey Funnel line was it?"

Southgate nodded glumly on hearing the name, then added.

"Yes, them and I've also had it with the Black funnel line too. Maybe I'll get onto the Blue Liners after this contract, providing old man Macaroni keeps his word."

"Sounds like you've had a bit of an outing. Maybe your old instructor had it in for you. Never mind Peter, once we get States side of the pond, all will get much easier for you." Larter said with empathy, for he also knew the penalties of rubbing up management boards the wrong way and too often.

John made his way down into the bowels of the ship to make his rounds report to, and still to be met, his chief engineer.

So you're 3rd Engineer Grey!" the chief engineer said with amazement, looking John up and down slowly.

"I was expecting someone almost twice the size of you, judging by all the trouble you seem to get into. My name is Chief Jones." the chief announced slowly, puffing gently on a large tobacco pipe, with a bowl almost as big as the proverbial dustbin. John said nothing but let the chief rattle on.

"You appear to have a fine engineering record according to all the accounts from your previous chiefs. All except one, that is, and it's his account that I shall judge your performance on. Just in case you wonder just who that person is, then it's my old shipmate Chief Engineer Creswell." Jones sneered.

"You are at liberty to take whose word you like, which means that you have no mind of your own to make or form your own professional judgement." John said quietly.

Jones's face went bright red then back to its pallid state before he spoke in a low and hushed manner.

"From the outset, you are in deep waters all ready. Just for you to know, I'll accept only the best from you. The first sign of shenanigans from you, and I'll personally throw you off the ship even if we're still at sea. Do you get my drift, Grey?"

John groaned inwardly at the prospect of the spectre of Cresswell re-appearing yet again into his life, but decided to start slaying some old ghosts from his past.

"I have a very responsible job to do on this vessel as you already know chief. Should I, in the course of my duties, find that I am hindered or obstructed in these duties, then in the aftermath of some shipping board of enquiry where its found that you have done so, I personally will have no compunction whatsoever, in blowing the whistle on you. In the meantime chief, all I'm here for just now is to give you my initial daily report, verbally, and my customary daily written one at 1200 hours tomorrow." John replied civilly.

Jones looked at John, as if hoping looks would have killed him on the spot.

"Oh very well! Just get on with it as I'm a very busy man." Jones said sharply.

"But I'll expect a full diagrammatic explanation in writing by 1200hours tomorrow morning."

But John knew not to fall into this trap, instead he made his report in the vernacular manner, then added that he needed certain requirements to see to the wireless office generator sooner rather than later.

Jones heard what John needed and nodded his approval by telling him to draw whatever he needed from the engineering stores, and then report back when his repairs were done.

With that final dismissal from Jones, John left him and made his way back up into the more pleasing atmosphere of the ships saloon and accommodation deck.

"Hello 3rd! I'm the 2nd Engineer Tansey Lee." a tall, slender, black haired man announced, meeting John coming into the dining hall.

"Evening, and hello! I'm John Grey. Sorry about my delayed boarding, things got a bit bogged down the other end. What have you got in mind for me? What kind of accent have you got?" John replied apologetically, shaking Lee's hand in greeting.

Lee looked at John's unassuming manner and body language before he decided to comment further.

"Apologies accepted, although you've probably had a run in with the chief by now. Not to worry, you're here now and that's all that counts. Besides, the person who stood in for you was more than glad to see you. We call our chief 'Spanners', because he can just look at an engine and tell what is or isn't wrong with it. Must be psychic or got a divine gift for anything mechanical. Anyway, no doubt you'll find out more about him as the voyage progresses, but happily you are still under my jurisdiction. And by the way, I'm a South African from Durban." Lee said jovially and promptly changed the subject, seeing that John was eyeing the food-laden plates that were being served at the various tables.

"I suppose you're hungry and in need of some sustenance. I'll show you to your table and leave you there to the tender mercies of our steward. After you've had your supper, call by my cabin as I've got some paperwork for you to handle." Lee added.

"Thank you Tansey, but I have a generator to fix for the Wireless Office, so I might be some time."

"Oh! Indeed there are a number of things that need fixing on this ship, believe you me, but we've got plenty of time to see to them, providing king Neptune lets us, and long before we return to Belfast. Come by my cabin and see me when you've finished. My cabin's just along the passageway from your own, and is opposite the 2nd mate's. Any problems with it just see the steward."

John nodded his answer, before sitting down at a table that indicated just where he was to sit, and got waited upon by a steward with more feminine ways and a high-pitched voice, which totally belied his big muscular body.

"Here you are sweetie! Anything else you want, just wave!" the steward lisped then minced off to see to the other diners. John called after him.

"Er! Excuse me. But who are you, for me to 'shall we say' wave to?" he asked him, feeling a bit peeved at such a strange introduction.

"Well! Since you have asked me nicely, my name is Julian, but you can call me Julie." the steward replied nonchalantly, puckering his lips up and blowing a kiss to him, turned back again to continue his work.

John simply nodded his head at the steward's reply and declined to ask for any other service from him. He had already heard of such men as described by his two close friends, but never had the experience of meeting one like the steward, until now. The phenomenon of homosexuality was something else for John to encounter for the first time, and to see it first hand for himself. He decided to keep an open mind on the subject, but also to distance himself from it so as not to be affected by it.

When the limp-wristed steward finished clearing John's table and left him to his own devices, he stood up and slipped out of the dining room, thus avoiding any further attentions from this strange person.

He had some serious work to attend to which his predecessor either had no clue how to attempt, or was just too lazy to see to it. He settled on the idea of the latter.

"I'm ready to start your jenny repairs now, Bruce." John announced quietly, stepping inside the warm radio shack.

As he shut the weather out, he stood listening to the radios whistling and twittering morse code being tapped out or sounding out all around the room from the radio receivers.

He knew from experience that when he saw Bruce or his 2nd with their earphones on and busily writing on a long empty page, he would get no reply until they had finished, and decided it was the opportunity to enjoy his customary after dinner cigarette.

After a few minutes watching these officers deftly tapping on their morse keys and finishing off their writing, Larter took off his earphones, and asked John to repeat himself.

"I've got the Electrical Officer to rig up a spare line from a bridge connection to your junction box, ready to clag on when you're ready Bruce. I'm also ready to repair your jenny." John said politely.

"Thanks! We'd better be sharp about it because we're in for a big heave, and I'll probably need as much transmitter power as I can get. Here read this!" Larter said quickly, handing John a hand written signal, which he started to read.

"Sorry Bruce, its double Dutch to me, and no offence to Helena either. What do all these numbers and strange words of yours mean?" John chuckled, handing back the signal pad.

"It's from my old pal Bob Goodman, the Chief Telegraphist on the mid point weather ship off the coast of Cape Farewell. According to him, we're in for one lulu of a storm that's coming straight for us. It's his opinion that it's a storm unlike anything the UK has ever seen since god knows when, and Bob really knows his stuff to be able to tell us accurately enough." Larter said sombrely.

"We've been in many a big heave before Bruce, so what's so special about this one?" he asked, watching Southgate plotting a graph across a sea chart and muttering some numbers when doing so.

"Not in this ruddy tub you haven't. See these? The NW150 and SSWEL 60/80?" Southgate asked, showing John the writing and what he'd drawn on a sea chart, whilst Larter quickly checked the data.

"Yes, but unless you give me a clue I'll never work it out!" John chuckled.

"NW150 is the direction the wind is coming from and 150 is the rate of knots it's travelling at. SSWEL 60/80 means that there will be a sea swell of between 60 and 80 foot high.

The wind will force its way through what's called the North Channel between the Mull of Kintyre and Northern Ireland, then either track its way down the Irish sea or turn to cross the land around the Morecambe Bay area and then head down the North Sea. It is predicted to gather into a much bigger and much colder force once these 5 digit groups meet, and by that I mean NE100 – CF10+" Southgate concluded glumly.

"So by those digits, does it mean that it will meet another strong wind from the NE of 100mph and get between those figures, presumably minus or plus 10 on both scales?" John asked politely, trying to read the sea chart and the figures just appended to it.

"Yes John! That's about the size of it! In fact it's what another old oppo of mine Scouse Kearns, would call 'a perfect storm' as he's already seen one earlier on its way towards the Yank coast off Florida." Larter said ominously, showing John his completed calculations onto the sea chart.

"Bob had already given us his original report for the shipping areas, Bailey, Hebrides, Rockall, Malin and Irish Sea, which the skipper has on his chart table. But this is his update report, which gives us an early warning of about 8 hours. In turn it also means that unless we're in the lee of the Mull or at least Rathlin Island on the other side by then, we'll be slap bang in its way." Larter said quickly, adding a few adjustments on the sea chart.

"Right then, better get started." John agreed, as Southgate took him to where the generator was housed.

He managed to find the fault, have it repaired then tested it within half an hour, much to the satisfaction of the two radio officers.

"Knowing 'Mad Monk' Blayden, I've a feeling he will take us right through the middle of this sea swell, which is worse than any tidal wave. Unless as I've said, we'll be lucky to survive this storm." Larter said gravely.

"'Mad Monk'? That's a strange name Bruce. How the hell did he get that?" John asked with bemusement.

"He's a bible thumper and doesn't allow drink on board for the crew, and he hates people smoking anywhere near him. And that's just for starters! When we have more time I'll swap some of our latest ditties with you John." Larter said with a knowing smile.

"C'mon Paul, better get some jury aerials ready whilst I take this to the skipper. John, if I were you, I'd get as many pumps ready and operating as you can, especially for'ard, as this tub has a dodgy bow just like the old 'Brook' had." He added

"Thanks for that Bruce. I'll get onto it." John replied swiftly and left to get himself prepared.

"3rd Engineer to the bridge!" came the terse voice over the ships tannoy system, which John knew was his cue to take part in whatever the captain had in mind to prepare his ship from the cruel seas.

John arrived onto the bridge in answer to his summons, but was disappointed to find that his other good friend Sinclair was not at the helm.

"3rd Engineer. I need you to get some pumps ready in the for'ard holds then report to the 1st mate on the cargo deck. . You'll have to dismantle all the derricks and ensure that all upper deck ventilation pipes are sealed off, save those that are obvious to the engine room needs." Blayden said gruffly.

"Have two pumps ready in each of the cargo holds and have already started to shut down the for'ard watertight hatches, captain!" John said almost absentmindedly, his mind leaping to an earlier such incident, which he almost repeated verbatim.

"You have? Good work. Now get down on deck and help Danbury the 1st mate to secure all the cargo hatches, especially the for'ard ones. All upper deck machinery and fittings must be tightly secured even if you've got to weld some of it down. Got that?"

"Aye captain!" John replied aloud, and raced down the gangway ladder towards the main upper deck.

"1st Mate?" John asked politely, when he approached a stout, middle-aged man who was instructing a group of deck hands on what was needed.

"Yes! Who is asking?" he snarled.

"I'm 3rd Engineer Grey, sent down by the captain to help you." John replied, unruffled by this man's abruptness.

"Ah 3rd! Good of you to turn up. We've got some work cut out for us and pretty sharpish too." Danbury started, and then continued to rattle off the jobs to the anxiously waiting seamen. It was several minutes before he turned and addressed John again, by waving him over to join him.

"We have a couple of broken hatch clips that my men can't use to secure the heavy duty covering to. If we don't get them fixed or at least a strengthening bar across the weatherboards, then this hold will flood up with the first heavy wave that comes over our bows. As this is the lead or first hold to be hit by the sea it's the most important one of all, and what I call the 'TITANIC Syndrome'." Danbury commenced.

John listened to the myriad of jobs that needed doing before he gave any answers to the man.

"Send a hand down to the engine room and get four bottle screw type clips. When I undo the deck bolts off the for'ard derricks, have the men to place the booms fore to aft along their corresponding cargo hatches. When I've fixed these new hatch clips you can secure the sliding covers into position. The cargo booms will act as a sort of tent poles for when the hatches get covered with the tarpaulins to form a secondary watertight skin over them. All must be doubly lashed down when the men have covered the hatches with the tarpaulins.

That will apply also to the after cargo hatches. I have two of my men with welding equipment to weld down anything else you need fastened down onto the deck, otherwise its all down to the seamanship of your men, 1st mate.

You'd better have your cargo holds properly stowed and secure and no crew in them, as I shall be shutting down all water tight bulkheads, hatches, and all unnecessary ventilation fans." John advised quickly and precisely, which drew several nods and grunts of approval from Danbury.

"Sounds good to me. We'll have to ensure all upper deck windows and portholes have their deadlights fitted too, and extra strapping onto the lifeboats in case they get swept away." he concurred.

The ship was starting to roll and yaw heavily as the winds started to create a mountainous liquid landscape for it to climb its way over, for the men to finally leave the upper deck and into the safety of the midships superstructure.

John shut the last heavy door that ensured the best watertight integrity the ship could provide against it being lost in this 'once in a century' storm that was forcing its attention upon her.

Man had learned many a bitter lesson on watertight integrity, as many a good ship was lost due to its lack of understanding of or for its provision. But as time has marched on, many a ship was saved through its strict code and of the mariners who used it in time to save it, and to live and tell their tales of outstanding valour.

"All upper deck machinery secured and pumps ready for action captain!" John announced, when he reported back onto the bridge.

Blayden was huddled over his chart-strewn desk, busily mumbling figures and angles to himself, drawing bold lines across his sea chart.

"Very well 3rd! Lets hope this new fangled so called leak proof system our illustrious board has fitted this ship with, works. From now on until the storm passes, nobody can cross the upper deck for fear of being swept overboard, and nobody can move from stem to stern within, for fear of some rogue wave breaching the bulkheads to sink us. And that won't be too hard to do to this ancient bucket." Blayden muttered almost to himself and braced himself for the next bone shuddering movement of the ship.

"The 1st mate told me about your idea of stripping down all the cargo masts and lashing them onto the cargo holds to provide a second cargo hold cover, is that right?"

John braced himself for some sort of onslaught from Blayden when he affirmed that was so.

"Well it seems that you're little idea is paying off nicely 3rd. Look out of the storm window onto the foc'sle." Blayden said, staggering across the bridge deck to show John.

The ship had just breached the top of the next wave in its path, only to slide down into the deep trough on the other side, before dipping itself into and burying its nose deeply into the wall of yet another skyscraper wave in front of it.

The ship shook and shuddered as the wave washed right over almost all of the for'ard part of the ship, before its remains dashed itself onto the bridge superstructure. The bows started to lift itself up slowly against the weight, for it to rise right out of the wall of water only to commence the cycle all over again, leaving the stern end to follow as best as it could.

Every time the stern got raised out of the water, the ship shuddered again due to the propeller racing free before it bit into the water again to propel the ship that much further along the wave dotted line that was its course.

John could not distinguish which bit of the water was fresh from the sky or salt from the sea spume, for him to discern where the horizon was.

'Nothing but water everywhere captain! Lets hope our bow and bridge superstructure can stand the pasting, as I feel sure our decks are only getting a good wash at the moment.' he thought, looking around the bridge.

Blayden interrupted John's thoughts, with a sharp command to the helmsman.

"Bosun! Keep the bow portside into the waves. And don't stray more than five degrees either side of base course!"

"Aye aye Captain!" the Bosun responded, wrestling with the big steering wheel, and cursing under his breath and struggling to keep on his feet.

"If you can't manage on your own Bosun, may I suggest you tie a strop around one of the spokes nearest your middle course, so that the wheel can only go that far and no further." John whispered gently into the ear of the Bosun.

"I've tried that, but the steering is too narrow in this weather. I need to have at least a ten degree zig zag to manage it otherwise the rudder would only snap or the steering gear get destroyed."

Blayden heard the Bosun's reply enough to demand that John leave the bosun to get on with his work and for him to leave the bridge.

John did just that by going out the back way and made his way to the wireless office.

"Hello John! What brings you here?" Larter greeted affably.

"That's one hell of a storm out there Bruce. I have a feeling that we're not going to make the other end of it, unless we heave to in some sheltered waters somewhere."

"You're right there! We've picked up several Distress calls within the last hour and there's more adding to it and coming from the north of us. From their call signs, they appear to be a large fleet of trawlers either from Fleetwood or Campbeltown."

"Is that where you expect this, um, sea swell to come from Bruce? Only from what I've just seen it looks like we're riding through it now."

"Sea swell? Then you'd better look out, so let's hope you're wrong John. I'll let you know when I come back from showing the skipper this latest report." Larter replied before swiftly disappearing out into the maelstrom, slamming the heavy steel door behind him.

"According the skippers dead reckoning position he gave us over an hour ago now, it puts us slap bang in the middle of the gap." Southgate announced, pointing to a place on a sea chart, which showed the coastlines of Northern Ireland and the Scottish Islands. That means unless the bosun can steer properly and on a decent course, we'll be out of this lousy storm within the next few hours and be heading on our own NW course for Canada."

"Hmm! Given certain facts from the engine room and our present speed, I think you can add at least another 4 hours onto that. Besides, unless the steering gear is 100% I'd say that we'd be lucky not to bump into some god forsaken island in the middle of nowhere and to our starboard."

"I'm afraid you've got me there John! All I know is that there are several mariners out there somewhere that would be glad of our help." Southgate admitted, writing down yet another S.O.S. distress call into his operator's log.

John listened for a while to the morse code that seemed to fill the sound-proofed room, and observed the hands on the clock move slowly on its way around its face, until a blast of cold wet air heralded Larter's return.

"It looks as if the skipper has either found some land not charted on the map or his navigation is somewhat suspect." Larter said alarmingly.

"I'd better get down to the compass room and also have a look at the steering tackle and see that all is well, or he will pin all the fault on me." John moaned.

"Well whatever he decides, let's hope he decides to hide behind that land and keep us from this gawd awful weather!" Southgate stated flatly, as John donned his foul weather gear again and proceeded to step out into the storm raging outside.

"See you both then! A man's got to what a man's got to do!" John sighed and made his way back into the bridge area.

"What's your ship's head bosun?" Blayden shouted over the invasion of noise coming from the bridge door that John had just entered through.

"340!"

"You're supposed to be on 350. How long have you been on that course Bosun?"

"I'm tracking my base course of 340 but the sea conditions are forcing me on an alternating course between 345 and 355, also that you wanted me to keep the oncoming tide to port, captain!"

"I asked how long you've been on this course. In fact, when was your last change of course?"

The bosun asked his messenger to search the bridge narrative log to respond.

"Our last course change was at 0300 from 285 to our present course of 340. Our speed was 20 knots but got reduced to 15 at 0345, but we're now at 10 knots and barely keeping way on the ship, captain!"

Blayden swore at this information as he worked feverishly to calculate his position in relation to the landmass ahead of him.

"Take a slow turn to starboard onto a new course of 015.

Use no more than 5 degrees of starboard rudder. I want to get close to that land mass and shelter there until either this infernal weather abates or when I can get a proper star fix to get us back on track."

The bosun repeated his orders and promptly obeyed with the time-honoured reply, "Aye aye Captain!"

Within moments, the ship was starting to roll heavily and shake itself from stem to stern as each massive wave pushed against its now much broader profile.

Everybody was hanging on to whatever they could, just to prevent themselves being dashed around, including John, who held onto an object that dangled his body outwards and almost at 35 degrees angle from the upright. He looked at the inclinometer and saw that the pointer had crept way past the so-called danger line before it mercifully swung back the other way again.

This lasted for nearly two hours until the ship managed to creep into a sheltered bay that was all peace and tranquillity in comparison to what they'd just come through.

Blayden looked out of the now uncovered bridge windows and commenced to take some prominent points of land to fix his bearings.

"It appears bosun, that we've been blown off track by some 40 miles in the last 4 hours, and that piece of land should be Rathlin Island on our port sided, but in fact its Tiree on our starboard side. Midships. Steer 020. Speed 8 knots. 1st Mate, we'll anchor here in Hynish Bay until this infernal storm blows itself away. Get the hands on deck to drop anchor then prepare an anchor watch. 3rd engineer, get yourself on deck and see to any damaged deck machinery. Report to me when done." Blayden commanded rapidly, despatching his officers to their duties.

"It looks as if we'll need another paint makeover 1st mate." John remarked, beginning to assess the damage to his 'outside' machinery.

"At least it's only paint, 3rd. Look at the bow! That's a dockyard job if I ever saw one." Danbury said in amazement, pointing to the buckled plating on the foc'sle.

15

John just smiled and shook his head.

"No such luck 1st. Just a few deck plates in need of straightening, and a light plate over the top of them to keep the water out. By all accounts our skipper will have a word with his boss upstairs, sacrifice our speed money and all that, just to keep this ship moving." John replied, looking skywards towards the silvery sheen of daybreak trying to force its way under the blankets of dark rain clouds.

"It appears that we need extra tarpaulins over the after hatches. There must have been a big wave to hit us for it to smash one of the lifeboats to shreds. But at least the vent shaft casings are still okay 3rd."

"Yes! All in all, we've been lucky. But we've still got the internal inspection to do."

Both men made their way down into the ships hull and made their systematic checks of the ships innards, which took them a further two hours before they were satisfied enough to make their report to the captain.

"I am heartened to know that both your reports mean that a good and thorough inspection of my vessel has been conducted. We have some repairs to effect and the ship looking like one again before we get under way again." Blayden announced, finishing the writing down of the points that Danbury and John had mentioned.

"It appears that we arrived just in time under the lee of this island to escape that sea surge. We'll stay at anchor and ride out the storm as I intend remaining at anchor for another day. So get the ship opened up for access again 3rd before you breakfast yourself. 1st mate, you get the off watch crew to clear the decks of all debris. Have the cargo booms erected again and get this ship painted in its customary colours. That will be all." Blayden ordered flatly.

"I'll be in my cabin if you need me, but make sure you have some reliable hands on anchor watch and keep a lookout on the bridge." Blayden added, and marched off the bridge.

Chapter II
Just a Tramp

The ship was still being buffeted by the winds as the much smaller waves slapped angrily against its sides, when the puff of smoke from the funnel announced that she was now ready to resume her voyage again.

The *Inverlaggan* weighed anchor in the early morning of the second day and left its temporary shelter to venture out into the now much calmer waters of the Atlantic that was creating mayhem and death to all mariners afloat, only some few hours before.

"Bosun, Port 15 and steer 320. Tell the engine room make revs for 20 knots." Blayden ordered sharply, as the ship responded to its commands.

John had completed his morning deck inspection and was on his way to enjoy his breakfast, when the 2nd engineer met up with him.

"Are you still experiencing difficulty in sorting out the brake and locking arrangement of the steering gear, John?"

"Not really, but whoever modified it could not settle on steam or telemotor controls. One is either telemotor or mechanical control and its neither fish nor fowl at the moment. On top of that, it's taking more than the standard 30 second transfer from hard a port to hard to starboard. So it will take me a few days to get my head around that problem, but really it should be the chief's pigeon not mine, Tansey." John replied civilly, and then added.

"Anyway, why are you asking?"

"I have been given a few hours a day to help you with your duties on this leg of the voyage, but you will have the aid of a junior engineer as your understudy for the entire duration. So after your breakfast maybe you'll come and see me down the engine room for a brief conflab with the chief."

"That's fine by me Tansey, say 0800hours." John replied,

17

sitting down ready for his customary breakfast of hot buttered rolls with bacon and sausage and a mug of tea.

"Where have you been sweetie? You haven't slept in your cabin since yesterday, have you been bad in the sick bay?" the gay steward asked politely.

"Been very busy, steward. No peace for the wicked it seems." John replied nonchalantly.

"Busy as that! And here's Julie thinking you'd been avoiding me, silly me! Never mind, here's your favourite sausage meat rolls and tea!" the steward said, emphasising suggestively the words 'sausage meat' and placed John's breakfast down gently in front of him.

"I haven't had time to read the Bill of fare yet, but as a guess, are we having chicken again today? Only this time maybe I'll get a decent leg portion if it's possible." John asked hurriedly, devouring his rolls.

"Oh you're a leg man are you, and here's me thinking you were all breast! Yes, it's 'cock au van' but I'm not sure about the van. But for you sweetie, I'll do my best." the steward lisped, emphasising the word 'cock' then left John to his meal, and his after breakfast cigarette.

After his repast, John made his way down to the engine room and into the engineers' office, where he met Jones, who was in company with Lee and 2 other officers.

"Morning chief! Morning everybody!" John greeted cheerfully, but only got scowls from the chief.

"Right! Now we're all here!" Jones said sarcastically.

"Maybe we can get some work done around this ship." he added, pulling out a large detailed drawing of the ships mechanical world.

"This ship is one of the oldest in the fleet and has survived the war by sailing the Canadian lakes from Port Arthur to St Johns in Newfoundland and back again, generating much wealth for its owners. I know as I've been on board ever since I joined her as its junior engineer. However, since then she has been left to slowly retire, and only necessary modifications or repairs carried out on it to keep it seaworthy. It is our duty to ensure the ship remains functional and as comfortable as possible, therefore you will all have to be fully genned up on the various manuals for the equipment that you find yourself maintaining during this extended voyage." Jones commenced.

"If this ship is as ancient as some of the equipment suggests, then why hasn't it been scrapped, chief?" John asked quietly, and as innocuously as possible so as not to upset this volatile mannered man.

"As far as I'm concerned, that's none of our business, especially yours 3rd. Just concern yourself with the job you're paid to do. But if you must know, the lords of the management board have decided that this ship will still keep its earning power by trading around the rim of the Atlantic, and to whoever hires it. It might be ancient, but this 450 feet long piece of motorised metal can carry a decent cargo of some 20,000 tonnes." Jones growled.

"So it's just a tramp ship now, whoring its way around the world. Let's hope we get our proper speed money and other bonuses during that time." Lee commented.

"Be that as it may, 2nd. But by the end of this voyage in some 6–8 months time, each one of you will be a much more qualified engineer than you are standing in front of me just now."

"With all this outdated machinery, some hopes!" John muttered under his breath.

"You said something 3rd? Speak up, what did you say?" Jones demanded.

"Judging by all the outdated machinery, what provision is made to replace an item that can't be fixed any more?" John asked boldly.

"You are a fitter and turner by trade, yes? Unless you can make a new one or get something to replace it, then you'll just have to re-fix it so that it does work again." Jones stated ominously.

"Maybe that's why the skipper is still using a sextant as he can't afford to buy and use the new navigational radar that most other ships seem to have these days!" John replied.

"That's enough from you Grey! You're here for instruction on some new duties that you'll be required to perform whilst under my authority, and quite apart from what the captain wants off you. So pay attention everybody." Jones snorted, before reeling off orders and detailed instructions to his junior officers. The meeting lasted two hours before Jones finished his meeting.

"I want an appropriate daily report from you Grey. And just so there are no hard feelings between us, you can call on me instead of the 2nd, if you've got a problem doing your job. As for you 2nd, I want to review the junior engineers instructional logs every four weeks as from today. Any engineer officer of whatever rank, not complying with my instructions or ships orders, or found incompetent to do the duty he is being paid for will be put off at the next port of call wherever it may be, without pay or compensation. Apart from that, have a good and profitable voyage." Jones stated belligerently, and left the engineers office to his stunned officers.

"That gentlemen, is what is called 'The Riot Act'. Make sure that each watch is a good one and your stokers on the ball. So be on your toes and on best behaviour, at least until we get to Barbados." Lee stated, before he ushered everybody out of the office.

Chapter III
Hot Water

The infamous mountainous waves of the Atlantic had subsided to only house size proportions as the ship swam her way on a westerly course that took them into the realms of the floating giants, where many a good and innocent ship had met its doom.

"All hands off watch to prepare for…" the ships tannoy announced anxiously, but John did not hear the last part, as he was too busy and engrossed in his work of making a new machine part on his lathe, for the ship's steering gear.

He was just finishing the part and testing it for accuracy with his gauges, when a sailor tapped his shoulder in a heavy-handed manner.

He turned round and told the sailor that if he ever did that again, he would never live to regret it.

"Sorry 3rd. I did shout on you, but you didn't hear me. Anyway, the skipper wants you up on the bridge."

"Tell him I'll be there as soon as I've completed this part for the steering gear."

"No 3rd! You're to come with me. The skipper's orders." the sailor insisted.

John stopped his lathe before wiping his hands on a clean rag.

"Very well. Take me to your leader." he sighed, following the sailor up and out of the engine room eventually ending up onto the bridge.

"You sent for me captain?"

"3rd! You should have been on deck at least 15 minutes ago. Where the bloody hell have you been?" Blayden asked, angrily.

"Making a new part for the steering system captain." John replied casually, ignorant as to what he was supposed of have, or have not done.

"Be that as it may, but that's no excuse for not obeying my deck orders. Get down onto the for'ard cargo deck and help

Walters the 2nd mate. He'll tell you what is required." Blayden stated gruffly, and dismissed him with a wave of his arm.

"What's the score 2nd mate?" John asked, arriving to stand next to Walters.

"We're slap bang in the middle of an armada of massive icebergs, the size of skyscrapers, that have decided to come down and mug us innocent ships. Which in the custom and tradition of sailors, means that we have to post several lookouts all around the ship, and need some sort of heating system for them to stay on watch."

"Oh is that all! So what's happened to the navigation radar for the skipper to get into such a pickle? Do you mean to tell me that you and the skipper are asking an engineer to sort out the seamanship of the vessel and that of your own men?" John asked sharply in disgust at being summoned, and started to shiver with the cold, as he was not dressed for going onto the upper deck.

"Unless the skipper can extricate us out of this mess of his own doing then I suggest that you get your men to stuff some hot water bottles under their jumpers, and issue them with extra cold weather gear. That should do it 2nd mate! If that's all then I'm off back to the engine room."

"It's not as easy as that 3rd. For a start there's no cold weather gear on board, let alone hot water bottles. We're only equipped for the Caribbean, not the Arctic."

"Well then what do you want off me, for Christ sake? I'm no magician you know."

"What the captain wants is a hot water hose system rigged, something like a piped heating system. It should also have a sprinkler system to help reduce the ice building up on the cargo masts and main decks."

"Is that it?" John replied in amazement, and then added.

"Okay, here's the situation. Have some of your men break open the deck fire hoses. Then have the hoses run in a circle around the upper deck. Wherever you find a hydrant valve have the hoses connected up to them. Let me know when you've done that.

I'm going down to see the chief engineer to get the hot water pumped through it. Meet me here in about 10 minutes 2nd."

Walters nodded in agreement as John scurried back down into the warmth of the ship to get himself suitably attired for the upper deck and sort out his end of the problem.

John returned on deck shortly afterwards and met up with Walters, who was busy testing the hoses for their effectiveness.

"I thought there was supposed to be hot water in these hoses 3rd. These hoses are stone cold." Walters moaned.

"Give them time to warm up 2nd. But don't expect them to be much hotter, or your men would scald themselves with them. The water will only be about 20 degrees above atmospheric temperature, which is sufficient to melt any ice or snow off the ship. As I've said, the men will just have to put extra clothing on underneath their foul weather clothing."

"Would you fancy staying on deck in this wet and freezing weather 3rd? I don't think so." Walters said with disappointment, as his sailors started to moan about the rapidly deteriorating weather, and stamped their feet about trying to keep them warm.

"I suggest you tell the skipper to rotate the lookouts every hour and issue them with hot drinks before and after their shift."

"You must be joking, 3rd, I'll do no such thing. The captain would...." Walters started to say, but only spoke to the back of a person disappearing from him.

John left Walters in disgust, and went to seek out Larter, whom he knew would now be in the saloon.

"Bruce. I've just been bollocked by the skipper for not attending his deck orders. And by that, I mean me providing hot water and provisions for the seamen on iceberg lookout duties. What's the score on this new fangled radar that's supposed to be on board?"

"Calm down John. Paul is the boffin for that type of radar, but from what I gather is that it's no use in rain or fog. Just a blanket of blobs everywhere. It only responds to solid objects such as mountains and large bits of metal such as a ship."

"Well at least it's got its priorities right, Bruce. But what about these bloody great icebergs that somehow has ambushed us?"

"As its only solid water, it would only show up on the screen as a mushy blob. If it were a tidal wave, it would show up as a big line right across the screen. But if we were to enter a harbour, it would show all the land features and any buoys or ships in the harbour as we enter it. But only up to about 10-15,000 yards or so ahead."

"That's only about 7 sea miles. A dirty great tanker takes five of that just to stop. Not much room for any further manoeuvre after that I dare say."

"Well, yes John. But then who are we to question the actions of the captain." Larter said, offering John a glass of lemonade. John took the drink and tasted it but wrinkled up his nose at it.

"Sorry John. It's the best on offer whilst at sea. Captains orders." Larter said apologetically, raising his glass of the same.

"Cheers John!" he added with a smile and continued to smoke his cigarette.

"Just as well we've no passengers on board for this part of the voyage, or there would be riots let alone mutiny." John retorted, finishing off his drink.

"Must get back to the engine room, I've got a new part to finish off and install into the steering system or we'll end up in Norway let alone Nova Scotia."

Larter looked at his watch and scrutinised it.

"Aye, and I must get hold of Bob Goodman and the new radio beacon he's trying out. Lets hope he's still on watch!" Larter said with a yawn, and left the saloon with John.

Both men went back to their own part of ship in the knowledge that somehow, trouble with a capital T, would call on them sooner rather than later.

It was shortly after lunch when John had just installed the new part to the steering system when his junior engineer assistant tapped him on the shoulder in a frantic manner.

"What's up Menzies, we've sprung a leak or something?" John asked roughly, rubbing his shoulder in pain.

"3rd. The tannoy has just announced the 'Standby collision Starboard side."

"So what of it? Unless we get this gear back to full working again then there'll be no need to worry if an iceberg does decide to call on us for tea." John said sarcastically.

"But 3rd! Aren't we supposed to be on deck helping out or something?" Menzies asked with panic in his voice.

"Oh that! Yes, I suppose we'd better get up somewhere safe. You go and get the lifebelts from that locker over there and take them up on deck. Wear one yourself mind you!" John replied, pointing to the emergency stowage locker above them.

"I'll be right behind you."

Menzies did not wait for any further invitation as he hastily opened the locker, grabbed the lifebelts, and rushed up the ladder and out of the compartment.

John completed his test inspection, wrote the details into the maintenance log before he too left the compartment and sauntered up onto the main deck where he saw Menzies helping a couple of stokers sweeping some ice debris off the after cargo deck.

"Shades of the *Titanic*, Menzies!" John stated, looking over to a towering iceberg only some yards away from the ship.

"That man there! Come here and lend a hand on this fender starboard side." an irate voice shouted to him.

John looked around and pointed to himself.

"Yes you! Don't just bloody well stand there. Get over here on the double."

John flicked two fingers up at the man then went forward and climbed up into the bridge to see what really was the matter for everybody to panic

"3rd! We need extra power to No 1 cargo winch. I have grappled myself onto that berg on the port side to try and lay off the bloody one on the starboard side that seems to want to join us without a boarding pass. I'm not taking passengers on yet, so see what you can do!" Blayden shouted, pointing to the for'ard deck.

"On my way captain!" John replied swiftly, descending the bridge, only to meet up with the owner of the raucous voice that shouted to him earlier.

"You! I thought I told you!" was all he said before John showed him his rank and trade, which reduced the man to gaping and stammering.

"Now then matey! Just who the bloody hell are you to scream at me?"

"5th mate Crabbe. Sorry 3rd, I though you were one of those lazy sailors from the after section."

"Well then Crabbe. I suggest you grab hold of that brush and sweep up too. Show the men that you can work just as well as shout at them! My orders only come from the chief engineer or the captain, not the likes of you." John stated angrily.

"Er, Yes why don't I!" Crabbe stuttered, and started to sweep up with the very broom he was about to give John.

It was only when John saw the extreme difficulty and danger the ship was in, that he appreciated the urgency and panic among the crew on deck.

He saw there was a huge iceberg just off the starboard bow and one much bigger on the port bow but still some chains away, with several heaving lines with grapple hooks clinging onto it. The sailors were trying to wrap their end of the lines onto the anchor capstan, which was trying to pull the ship towards it.

There was yet another iceberg on the starboard quarter still leaning over the ship, shedding tons of ice onto it, and although some yards away, it was still coming towards them.

John met up with Danbury on the foc'sle who was beside himself with worry directing the men to do this or that as he lurched from one crisis to another.

"How the hell did we get ourselves boxed in this lot 1st mate?" John asked aloud, and whistled at the sheer size of the icebergs almost on top of them.

"We came out of a fog bank about ten minutes ago to find these littering the place, 3rd! We need extra hoses to flush off the thick coat of ice that's forming on deck. We also need extra power to the cargo derrick winches, because the captain hopes to use those bergs on the port side to pull us out of the way of them on the starboard side.

That big one on the port bow has some decent sea room for us to tuck ourselves around into, providing there's no underwater obstruction to snag us as we go around it." Danbury explained, pointing to each obstacle.

John went over to the winches and capstans and within moments he had them working at a greater capacity than what would have ordinarily be required from them.

"You can't work them for more than 10 minutes per hauling time 1st Mate. Pull for 5 minutes, then slacken off for two minutes before pulling again." John announced, when he arrived back to join Danbury.

"What about the hot water hoses?"

"They only have a 20 degree above atmospheric temperature to melt the bits of berg sticking out towards the ship. They have a 400lb pressure on them to provide a good head of water for you. But don't ask for more or the hoses will only burst on you and probably scald your men into the bargain. So be careful."

"Thank you 3rd. What I'd love to do is throw lots of dynamite at them to clear our path, but it would probably be just like throwing snowballs at them." Danbury concluded, miserably.

The ship was pulled slowly towards the big berg, before she was steered around behind it and into a patch of open water.

Blayden was sermonising, waving a large bible and shouting at the top of his voice at the bergs from his vantage point on the bridge, as he cleared each obstacle.

"Get thee behind us you miserable purveyors of the devils work! Oh Lord! We are your sinners but think of thy work that still needs to be done!" Blayden ranted.

For several hours the ship slowly but gingerly extricated herself from these floating walls of death, and Blayden finally stopped his fire and brimstone sermons.

"Bosun! Port 15, steer 270, speed 20 knots!" he whispered hoarsely, before leaving the bridge.

John stood for several minutes behind the new radar display unit to watch this man openly defying the perils of nature, before he decided to go into the radio shack and speak to Larter.

"That man is cracked. No wonder he's called the 'MAD MONK'." John opined, sitting down heavily on an empty chair next to Southgate.

"If the power of speech was ever harnessed and sold by the tonne, the skipper would be the richest man on earth." Larter replied, and took off his headphones.

"Amen to that!" Southgate intoned sarcastically.

"How far behind schedule are we Bruce? Maybe we'll have to go full speed to make up the diff?" John asked.

"Despite the bad storm we've been through, we're actually still afloat and making headway, so the board of governors have allowed us 3 days grace. Mind you, if we meet up with the Newfoundland fog banks as well, then we can forget it. The skipper has got his knackers in a vice now, and getting squeezed by the governors. So he'll need as much speed as he can get. That means that your stokers will be working overtime to keep those engines on the go. On top of that, we've been diverted to Halifax that's why we've been dancing with icebergs lately."

"Then if this first leg to Nova Scotia puts us behind, giving a knock on effect to the subsequent legs of the voyage, it will mean that we've sailed thousands of miles and wasted our time for nothing. We'll be paying their lordships instead." Southgate observed.

"Hopefully not. But if by the time we get to the bottom leg of our voyage, then they will just re- route us or bring us home before time." Larter stated.

"Aye! Just like what happened to the old *Brooklea* at Bermuda, eh what Bruce!" John replied with a nod. *

* * *

It took the ship almost eight days to traverse the North Atlantic; no thanks to the increasing fields of icebergs they kept meeting. All of which meant that the radio shack was in constant use in reporting these finds to the rest of the maritime world, for fear of yet another famous iceberg sinking.

The *Inverlaggan* managed to complete her last dangerous and even more perilous passage through the notorious fogbanks of Newfoundland.

She arrived in the very early morning off the coast off the peninsular of Nova Scotia, as the first piece of land that is part of arguably the biggest, and the most beautiful and most striking country in the whole world, Canada.

John stood in his accustomed place on the foc'sle awaiting his summons from the usual panic created by frustrated sailors, but his attention was on the sights as the ship slowly entered the world's second largest natural harbour of Bedford Bay.

He saw the different coloured harbour lights indicating only what the pilot or ship's captain could understand, but from what he saw, he could understand that on the opposite side to where he was to dock, Halifax, there was an equally important port just across the harbour, that of Dartmouth.

Halifax is the capital of this 350-mile long stretch of land, joined to the mainland of the American continent only by a narrowest of causeways and forms part of the country of Canada. It was colonised by the British only a few years after the famous conquest over the French colonialists at Montreal by the British Army commanded by General Wolfe in the 17th Century.

It was thanks to the pioneers from the 'Sceptred Isles' of the United Kingdom from the 17th century onwards and much to the chagrin of the erstwhile French settlers that this beautiful expanse of land was really opened up and, to have and enjoy such a rich diversity of life that exists today.

This is where John and his shipmates were to spend a brief time before sailing off to much warmer waters[1].

---

[1] See *A Fatal Encounter.*

Chapter IV
All Change

"**W**akey wakey, 3rd! You've got 30 minutes to muster in the dining room." the steward whispered, but shook John roughly to waken him up.

"Wha! Wha! 30 minutes?" John said in alarm, waking out of his deep sleep.

"Morning 3rd! Had a good nights sleep did we?"

"Oh it's you steward! What's the bleeding time?" John asked, rubbing his eyes and tried to accustom his sight to the pale yellow light that shone, seemingly search-like, from above his head.

"It's just after seven bells of the morning watch 3rd."

"Bloody hell! I only got turned in at 0400hours. What the blazes am I required to do now that we've arrive alongside, steward?"

"Let's put it this way. I have an early morning breakfast tray for you. Get this down your neck and get yourself prepared for an early meeting on the bridge with certain luminaries of the shipping line. The skipper and other officers will be there, so you won't feel out of place."

John climbed out of his bunk and washed his face and hands in the cabin sink, before sitting down in the swivel chair at the writing desk that was opened to where his breakfast was placed.

"These rolls are nice and fresh, steward?" John asked, eating his hot buttered rolls stuffed with large rashers of bacon.

"Yes! I got them off a friend of mine who runs a snack bar on the corner of the jetty we're tied up alongside of."

"Whatever steward. It's certainly a big improvement to the slabs of concrete we've been given these last few days. And before you pipe up and say anything against your friend in the galley, I do appreciate that the ovens had packed up on day one, and I was not to be able to mend them. So please spare me your moans and groans."

"Glad you appreciate what we chefs and stewards go through 3rd! But then, when you've got a chance, please mention all this in your meeting." the steward concluded, and finished off his chores around the cabin, before leaving John to get himself organised for the day.

"Good morning everybody! It appears that our shipping line has kept up its promise once more, despite all that mother nature has thrown our way. But then that is why each one of you have been chosen for such a voyage." Belverley greeted when he entered the saloon to the gathering of the ships officers.

This opening statement of the meeting was to all intent and purpose made to gee up the ships officers. But to most, it was a statement more of patronisement than thanks for the hard work produced by each man.

"We have a change of schedule for you, which will not only involve a different cargo manifesto, but a change of voyage that we could not foresee prior to your sailing from Liverpool. The papers have been prepared for each man to sign to enable the continuity of the ship and its present crew. Should any person feel that they are unwilling to undertake this new voyage, then please let their intentions be known at the end of this meeting, in order for us to find alternative arrangements.

However, as each one of you is under special contracts and have already signed your Articles in the pursers office, to join this vessel, perhaps we can dispense with the niceties, and get on with what we're about to undertake." Belverley stated, and went on to outline the future voyage the *Inverlaggan* was going to do.

"There goes our run ashore John. Our cargo needs special regulations and handling let alone clearance from the politico ashore." Lee whispered to John, as Belverley droned on about what was what, when, why, and by whom.

"What, not even an hour ashore for a first look around and maybe get some 'rabbits'?" John whispered back.

"No. Just load up and bugger off. Like as if we're lepers!"

Belverley finished his summation and was about to leave when he looked over to John and beckoned him with a curled finger.

John saws the signal and came dutifully towards him, but

guessing what he was summonsed for.

"3rd Engineer Grey, glad you finally made it on board." Belverley greeted, as John stood in front of him.

"I have every confidence in you to come up with some sort of solution to provide the ship with an appropriate stowage method for a cargo that this ship was not built for. However, here are some diagrams for you to consider, work upon, and offer me some working arrangements so that my ship and its cargo will arrive at its next port of call in one piece." he added, giving John a large roll of technical drawings.

John took the package and unrolled it to see just what Belverley was talking about, before committing himself to any response. He examined the drawings carefully, then handed them back to Belverley, saying.

"I'm just a 3rd engineer, not a magician, Mr Belverley. I suggest that you give them back to your commodore or his sidekick Cresswell, to make out some proper plans for me to work upon. Those are useless and unworkable, and there's no way I will rewrite or amend them." John said and turned away in disgust.

"Don't you dare dismiss me Grey!" Belverley snorted angrily.

"You are forgetting just who you are, and just how you got to the rank you 're enjoying now."

"Glad you mentioned that Belverley. Because if it wasn't for me, you would be at least two ships less in your fleet by now, and your line wouldn't be enjoying the prestige gained from my efforts with the SFDs'."

Belverley must have realised what John was saying was the truth, so softened his tone of voice and manner.

"Now let's not get too bogged down with bygones. We both know we are just as ruthless in our objectives to achieve a common goal, and that is of providing ships of excellence for good of the shipping trade. So don't be too hasty on this, as it is not in our interest to do so. Just look over the plans, and if necessary, get a second opinion from another person whom only you deem worthy of asking from. But whatever you do, I need your workable solution by tomorrow morning." Belverley concluded with a nod of his head, and slapped the large roll of drawings into the crook of John's arm for him to grab hold of, and left without further ado.

"Hello Grey! Your friend Mr McPhee is ashore in the dockyard. Suggest you see him." Lowther whispered in John's ear, and winked to him as he passed and followed Belverley out through the saloon doorway.

"I'm the chief engineer around here Grey. What have you got there that needs my attention?" Jones snarled when he came up to John.

"Yes, show us what Lord Belverley gave you." demanded Blayden, arriving almost in unison with Jones.

John looked at the two irate men, then stuffed the bundle of drawings under his arm and left them speechless when he departed abruptly to make his way back to his cabin.

On his way, he met the steward coming along the passageway and asked him to do him a favour, which the steward agreed to do.

"I'll do my best 3rd, but I've got several friends ashore to meet up with. In fact why don't you come ashore with me, I'll show you the sights and all, trust me." the steward replied.

"Sorry steward. Shore leave cancelled, and I've got too much on at the moment. But if I've not heard from McPhee in two hours, then I know you've either jumped ship, or you've found another like minded friend."

"Jump ship? Not me sweetie! We've got some lovely passengers coming on board later on, which means lots of lovely tips and with luck not only of the money kind either." the steward quipped suggestively, pursing his lips, and smoothed down his hair, before leaving John alone in his cabin. John looked at the departing steward and wondered just how such men existed, before he shut his cabin door and got himself organised for this unwelcome intrusion into his daily life on board.

A loud knock on his cabin door interrupted John's thoughts, as he beckoned the caller in.

"Hello Grey! Got yourself another load of grief from you know who, then?"

John recognised the familiar voice of McPhee, and stood to welcome him into his cabin.

"Hello Fergus, good of you to come. Mountain to Mohammed this time round, I fear!" John greeted.

"Something like that John. Now what seems to be the problem how can I help?"

John showed McPhee the technical drawings of the ships' design, then what is required as per Creswell's drawings, then he showed his own rough drawings and notations. All of which took a good hour to follow through, and for McPhee to give his considered opinion.

"Well John, it seems that you've spotted the basic flaw in Cresswell's designs for the false decking, and apart from an extra bulkhead here and here, everything you've done seems okay." he explained, and drew a couple of lines on John's drawings.

"But that will add an extra hundred tons to each deck, and therefore less cargo carried, as far as the captain is concerned."

"You did say a unit of the Canadian Cavalry? Never mind horses, they are easy to carry, but they'll have at least sixty assorted vehicles, some of them armoured. Then add their several hundred tons of ammunition and other pyrotechnics, plus their fuel and stores. That's why you need the re-inforced decking. Then of course there are the 250 men to consider below decks, John."

"No, we've only got 50 soldiers as the rest will be on board a trooper that's accompanying us."

"The officers will be in the passengers cabins, so you can put the men into one of these extra spaces I've shown you. Never mind about messing and toilet facilities as they can use the crew's facilities. But you'll have to rig up a vent system for them otherwise its going to be stuffy and like a furnace in there especially when you get to the Carib and beyond."

John took a little more time to study his amended drawings, before he drew the sketches and measurements onto fresh pieces of paper.

"Here you are Fergus. These are your copies to keep with all the others I've given you. We'll just leave Cresswell's drawings untouched but use mine as ' adjustments made' for the purpose." John said at length, and winked to McPhee.

"Well said John! You're on your way to become a good engineer one day, and maybe a good ship designer yet."[2]

"Thank you Fergus. Here's a glass of cheer!" John replied, reaching for his secret supply of whiskey and pouring out two glasses full of the light golden liquid.

"Now where have I heard that one before, young man!" McPhee chuckled, taking hold of his glass and drunk deeply from it.

The two men talked over a few more technical details for a while longer, before McPhee stated that it was time for him to get ashore again.

John accompanied McPhee to the gangway and waved him off as his launch sped away from the ships' Medway ladder. (A flight of wooden stairs leading down the outside of the ship to assist passengers boarding/disembarking from launches or other smaller craft.)

"Who was that you waved off John?" Lee asked, as they met in the doorway of the saloon.

"That was the naval dockyard superintendent Mr McPhee, do you know him Tansey?" John asked in reply.

"Slightly. Met him in Gib a couple of years ago. But what was he doing on board, as he never came to see 'Spanners'."

"I heard he was over here, and asked the steward to phone him to see me. He's helped me to sort out the new decking arrangements we'll be needing in the morning."

---

[2] See *Future Homes.*

"That sounds grand! But how did you get to handle this pigeon, its strictly dockyard shipwrights territory you know?"

"Oh, don't ask Tansey. It's a long story, but sufficient to say, there's a lot of paper work that needs sorting and I'll need some help with, and for getting the work done. So if you care to come to my cabin later, I'll show you what's what."

"Fair enough! See you in about an hour then." Lee stated, as John left him.

Within the hour, Lee was knocking on John's cabin door.

"Thanks for coming Tansey. Here're the drawings that I was given by Belverley, and here's what we'll be needing." John greeted, when Lee entered his cabin.

Both engineers poured over the drawings and discussed some vital technical problems they had encountered, which took them well into the evening, before they decided that was all they could do prior to the construction

"Right then John. Lets see if we can get something to eat. We'll have an hour off before we start."

"Sounds right by me Tansey, but we've got to see the captain and 'Spanners' before we do, else we'll into deep water, if my memory serves me correct."

"Leave that to me John, just you get your welding team ready. Now let's go eat."

Chapter V
Whizz Bang!

John had Menzies and the welding gang mustered on the for'ard cargo deck and talking amongst themselves, when Lee arrived with Walters and some sailors.

"We've got a barge coming alongside with the extra decking that McPhee has sent over for us. He said that he'll come and inspect it with the captain and when you've finished. But we've only got until 0700 to complete it." Lee announced, arriving alongside John.

"Thank you Tansey, glad to hear it." John replied, and then gathered all the men around him to explain what was required from them. John asked Walters if there was anything to add.

"Yes 3rd! My instruction states that once we've loaded the ammo and put our first false decking on, we'll be moving over to a jetty to take on board the vehicles and the rest of the stores. We should be alongside by 0300 and start loading the vehicles 0730. We've been promised help from the dockyard for that, so hopefully we can do it a bit quicker than our own lifting tackle."

"Good, because it means that we can all have a few hours rest before John starts the partitioning of the holds for the vehicles. That means the inspection cannot take place until the entire cargo is loaded." Lee concluded, which galvanised the crewmen into action, with their allotted tasks.

The for'ard derricks were swiftly bobbing up and down, swinging back and forth unloading the extra decking, before they started the serious task of taking on board the two barges of live ammunition.

"Lets hope none of this drops into the hold or we'll really have a holed ship 2nd!" John said jovially to Walters, who was directing the operations from the foc'sle.

"It's not so much the crated ammo, it's the boxes of whiz-bangs, 3rd. One nasty jolt and the whole lot would light the sky like a Christmas tree."

"And you expect my men to work with blow torches with them around? Can't we stow them as deck cargo. That way, we can get the first false deck sealed and re-inforced for the armoured vehicles."

"Ordinarily yes, but we don't have strong boxes rigged on deck for them. But by the looks of it, they're already in stout containers, look." Walters replied, pointing to a large box being lowered into the first hold.

"Better stow them in No4 hold aft, that way I can partition them off more easily. Not only that, it keeps the explosives apart."

"Yes, that's fine by me." was the reply, as the 2nd shouted his orders to the winch-men and cargo handlers.

The ammunition was duly loaded and the barges taken away, before the ship got under power and steaming her way slowly towards an empty jetty ahead of them.

Ordinarily, John would be on the foc'sle for harbour manoeuvres, but was too busy below with his men. He went aft to see how Menzies was getting on in the after holds.

He inspected the work done and was satisfied with him.

"Well done Menzies, that's it for now. We've got the brackets and the drop down flaps ready. All the sailors have to do is drop the partition boards into those grooves, then drop the flaps down on top of the vehicles as each layer is completed. Make sure your men stow everything away before you get turned in. I'll see you at 0700, probably in the dining room." he advised.

"Cheers 3rd, the men did work well. Had a bit of a problem with the welding gear, but all sorted once we got new rods and full gas bottles. See you later then." Menzies said cheerfully, leaving John to have one last look around before he left to see Lee.

"Tansey! All drawings and modifications completed. The full picture will take place as we load the rest of the cargo. Care to take a look?"

"Not necessary John. I'm quite happy with what I've already seen. Good plan of yours though. Don't forget to hand back your drawings and notes to for checking when he inspects it all."

"He'll only get what was on the original drawings, but should see the alterations as you did. He'll probably bollock me for not sticking to the drawings, but will appreciate them non-the-less."

"Need I remind you its company policy to hand over all inventions and other suggestions. But then, it's a fool that does that." Lee said with a smile, but let the matter drop.

"See you at 0700 for the ongoing inspection John. Your friend McPhee will be here to see that all is well before announcing us fit for sea."

"3rd! Its 0645, and you're required by the 2nd mate." the steward announced softly, shaking John awake.

"That time already steward? Any chance of a cuppa?"

"I'll have one ready for you in a minute. Did your friend show up after?"

"Yes, and thanks for that steward. We had a good meeting. "

"I gather from the grapevine that we're sailing very soon, and my friends ashore told me that there's some lovely soldiers coming on board, just for the ride. How lovely, they can ride my boat anytime."

"Don't get too excited steward, they're probably a bunch of hairy arsed marines out to do somebody no good. Anyway how did you learn that info? So much for loose lips."

"Loose lips and everything else too I hope." the steward replied, giving John his cup of tea.

"Here you are. It should do you until breakfast at 0830."

John took the hot steaming cup of tea off the steward and sipped it slowly to savour the flavour of his favourite tea, Indian Prince. He ate his buttered toast as he was dressing until he was dressed for the day, and drank the last from his cup, before he donned his cap and made his way out onto the weather deck and the gangway head.

"Morning 3rd. Our cargo will be arriving by train shortly, so we have the chance of getting organised." Walters greeted cheerfully.

"Morning 2nd. It looks like a lousy morning for it too. Any sight of the inspection team yet?"

"The captain and the dockyard team should be here soon. Probably will watch what we'll be up to as the cargo is loaded." John nodded his reply and left the gangway to Walters and went forward to muster his stokers working party.

"Morning Menzies. You know what to do aft. Make sure you have each deck level separation bulkheads fitted with their fire hoses. Once the main hold is secure, shut the main water-tight hatches, and isolate them off the circuits."

"Aye 3rd. But shouldn't we put suction hoses instead?"

"Due to the holds being put into smaller compartments, with low deck-heads within a larger compartment. If we get holed which we won't be able to do much about, but any flooding will be contained within that small area. But should there be a fire, then we could contain its spread to that small area, instead of losing the entire cargo. Its called good damage control, Menzies. The 2nd will be on the aft cargo deck if you get any problems, as I've got the chief my end."

"Cheers 3rd," see you later!" Menzies said with a nod and left with his working party.

"Morning 3rd, lets see what you've got!" Jones said gruffly, as John arrived with his arms full of drawings.

"Morning chief! All organised, and ready for the cargo. You will see just what is what when it's stowed on board."

"Yes, well it'd better be, for your sake. We've got the chief dockyard superintendent and the captain coming up the gangway to see it working." Jones responded, taking his dustbin sized pipe out of his mouth, and used it to point towards the gangway.

The inspection team took several minutes to arrive, as the first vehicle was being hoisted aboard.

"Hold that there. I want to see the hold first!" Blayden shouted to the dockyard crane operator.

The operator responded with a wave of his hand and stopped the crane, with the vehicle suspended in mid-air.

"Morning 3rd engineer Grey! Understand you've implemented the designed plans. Hope it didn't take you too long to do." McPhee greeted pleasantly when he arrived with two others who were part of his team.

"No problem. I have already sealed off the ammo, and am ready to show you how the box system works with these trucks."

"Good man. But I too must inspect your work. Chief Engineer, I have a copy of the plans, same as yours, so if you care to accompany me." McPhee replied before he and Jones joined Blayden by stepping onto a cargo pallet to be lowered down into the depths of the hold.

There seemed to be a pause in all activity until the three men re-appeared back onto the main deck again.

"Right 2nd mate. Get the cargo on board if you please." Blayden commanded, where-upon the 2nd waved his hands over his head to the crane operator to commence lowering the still suspended armoured vehicle.

As each deck level was filled, the cross struts, props, dividing walls and deck flaps were placed and secured, before the next layer of vehicles were lowered down. This went on until the entire first hold was completely filled and the hatches battened down. A large crate was put on top of the hatch cover, which stated that it was a light tank. When the second hold got loaded and secured in the same way, the inspection team clapped their hands in approval of what they'd seen.

"All is well so far 3rd. But we need an internal inspection too." McPhee said delightedly, but much to the annoyance of Jones.

"Some of what I saw does not appear on the drawings 3rd. Who gave you the nod to amend them or alter them?"

"Steady on chief. The plans are good, its just that 3rd engineer Grey saw he needed a few modifications added on to make them work as good as they are now." McPhee countered.

"As long as my ship is seaworthy and no possibility of cargo shift, then I don't care. My problem is where to put the extra men." Blayden muttered.

"I've got a specially prefabricated compartment for the men, as the officers were presumed to be staying in the passengers cabins." John replied swiftly, pointing his finger to one of the plans that Jones was holding out.

"We'll come to that later. How's your team doing aft Mr McPhee?" Blayden asked.

"Here they are now captain. My deputy will give you his report."

"Glad you've decided to put extra fire hoses in with the whiz-bang box compartment. You'll have to place extra steel bands around the deck cargo of oil drums, though. Apart from that, all is well as far as we are concerned." the deputy announced.

Blayden just nodded, but gave Jones a sideways glance at the mention of the fire hoses.

"Good. Then we can see what its like after the last hatch is secured." Blayden conceded as the inspection team walked back across the for'ard cargo deck and made their way up to the bridge.

It took a further two hours before the entire ship was loaded, and for the long, now empty train wagons to be shunted away.

John had his breakfast and was relaxing on the bridge wing looking around the harbour, and wondering what the place was like.

'Maybe next time' he thought, smoking yet another cigarette.

"Morning John, I thought I'd find you up here. We'll be taking passengers on board soon, but we're required in the saloon for a meeting with Belverley and company." Lee greeted, calling up to John from the bottom of the ladder.

John flicked his cigarette end over the side, and responded to Lee's information.

"Morning Tansey. We showed them this morning, and McPhee went away very happy. So what's the meeting for?" he asked, then swiftly moved down the steep ladder.

"Usual pre-voyage meeting from the mad monk, and probably the riot act from Belverley again, but better look lively John."

Both men arrived into the saloon and took their customary positions at the table before Blayden, Jones and the ship owners came in, in single file as if playing 'follow the leader'.

John managed to slip Larter's lighter to him and whispered in his ear, before everybody was called to pay attention to the speaker.

Belverley opened the meeting by praising the officers for their hard work and efforts to get the ship ready for sea in almost record time. He went on to explain the need for the change of cargo and that whilst the UK is still at war out in the orient, every ship had to do its share of duties no matter what.

When he finished he handed the 'chair' over to Blayden, who explained about the voyage and what was required of each officer, let alone the men. The dangerous cargoes on board; extra smoking prohibitions, and other such relevant items.

John looked at his watch whilst listening to Blayden drone on, and realised that not one drink could be seen at the table, save for glasses of water in front of everybody.

'Let's hope he doesn't start a prayer meeting too' he thought, slowly gazing around the room at the equally bored officers sitting with him.

Mr Lowther, who is Belverley's finance advisor, spoke of the extra pay each man would be earning, which drew a half-hearted cheer from the room, before Belverley concluded the meeting by wishing everybody good luck.

The speakers trooped out again as they came in, Blayden leading the way, but Jones stopped behind and called John over to speak to him.

"Grey. You have something for me, like a few drawings or something?" Jones prompted.

John was taken by surprise and answered in such a manner.

"Now don't play games with me 3rd. My mate Cresswell told me all about you. So come on, hand them over."

"Chief, I don't understand what you're on about for I have neither a drawing nor a something that you accuse me of." John lied, to protect himself.

"You must have something to be able to implement those alterations to the cargo deck plans. How else could you do such a stunt?"

"Chief! All I did was to go by the drawings, but had to improvise as I went along, otherwise we would not have had a successful inspection. I was not able to make notes or sketches as time was against me, that's why I haven't anything to hand over."

"I smell a rat here, Grey! I've got my beady eye on you. One false move and I'll get you, do you understand me!" Jones snarled.

"Now look here chief! We're still alongside the jetty; all you've got to do is call the inspection team back with their drawings, the same ones you've got. Maybe then you'll believe me and be satisfied." John said angrily whilst he looked intently at Jones' face.

"Besides, all you've got to do is make your own and add them to your set of drawings. That way it'll be a chief engineer that will take the credit, not a mere 3rd."

Jones stared at John for a moment and John could see the recognition of what he said in Jones' eyes, as the proverbial penny dropped into Jones' brain.

"That's for me to decide and for you to get on with your work. Remember, I've still got my beady eye on you Grey." Jones snorted, then stormed off to join Blayden and the others.
John shrugged his shoulders and went the opposite way, to be met by Lee, and Larter.

"What was that all about John, as if I didn't know" Lee said with concern on his face.

"You still sailing close to the wind John?" Larter asked, when he arrived on the scene.

"I don't know what you mean, but I've got my beady eye on you lot." John replied, mimicking Jones phrase, which made the others laugh.

"Well, he means it John, so be careful. Just keep your head down and be on your toes for the rest of this part of the voyage, and all will be well. Trust me, because I know Jones better than he would like to think." Lee said quietly.

"Yes John, we don't want to come and rescue you after he's stranded you on some deserted beach or other. Saving its Barbados or anywhere else in the Caribbean." Larter smiled.

"And thanks for finding my new lighter, it was a special gift from you know who." He added.

"Just as well I know the inscription then Bruce." John laughed as they sauntered out of the saloon and off to their own duties.

John was on the foc'sle when he saw Menzies approaching him in a great hurry.

"3rd. We've got a problem with the soldiers cabin, better come and look." Menzies said anxiously.

"What's the problem 4th?" John quizzed.

"We've used a cargo vent system as opposed to a cabin one, I think."

John looked at Menzies for a moment and feeling very unhurried.

"Ah yes, I remember. It's a single stage axial flow fan as opposed to a double. Ideally it should be an Air Conditioning Unit (a.c.u.) but this ship is not yet fitted with such beasts." he explained.

"We don't have a spare one on board so use the phone on the gangway and get hold of Mr McPhee for me. Do it now as we've not long before we sail. I'll wait for you down there, but don't take no for an answer." John ordered, sending Menzies swiftly away to the waist deck and the gangway.

"3rd Engineer to the bridge", came the terse metallic voice over the ships tannoy system, which prompted John to comply.

He arrived into the bridge and was met by Danvers and an irate army officer.

"3rd Engineer, we have a problem to say the least with our guests accommodation in No 3 cargo hold..." Danvers started, but was over-shouted by the army officer.

"My men are being suffocated in that hell-hole down there, and that you, so I'm told, are responsible for it. Get if fixed right now or I'll shove a bayonet so far up your arse you'll be eating tonsils for a week." the red-faced man shouted.

John just stood and looked at this spectre that reminded him of Cresswell, then coolly turned to Danvers and said quietly.

"First mate, be advised that this matter has only just been brought to my attention, but is being seen to even as I speak."

"Well don't just stand there, get on with it man. My men are down there, not yours!" the army officer interjected loudly again, but was ignored again by John.

"Damn you man!" the irate man shouted as he started to draw his commando knife from its sheath strapped to his brown leather belt.

"What have you got in mind 3rd?" Danvers asked quickly and moved to restrain the man.

"Actually first mate, unless the dockyard has the spares that I need then there's nothing I can do about it. In fact neither can the Chief, nor all the kings men. And in case you ask, yes, I'm waiting for 4th engineer Menzies to come back with that information." John said directly into the face of the army officer, who tried to wrestle his way out of the grip of Danvers.

Menzies came sprinting into the bridge and in gasping breaths told John that McPhee would be bringing the replacement and other spares with him when he arrived in about 2 hours from now.

"That means we have a delayed sailing time, 3rd!" Danvers stated, pushing the army officer away from them.

"You sir had better take charge of yourself or you will not be sailing on this vessel. Now get below and tell your men to assemble in the saloon and wait until our engineers fix the problem." Danvers said crossly as the army officer left the bridge muttering to himself.

"Thank you Menzies, we'll get the old one stripped down and ready for those spares. But I wonder what the others could be, and why is McPhee coming on board himself?" John asked more to himself as the two engineers left the bridge to Danvers and his charts.

"This is a good time to learn Menzies, and don't forget to make some decent sketches in your log-book for the 2nd." John stated, with both men working in unison to remove the offending machinery.

A soldier approached them and told them that the spares had arrived and that some of his men were bringing it down to them. John thanked the soldier and told Menzies to have a rest until then.

When the new machinery arrived, it was much better than John had envisaged, in comparison with the old and almost clapped out machinery dotted around the ship.

"Here we are Menzies. Just follow my lead and do exactly what I tell you." John advised, and started to install the vital machine.

It took them about an hour to install and test, then finally wrap up their tools and clear away.

"That's yet another fine piece of engineering you've been taught Menzies. Hope you find it useful some day. Now, get the rest stowed away before you finish for grub. Report to me in about an hour, as I've got my report to you know who, including Uncle Tom Cobly and all." John advised with a wink and wiping his hands on yet another rag before he made his way along the passageway and up towards the bridge where everybody was waiting for him.

"Ventilation system installed, and working satisfactorily. I shall make my full report in the customary manner but in the meantime the men can now return to their accommodation." John stated loudly and calmly to the sea of faces before him.

"Well done 3rd! I've brought a few little extras for you that you will need, that I had noticed during my inspection this morning." McPhee said gleefully, and much to the chagrin of Jones.

"I'll expect a full diagrammatic account of what you did, and that will include any other spare part installation carried out on this vessel." Jones grunted.

"It seems you've struck yet again Grey. Circumvented yet another awkward moment, and one that perhaps our army friends will be grateful to you for." Belverley said evenly, puffing furiously from the large cigar dangling from his mouth.

'Now where have I seen those cigars before' John thought, standing to face the very people who were praising him now instead of trying to lynch him had he not succeeded.

"Perhaps we can get on with the business of sailing now gentlemen, so kindly leave my bridge for me to do my work." Blayden commanded, with a wave of his arm to dismiss them.

"3rd! Stand fast!" Blayden ordered.

"I've looked at the new plans and shall we say 'alterations' to my ship. It appears that you've strengthened my ship with these matchbox type of compartments. But what if I want to inspect one of them or get to a part of the ship for some reason or another?" Blayden asked, and then beckoned John over to a large scale drawing of the ship that he had spread out on the chart table.

"Apart from the ammunition layers in 1 and 2 holds which are sealed and tack welded down, you are able to move through the rest of the holds, but in maze-like fashion. I have made a detailed drawing of how to negotiate them, which the army engineer has, but which would be used only for their equipment checks and any maintenance needed. That type of access is only about 5 feet high and two feet wide in places, but to access stem to stern during foul weather, I have made an aisle 6foot high by 3foot wide, each side of the holds. Using the starboard side going for'ard, and port- side going aft." John replied, tracing the routes over the drawing with his finger, for Blayden to see.

Blayden nodded as he looked more closely at the drawing for a little while.

"You've done well Grey, but you'll have to mark on this drawing exactly where it goes and where it stops." Blayden said, offering his pen to John to use.

It took only a couple of minutes to alter the drawing before the pen was handed back.

"There, that should do you. Now I can get on with my own work too captain?"

"Yes 3rd. That will be all." Blayden replied, dismissing him with the customary wave of his arm.

Chapter VI
A Pack Of Cards

Yet again the North Atlantic decided to play with the man-made object that dared to enter its back yard, sending big lumps of waves to wait and gang up on the ship when she left the calm waters of the harbour.

The ship turned due south from Halifax and out into the vast open spaces of the black and grey marbled ocean, to swim her way to much warmer and friendlier waters of the Caribbean. But the Atlantic was always there to see that some ships never arrived at her destination port, in its own way of culling men and ships to keep the numbers down.

John was finishing his evening meal after his deck rounds when Lee sat next to him with a ream of drawings and notes.

"Hello John, guess what I've got for you?" Lee teased, dumping the pile down next to him.

John looked at the pile, then at Lee and smiled.

"I wondered when you'd give me this lot. Judging by the topic of the first diagram, it's the ships ventilation system, and the notes are probably from the chief for me to follow. Is that so Tansey?"

"More or less, except that the bottom lot are from McPhee. I've looked through them all and will let you handle it. Any problems then give me a shout, as I've got a few headaches of my own to sort out."

"Have I still got Menzies in tow, or am I solo?"

"No Menzies has been given engine-room watches for this leg, but I can spare you a stoker or two as and when."

"Pity, because I thought I was getting somewhere with him. Still, he needs his watch-keeping certificate more. I will need one stoker full time, Tansey. Probably a good welder, if that's possible."

"See what I can do John, but keep me informed. See you later." Lee concluded, leaving John to finish his meal.

As John was leaving the dining room with the bundle of papers, the ship lurched as if to remind everybody on board that she had hit yet another mile-stone. He staggered and fell heavily to the deck, with his papers fluttering around and scattered everywhere.

Fortunately for him a soldier who was only a few feet away on his way into the dining room, stopped and helped John back onto his feet.

"You all right?" he asked, as John brushed himself down and rubbed his elbow.

"Yes thanks. My arm took the fall, but I'll be okay in a moment. All I've got to do now is pick up this lot and try to make sense of it." John replied, feeling more foolish than hurt.

"I've heard of a shuffling a pack of cards, but you've certainly mixed your papers up good and proper. Here, I'll give you a hand."

Both men picked up the papers, which were put into their own little piles of drawings and notes, before they were satisfied.

"Thank you for your help, maybe a glass of wine in the saloon afterwards?" John offered.

"That sounds good to me. But first, judging by your paper-work are you an engineer?"

"Yes. I'm the 3rd engineer on board. John Grey."

"Pleased to meet you Grey, I'm Staff sergeant Ford, of the Royal Canadian Engineer corps. You must have been the one who fixed my lads Billet for them."

"That's my job on board. I see to all machinery that is not within the confines of the engine or motor room. This paper-work as you call it, is my headache for our trip south. It outlines my work to be done, which in turn, creates yet another mountain of paper-work for the chief engineer and the ship owners."

"How many men do you have to do all this, 10, 20?"

John chuckled, but still winced at a sudden pain down his arm.

"On my own, but with maybe the odd stoker to help. To you that means a mechanical engineer."

"Yes, I'm familiar with the phrase, and in fact I'm more at home 'at sea' than on land. That's due to the fact that my old mans' got a marine engine and engineering concern up in the Great Lakes. But diesel, or in fact, steam engines that run on land is almost the same as those that run at sea, so I chose the solid ground ones instead." Ford explained.

"Can't fault your logic there Ford. Must go now, and thanks for helping me."

"Call me Ben. I'd be grateful to you if you'd let me help you. Maybe I'd get to see some different machinery other than tank engines or a tank carrier's gear box."

John turned to Ford, and thought for a moment on the prospect of having his own private repair team other than welders.

"That sounds good to me, er, Ben. But I'll have to clear it with my chief engineer. I'll see you in the saloon in about an hour for that drink and let you know."

"Why, that's great. I'll be able to get some of my lads off their backsides and earning their way instead of lazing around fretting their way back to land. See you then."

John dumped his pile of papers onto his little table-cum-desk and made straight to Lee's cabin to see if this new idea would be allowed.

"Come in!" Lee responded to John's knock.

"It's me Tansey. I need your advise on a certain protocol." John started, and then explained his mission.

"There's no problem there John, at least I have no objections and I doubt the army would either. In fact, will jump at the chance being several stokers short on this trip, due to some of them jumping ship in Halifax. That was my headache that I told you about. The other thing and why he would agree to it, is that should anything go wrong, you take the can and would end any career as an engineer you might have in mind. That said, I wish you luck, but don't forget to have a word with the army boss on board, and a special clearance with your friend McPhee."

John thanked Lee and went to seek Jones out to get this new arrangement of working on board, underway.

"3rd! Just the man I want to see." Jones stated bumptious.

"It seems that we did well back in Halifax, and thanks to McPhee being around, we have some very nice pieces of machinery for you to install, before we arrive the other end. Unfortunately for you, you'll have to do it all yourself as I can't spare anybody." he announced with a smirk.

"Yes, I got your package from the 2nd, and am about to wade through your instructions. But I've really come to see you about something that I need your permission to do." John said calmly, and then explained what it was.

Jones sat in his big armchair, puffing away at his pipe listening to John, nodding his head at the points raised.

"I've no objections 3rd, because of two things. One is that with the help of some real engineers you will be able to complete these tasks much earlier. And two is that should anything go wrong, and bearing in mind we've got Mr McPhee on board, you will take the rap for it. In short, you're days at sea would be over, or you'd never get any higher than a 3rd for as long as your arse looks downwards." Jones replied sarcastically.

"Well as long as I've got your permission, and that of the army, that's all I need. I'll still keep my daily rounds and my daily reports going, but you'd have to come and inspect / accept my work once the machinery has been installed."

"That's fair enough Grey. Before you go, we'll be meeting the ship owners in our next port of call, so be prepared if the shit hits the fan. That will be all." Jones said, dismissing John with a wave of his pipe-filled hand.

John arrived into the saloon feeling elated at the prospect of having his own gang of men working for him, and also a new working practice that he would write down for any future occasions, if it ever happened again.

"Hello John, grab a pew. What're you having?" Larter greeted, as he stood up to go to the bar.

"Usual for me Bruce, and get me a packet of Woodbines please, I could do with a good smoke." John requested, sitting down in one of the very few empty chairs in the saloon.

He looked slowly around the smoke filled room to see if Ford was present, and noticed that there were several other passengers on board other than the army.

Larter arrived with John's drink and sat down heavily next to him.

"Where the dickens did these passengers come from, Bruce?" John asked, full of surprise.

"It seems that the army brings all its baggage with it, family included, John. In this corner ladies and gentlemen, are the officers with their ladies, over in the blue corner are their senior ratings and their wives, and in the red corner are the squaddies with their women." Larter said in the manner of what a boxing match commentator would announce.

"We get what's left!" Lee finished, arriving alongside Larter.

"Hello Tansey. You were right about 'Spanners'. I've been given the go ahead, and intend starting sometime tomorrow."

"What's this John?" Larter asked with raised eyebrows.
John briefly explained what he was planning and got a pat on the back when he finished.

"I always said that you'd be a good engineer John, that's why me and Andy agreed to help you a long way back in Belfast." Larter said pleasantly, which gave John a tingling sensation running up his spine at the very mention of their first meeting that seemed several lifetimes ago.

The three officers talked quietly whilst enjoying their holiday for drinking, as Blayden only allowed it whilst passengers were on board.

"Engineer Grey?" a gruff voice asked from behind him.

He turned around and saw the now very calm officer that he had met on the bridge, and stood up to face him.

"I am! Who are you and state your business?" John said evenly, and wondered why he had picked up that stock phrase of questioning.

"I'm the Officer in command of this unit. I met you earlier today if you remember."

"Ah yes. The man with the toothpick stuck in his trousers belt. What can I do for you?"

"More to the point, what can I do for you? I understand you've been talking to my regimental engineer, Staff sergeant Ford."

"Yes, go on." John prompted.

"I think it is a good idea you've concocted with him. It will keep my men occupied during this long transit. We have some of our own tools and equipment separate from those crated up in the cargo holds, should you need them. Just keep me informed, that's all I ask."

"That's kind of you, but I have all the tools I need, it's just the skilled manpower I hope to use. I hope to see Sergeant Ford later on this evening and to start after lifeboat drill in the morning."

The man nodded his head and returned to his table, as John sat down with his own friends.

Ford arrived some time later and had a drink with John and his friends, before they got down to business and finalised a plan that was agreeable to both men.

Chapter VII
Deal

The night was a very uncomfortable, storm-tossed one, and the passengers were feeling uneasy, let alone being very seasick. All the passengers were made to wear their life jackets, which also made life more difficult for them, but at least they were in the warm and safely tucked up in their cabins.

The ship shuddered and shook as it corkscrewed its way through the waves that was just yet another night at home for the ocean. The crew were kept busy all night, trying to keep the deck cargo from leaving the ship without permission, as they slung yet another steel hawser over it and lashed it all down even tighter. Or making certain that no between deck catastrophe would befall them, especially as there was a good 50 tons of whizz-bangs on board, let alone the 1,000 tons of high explosives and ammunition.

This kept the crew on edge until the dawn of what was a lovely and bright day, and where the sea had somehow got tired of toying with the ship and gone to lie down for a while, as the water was almost as smooth as glass.

John woke with a start, feeling the steward shaking him roughly.

"It's 0700, 3rd. Time for ship's officers breakfast slot!" the steward announced wearily.

"Then I'd better get it before the rest of the gannets arrive. What's on the menu?"

"Usual fodder, but there'll be lots of passenger grub available, as most of them won't be having any."

"Need I ask, steward. Probably got their sea-sickness bags lashed to their faces instead, yes?"

"Yes, poor lambs. But at least I can get my head down for a while, as I've been up seeing to them. Like flaming Florence Nightingale I was. Up down, up down, back and fore to the sick bay for tablets, bandages for nose bleeds or treating cuts and bruises at they got banged about in their cabins. Glad it's a nice peaceful morning for everybody to get back to normal, before it hits us again."

John realised that the ship was in the eye of the storm and he had only a few hours to get his work done, and start his new project.

"Thanks steward. Never mind my cabin, I'll see to it later. Get your head down as you said."

The dining room was almost a wreck, with tables and chairs strewn everywhere and covered in broken china and cutlery, as John picked a chair up and carried it to a large table where other officers were tucking into their food.

"Morning 3rd, we've got a decent selection this morning. Recommend the poached egg on your yellow peril." Southgate breezed.

"Morning all!" John greeted.

"Naw, I'll stick to my bacon and sausage rolls thanks."

"We've got a problem with No 3 hold, 3rd layer down. The decking is buckling, and I think perhaps it's those duff welding rods we used that is causing it." Menzies informed.

John looked puzzled for the moment before he recalled what Menzies said about it yesterday.

"Thank goodness you know the problem 4th, perhaps you'll see to it after your breakfast?"

"Sorry 3rd, I'm required down the engine-room as soon as I've finished my breakfast. Maybe the army boys might help out if you ask them."

"Yes, that's a good idea." John replied then spoke to the steward as he served John's food.

"Steward, do me a favour and ask staff sergeant Ford, I think he's in cabin 21, to come and see me. Now if possible."

The steward nodded his head and went on the requested errand, then came back a few minutes later with Ford.

"Morning Staff, glad you were able to see me. Sit down and have a good early breakfast while you're here." John greeted, dragging another chair over to the table and the steward set him a place.

"Morning 3rd, yes that sounds nice." Ford agreed with a nod in acknowledgement to the other officers at the table.

Ford ate his breakfast whilst John Lit enjoyed a silent, after meal cigarette, until Ford was finished for him to light up too.

"I am due to go on my morning inspection and I thought you might like to accompany me. But first, we have a problem with an internal deck in No 4 hold that needs some welding. Have you got any welders in amongst your lot Ben?"

Ford nodded and quoted a few names, enough to satisfy him.

"When you're ready, we'll go so that I can show you what is needed. By that time, the men will have had their breakfast and you can fetch them."

Ford stood up, drunk the last of his tea, picked up his cap and said: "Let's go John. I believe in getting things done first as last. That way it saves a lot of trouble and maybe a few lives into the bargain."

They made their way down to the soldier's accommodation where Ford detailed off 2 soldiers to come with them.

When they arrived at the problem that Menzies had reported, John took a quick assessment and told Ford what was required and where to find the welding equipment.

"Not a problem John. My two lads are the finest welders in the corps and will weld all day if necessary. Leave it to them." Ford replied, before he gave his orders to the two men.

"And now for the main course John. Lets do your rounds!"

John chuckled and thought of his mystery trip around his first ship with 2nd engineer Day, but moved swiftly back up onto the main deck where he would begin.

John took Ford from stem to stern, inside and out and ended up on the boat deck, where they stopped for a smoke and a breather.

"I see you took some notes. Lets hope they'll come in useful some day. Is there anything you need to clarify or were my explanations sufficient?"

"By heck John, a good instructor you'd make I'd say. Mind you, just as well I know a few things about machinery too. One thing though, and something you might appreciate. Your capstan needs modifying, or you'll spend ages and lots of money in repairing it all the time. Here's a drawing that I've prepared for you. A bit crude but you'll understand the main gist of it." Ford replied, handing John a small drawing and instructions.

John looked at it and instantly recognised what Ford was telling him, but asked about it none the less.

"Simple, all you need is a neutral gear. That will stop the undue wear and tear on the brake lever. Our tank transporters have 29 gears for the driver to cope with, so I think your sailors can cope with just one extra to make up the 5 needed."

"Indeed Ben, if only it was that simple." John agreed then looked at his watch.

"It's 9.30 and time for me to make my report to the captain, but I need to know about that welding job first."

"On my way. Meet you here in about five minutes?"

John nodded and watched the man hurry down the companion-way ladder before he poked his head into the radio shack.

"Morning Bruce, Paul! What's the weather like for today?" he asked politely.

"We've got about another three hours before that storm hits us. Ordinarily this leg is only two to three days, but we're miles off course and we'll be about a day late arriving at Bermuda." Southgate announced, taking off his headphones and throw them onto his desk.

"Bermuda? I thought our first stop was Barbados." John asked non-plussed, then realised that McPhee and his assistant were to disembark there.

"So you reckon another three days on top then, Paul. Well let's hope we sail into some good weather to give me a chance to get our vent system sorted and before McPhee leaves us."

"Amen to all that, John!" Larter concluded, as he finished writing in his operator's logbook.

60

"Well, must go. Rounds report and all that." John sighed and left his friends to wait for Ford.

Ford came trotting up and told John that the job had been completed and to his satisfaction. The only thing was that the heavy tank-transporter had been damaged during the storm, which meant they were not able to get a certain part for it until they got their workshops operating again.

John told him that he'd make them a part if necessary, providing he had the right metals. Then asked Ford to wait for him until he came back from the bridge.

"Deck machinery satisfactory. 'Tween deck inspection found a buckled false deck due to weld failure. Work now completed and satisfactory, Captain"

"Thank you 3rd. Just as well you've got it done, as we're about to have round two of that storm. Boat drill might have to be cancelled until we get out the other end, so you can get on with something else."

John nodded and left the bridge but spotted McPhee coming onto it, and stopped to speak to him.

He told McPhee the brief outline of his plan and asked if he would 'sit in' on it, and make a report on the progress or outcome of it.

"Certainly John. Give me about half an hour and meet me in the passengers dining room." McPhee said with delight, as John nodded and finally left the bridge, to meet up with Ford again.

"Right Ben. We've got the heavy mob joining us shortly, so time to get your men detailed off and meet up with me in the passenger dining room in about 10 minutes. I'll go and get the stack of paper-work" John suggested.

Ford nodded his head and went to collect his men.

The dining room had been cleaned and put back to order again as John walked in, and met the soldiers sitting around a large table, taking their ease, with Ford sitting in front of them and making small talk.

"Men, this is 3rd engineer Grey" Ford announced, then introduced him to the other sergeants and soldiers.

John put his stack of papers onto a separate table, and picked up a pile of cardboard squares, ready to deliver his plan to the men, when McPhee entered the room, whereupon John introduced him to the soldiers.

McPhee sat in a large chair and invited John to commence.

"Now that we're all here, I can begin." John announced, explaining the outline of the task ahead of them. He asked for any questions before he carried on, until he came to the pile of cardboard.

"Here is the 'Ace', that will be you Fergus. Here is the 'King', that will be me.

The 'Queen' can be the drawings of the machinery. Staff Sergeant Ford, you are the 'Jack'. The 'Ten' is the test and inspection" John stated, laying each card onto the table in front of him, and explained who was who, did what, and when. He concluded by saying,

"Those are the cards, and that is the deal." then asked if there were any questions, but only McPhee offered one.

"In view of the weather conditions, and my limited time on board, what would your expectations be if this was a failure or at least you were not able to complete sufficient amount of work for me to offer my report?"

John thought for a moment, but was cheered on by the soldiers, who stated that they would make sure the work was done, which gave him the answer.

"I think you have your answer Fergus. I'll have some drawings and notations ready for you before your feet touch dry land, see if we don't." John stated bravely.

McPhee stood up and went over to the table, picked up his card and replied.

"Well, I'm in gentlemen. It's about time we had a good card game, and I think we can all play this one. Now I intend to show you how."

John smiled at the encouragement, watching the soldiers take their allocated cards.

"One thing though, everybody. The weather is going to be rough again and the boat drill has been brought forward now instead of being cancelled. I want you all to muster in the area of No3 hold, just behind your accommodation, in about 30 minutes. That will give you time to have a cuppa and a smoke up on deck if you want. But that's where we will operate from because that's where the spare machines are, and where I shall give your instructional session." John stated, but conferred with Ford on that matter, who agreed whole-heartedly.

Thus John had set the scene and the start of his new project that would, unbeknown to him, be yet another feather in his cap in years to come.

Ford accompanied John to the saloon for their break, before going below to meet the men.

As they reached the men, the tannoy system announced that there would be a boat drill in five minutes, and on hearing the ships horn all passengers were to proceed up to the saloon.

"This is a drill men, but if any of you wish to join your family in the saloon then do so now." John announced, but nobody moved.

"It's all right John, I and the rest of us are chosen because we are single." Ford said quietly.

"Fair enough men! We're all good swimmers then, so lets commence." John smiled and got four men to open the first crate of machinery and laid it out for everybody to see.

John explained the vital parts of the machine, and pointed to one already in use just above their heads, to show how they would be taken down and remounted.

The session was completed and questions answered just in time for John to dismiss them for lunch.

"After lunch, muster back down here again, in say 1 hour from now, and don't be adrift, er, I mean late." He smiled, remembering those words, being his very first order from Cresswell.

Chapter VIII
Queer Street

John went to see Jones about his daily report, but was told he was too busy to bother with trivial details at a time like this. He had a sick engine that need nursing, never mind the comforts of the passengers.

"I'll come back later then chief!" John replied, relieved, because all he was going to do was tell Jones that he didn't have time to write his report anyway. So he went down to meet the men again, who were waiting for him.

"Before you start, make sure you've got your 'Queen' with you." John announced. In return, he was met with whistles, and banter from them, but continued after they had quietened down.

"Thank you men. As I was saying, and don't forget the jokers. Also to make sure you have sufficient lifting tackle and mats to put around for padding when the ship starts to perform again."

When the men got organised into their teams, John told them to follow him so he could show them which machine to start with.

The first machine was removed and taken away for refurbishing, with the spare one remounted in its place. Once it was tested and given a 'Ten', then they moved to the next one for it to be removed.

John had the men removing, cleaning, repairing, and remounting each faulty machine for several hours before the weather hit the ship for six once more. So he decided to calla halt and asked card 'one' who was the cook-cum-waiter, to get some grub for them all.

"Best go and see the steward, Julian. He'll fix you up but be careful of his, shall we say, shirt-lifter ways." John advised, making a limp-wrist gesture.

His statement created more banter from the men, but the soldier that was nominated with card 'One' just smiled and said in a lisping manner.

"Oh that's okay with me. I'm sure we'll get along quite the thing."

John looked at the departing soldier and was convinced he too minced around just like the steward, but shook his head and brought himself back to his task in hand.

The soldier came back, carrying with much difficulty, a large kettle full of tea, a string of tin mugs and a bag full of sandwiches and biscuits, which the men immediately relieved him from his goodies.

John and Ford sat on some tables made from the wooden packing cases and took their food.

"If you are all in the same unit Ben, how come there are different shoulder flashes on the men's uniform?"

"We on board are the advance party of the support units for the battalion. Myself, the other sergeant, plus the rest of the men in the repair teams are engineers. Then your card 'One' is in the catering corps; card 'Two' is in the service and supply corps; Then of course you've got a few signallers, pay clerks, medics, and so on. All except for a platoon of combatants to guard us until the main body arrives. The major, whom you've already met, is the Adjutant of the battalion, and the commanding officer's right hand man. The main body of the battalion will be arriving by troopship, probably a few days after we do, with the remainder of our equipment hopefully within the next two weeks of arriving." Ford explained.

"A fighting unit off to war, but how is it you're taking the families along?" John asked in puzzlement.

"We are only a relief battalion to the one in Georgetown B.G. which is being sent out to Hong Kong for further onward deployment. We're a Canadian unit and able to relieve the British Tommies anywhere other than out in the Orient. Not that it bothers us much, as we had a belly full of the last two punch ups." Ford said sombrely.

John nodded his head and realised the truth in what was said, and remembered Larter's own remark on the devastating war that ended less than a decade ago.

When the men had finished their break, John went through what had been done and referring to his pack of cards procedures, before he announced that although they had done well, they still had quite a lot to do before the 'ace' was played. Then when everybody had cleared and stowed everything away and cleaned up he announced.

"I will ask you all now to resume the work when the storm has gone. All of you have worked well, and both Staff sergeant Ford and I are very pleased with what you have done. All the machinery tested and now in good working order. Therefore, at my own expense, each one of you will be entitled to four bottles of beer, which you will obtain from the bar in the passenger saloon. However, that will be after evening meals, but please use your noddle and don't get drunk. In the meantime try and get some rest as it's going to be long night. Thank you men. Staff, a word when you're ready."

The mention of free beer was given a hearty cheer, and the men left the now empty space, leaving John and Ford alone.

"Ben, I'm hoping No 3 has kept a running log on what we did today, as I will need it for my own write up for the benefit of my chief engineers report. Also I need all the completed 'Queens' and 'Jokers' to give 'Ace' an update on our progress."

"Number 'Three'? That's the corporal in team two. I'll get it from him and bring it to your cabin just as soon as I've spoken to my men. He's already given me the 'queens' and 'jokers' for you, as I too operate in a similar fashion." Ford said quietly, handing the bundle of papers to John, who took them and stuffed them under his boiler suit top.

"Right then, Ben. I think we'd make a good team, and it was nice to have good company for a change. See you later then." John replied, for Ford to smile and left to see to his men.

* * *

A loud knock on the cabin door, followed by the reek of tobacco as an irate Jones came through it.

"Where's my daily report Grey? And what the hell have you been doing with the ventilation system. I've had the captain on my back all day as a result of the passengers complaining to him about it.

To overhaul that system normally takes a dozen men a good week to do, and even then it's alongside the dockyard. But not you Grey, oh no! You think that you, a mere 3rd engineer can do it within a few days and during a ruddy great storm too. For Christ sake man, I hope you know what you're doing, and that everything works. If not, and I've already warned you about it, you're right up queer street, make no bones about it. What have you to say for yourself Grey?" Jones shouted vehemently.

John sighed quietly; put his pen down and stood up to face this irate man in front of him.

"Chief, for a start, I saw you lunch time as normal, but you told me to go away, saying something about a sick engine and not wanting the likes of me disturbing you. As for …" John started but was interrupted by Jones.

"I did no such thing Grey! It's your duty to report to me every day at noon, and as I have not been given it, you haven't been near me to give it. Isn't that the truth of the matter?" Jones accused, glancing around John's neat and tidy cabin, trying to locate it from where he stood.

John spotted the glances and decided to play the man at his own game.

"I gave you my report which you threw onto your desk. You were smoking and were sitting in your big armchair at the time. It probably got mixed up in with the pile of engineering drawings that you had spread out over your desk. You even had a large almanac opened with several notes pinned to one of the pages, although why I don't know. But it was given to you as normal." he said, and remembered what he saw in Jones' cabin at the time.

Jones' eyes narrowed, and gave John a sideways glance as if to believe him.

"Be that as it may, but I can't find it to read it. You better make another one out and give it to me with tomorrows." Jones said defiantly, then added.

"I want a report concerning your activities today. I have to offer the captain something to appease the passengers, so lets have it."

"Chief, I'm in the process of making one out, but as I'm due to go on my rounds, I will give the captain a verbal report, and you a written one as usual."

Jones gave John that sideways look again, scratched his nose and said belligerently.

"I'm watching you Grey! Don't think you can pull one over me. I've got my beady eye on you, and don't your forget it."
John whispered the same words under his breath as Jones used his catch phrase, but fortunately a knock on the door and the steward entering the cabin interrupted them.

"Oops sorry chief, didn't know you shared cabins with your juniors?" the steward lisped, bringing in John's fresh laundry.
Jones went bright red, and then sneered at the steward as he passed hurriedly out of the door.

"I don't give a fart what you faggots and shirt-lifters do, just don't do it near me." he said sneeringly, barging past the two men.

"Ooh get her! Right tantrum chops, I'm sure." the steward replied, pouting his lips and turned back to face John again.

"He's quite a sweetie when you really know him. Here's your clean laundry, 3rd. Dinner will be a bit late again, due to problems in the galley." he said.

"Yes, thanks. And thanks for seeing to the army lad for me. Those sandwiches were just the ticket."

"Yes, he's such a nice boy. He's promised to show me his pots and pans later. I might just do that after supper, anything to please that's me!"

John just chuckled and sat down to complete his reports.

"Well if you excuse me steward, must get on. There's a drink behind the bar for you, from the men." he announced, for which the steward thanked him and left him to it.

The weather prevented John from doing his upper deck rounds, but made sure all was well with his charges before making his usual verbal report to the captain, who was in his day cabin talking to McPhee.

"All 'tween decks satisfactory except for a leak in the bow section. There appears to be a couple of sprung rivets, but I've put some quick acting cement around them to minimise the leakage."

"Never mind the confounded leaks, what have you being doing with the ship? I've had complaints all day from the passengers." Blayden roared.

"Now now captain! Grey is doing his best for them, surely they could put up with a minor discomfort until he finishes?" McPhee said disarmingly.

"Speaking of which Mr McPhee. In project terms, here is my written report along with the corresponding 'queens' and 'jokers'. They represent about a half of what is to be done, but I need you to give me a 'ten' on them as soon as possible." John replied smoothly, handing McPhee the paper work.

McPhee took the bundle and flicked through them and studied John's report before replying.

"I see what you're doing. You are using just one machine as a replacement, and using the old one after its been refurbished to cover the next one. Like a rolling refurbishment, instead of piece-meal shutdown as is done in the dockyard. Very clever indeed Grey, and I see you've concentrated on the passenger accommodation and the crew's accommodation first. Hmm! I want to inspect that right now if you will. I think you'd better come too captain."

"If need be, then I will." Blayden said angrily following the other two out into the bridge and down to the inspection areas.

After they had finished and returned back to the captain's day cabin, McPhee turned to Blayden and told him that what John had done was top quality work and that he had saved the ship owners thousands of pounds in repair bills. Then briefly related what John did on the *Brooklea,* a few years ago.

Blayden was surprised at this revelation concerning his own ship, and seemed to mellow a little, by replying.

"Well as long as you give me a certificate to state all is well Mr McPhee, then we'll say no more on the subject. You, 3rd can go now and rest up until the weather abates, before I want to see you again."

John nodded his head, and winked to McPhee, before he left the cabin and made his way back down to the saloon, to enjoy an evening in good company and the captain's permission to have some very rare time off.

Chapter IX
Trumped

As the ship was still in the grip of the storm that refused to let go of her; John was catching up with his paper work and preparing for the next round of repairs. He even had time to have a second look at what Ford had given him about the foc'sle capstan, and decided that it would be worth his while following it up, but would wait until he was next in Belfast. Also due to the fact that there was less activity in the galley, managed to fix the faulty ovens.

After the brief but hectic burst of activity, his free time seemed to drag because was always doing something, going somewhere, or seeing someone, so as it was only early afternoon, he decided to go and see Ford and his men.

"Hello Ben, how are the men, still with us?" John asked cheerfully as he approached Ford, who was reading a book at the time.

"Oh hello John. Yes, the lads are okay, and thank you for their drinks. What can I do for you?" Ford responded pleasantly, putting his book down and sitting up to receive his visitor.

"I have come to see what I can do for that vehicle of yours. The one that you told me about, er, the Diamond T, I think."

"Ah yes, we need a part made, and have the metal required, but all the rest is still cocooned within the vehicle until it is unpacked on the jetty. That's what we do with them all. We load them up with stores, so that we can take more with us on board. Like a Trojan horse if you like, John."

"I'm glad you told me that, as I was wondering just how you managed to squeeze all your equipment into one ship where it would probably need two. Now I know." John said with a smile, then added

"Tell me or give me a drawing of what you want, the metal to be used and I'll make you one in the workshop. We'll do it now if you're not doing anything in particular."

Ford sprang to his feet and led the way down to the hold to fetch what John asked for, as both made their way down into the engine room and the small compartment that constituted the ship's workshop.

"And I thought it was cramped in my workshop, so how do you manage John?" Ford asked with a whistle, seeing the cramped conditions in which John was starting to work under.

"It's easy when you know how Ben. I shall be about 30 minutes, so if you want to have a look around the engine room, go and speak to the 4th over there."

"Yes, thanks John, I'll do just that. It's been such a long time since seeing such engines in working order. Normally I get to see them as scrap metal." Ford shouted into John's ear.

John just made silent gestures in the universal language of such noisy places, and saw that Ford knew exactly what was being said as he left the workshop.

After both men left the workshop with the newly made part, replaced the broken part with it, and tested it, they made their way back to their respective cabins to clean up and met back up in the saloon for tea.

"Hello John, have you seen 'Spanners' lately?" Lee asked with concern.

"Hello Tansey, haven't seen you since yesterday morning, and no I haven't seen him since yesterday afternoon. Why ask?"

"We need all the air we can get in the motor room as it's getting too stuffy to work in it, and 'Spanners' is after your blood because of it. Did you make your daily report today?"

"No Tansey, because I was given time off as sanctioned by Blayden. Mr McPhee has been satisfied with my work and has a report to give to 'Spanners' when he's finished with it."

"Bloody hell John! He'll have your guts for garters for sure. If you've got some sort of report to give to me then at least it will be something, and better than nothing. 'Spanners' is strictly by the book man, and always keeps…"

"His beady eyes on us lot." John finished, parodying the chief again.

Lee shook his head slowly, and told John to keep a low profile until the weather cleared and hope that 'Spanners" sorts out his own problem with the main engines.

Ford listened to the cross talk and waited until Lee had left before he started.

"He must be your 2nd engineer, so this 'Spanners' bloke must be your chief. He sounds a right tartar, just like my own boss on the troop ship. Haven't you told your chief what we did and what we will complete once this ship has finished bouncing all over the place?"

John didn't have time to reply, before he heard a bellowing voice that sounded even more ominous in the almost empty saloon.

"Grey come here you! I want a word in your excuse for engineer's lugholes. Come to my cabin right now!" Jones shouted, beckoning John to come over to him.

"Here we bloody well go again, Ben. Do us a favour and fetch McPhee, then bring him to the chief's cabin, er, just down from mine." John whispered, moving slowly towards Jones, and followed him to the cabin.

"Shut the door Grey! Then tell me exactly where you have been since I saw you yesterday, and don't lie either." Jones demanded angrily.

John related exactly what happened, whom he spoke to and what was said in return, before Jones interrupted him.

"Don't you lie to me Grey. You could never have done all what you said. I know you're lying because of the bad air exchanges in the motor room. I'll bet you just wanted a few days off whilst the ship is fighting its way through a bigger storm than what we first met on leaving Liverpool. Isn't that right, Mr 3rd Engineer Grey! I told you that I had my beady eye on you, and I've found you wanting. You are not fit to even grace a 3rd officers uniform let alone an acting 5th, which if I have my way is

what you'll be by the time we leave Bermuda." Jones ranted on for a while,
as John just stood quietly waiting for any violence from Jones, because he had already gone through such a scene before.

'I wonder if I'm in the wrong shipping company, with all this hassle I keep getting. I wonder if all the shipping lines are the same for Ford to choose the army instead of life at sea?" he thought.

Jones was still ranting and raving when McPhee walked into the cabin with his 'Ace' card in one hand, and a folded piece of paper in the other, which made Jones stop dead in his tracks.

"Evening chief! I hear you've got a spot of bother with this upstart 3rd engineer." McPhee said nonchalantly, but gave John a sly wink.

"Mr McPhee, what are you doing in my cabin, you have no right to be here." Jones snapped, but it cut no ice with McPhee.

"I have come to check on the work the 3rd did for the benefit of your comfort and that of the rest of the passengers." McPhee said evenly, as he waved his 'Ace' card at him. Then went on to tell Jones almost what John had told him earlier, before he handed the piece of paper over to Jones.

Jones grabbed the piece of paper, read it quickly then ripped it up, and grabbed the ace card from McPhee and shredded that too.

"That's what I think of your report. I'm the chief engineer on board not you McPhee, and what I say goes. Now bugger off the pair of you and let a man do his duty." Jones snarled, trying to usher the two men out.

"Now now Jones. I have made that report in double triplicate, for the benefit of the captain, your ship owners, the 3rd here, and naturally for myself. It stands whether you like it or not." McPhee said ominously, pushing John before him and out of Jones' cabin.

As both men walked back to the saloon, McPhee turned to John with a twinkle in his eye.

"That was the 'Ace' of trumps, John. Your plan is working nicely, and I have no doubt that you'll have the rest completed by the time you reach your destination. However, in future, make sure you have one just like it, or people like Cresswell and his cronies like Jones here, will make mincemeat out of you. Should that happen then you'll never make 2nd, let alone the dizzy heights of what your relatives did in H&W's."

"Thank you for your support Fergus. I shall make certain of what you've told me, and I look forward to my copy of your report, as I just might need it sooner than I think." John said, shaking the outstretched hand of McPhee.

"It's a pleasure John. One thing more though! You might do better joining a new company, if you do, do it well and become a 2nd, then how about joining my crowd in the dockyard as one of my able assistants."

"Maybe I will do just that Fergus, providing you're still chief dockyard superintendent." John replied earnestly, and parting company in the saloon.

The saloon was starting to fill up with some of the passengers who were brave enough to negotiate the still very rocky ship, as John was joined by Larter and then by Ford.

"Hello Bruce, I'm up for a drink, what'll you have?" he asked as Ford arrived, John introduced the two men before going to get the drinks for the three of them.

The three men talked and exchanged smokes and got the rounds in as the evening wore on, and were generally enjoying themselves, when Southgate came in and joined them briefly.

"We've got good weather ahead within the next two hours or so, according to the figures on the weather signal. So it looks as if we can put a spurt on and reach Bermuda before we planned." Southgate volunteered.

"That's good. Maybe we can have a couple more days of sunshine as well to warm our bones up. Even an extra day alongside whilst the dockyard fixes our bow." John replied.

"Shades of the *Brooklea* John. We can re-visit that café and perhaps you could look up your old landlady in that hotel you stayed in." Larter quipped[3].

John smiled and searched his memory to recall who it was and what the hotel was, until he was sure to reveal his knowledge.

"I remember, it was the Bermuda Heights, with a Deborah Thompson as the landlady." he said triumphantly.

Ford sat upright and gazed at John as the names were mentioned.

"Excuse me John, but you did say Deborah Thompson?" he asked, then went on to describe the woman and the hotel.

"Why yes, the very same, Ben. You obviously know of them, but how?" John asked in a similar nonplussed manner.

"Simple, she's a relative of mine, and we use it as our registered office, tax haven and all that." Ford replied, and explained briefly the family connections and the financial set up.

"Well I'll be blowed! Fancy that Ben!" John said incredulously.

"There you go John. It is a beautiful coincidence sometimes to meet someone far away from home, and who is belonging to the person you are speaking of. Mind you sometimes it can be fatal, if you've had a bad experience last time round." Bruce chuckled, and related a couple of incidents.

Ford was taking it all in and enjoying the tales as the drink started to flow more freely.

"So we've got an invite then have we Ben?" Larter asked jovially.

"Indeed. Keep it under your hat though, we don't want outsiders coming to spoil it."

"Sounds great Ben. Let's hope she has enough rooms for us."

"This time of year is no problem, but we have an appreciative set of customers who come back year on year."

---

[3] See *A Fatal Encounter.*

"Sounds a good business, Ben. I think I'll give that a try myself one day, providing Macaroni lets me go." Larter said cheerfully.

The conversation ebbed and flowed for a while longer until everybody realised that the ship had stopped its rattling and rolling, to be replaced by a quiet and gentle sway.

"Well Ben, we've got the weather now, so maybe we can start after my rounds in the morning. How about it?"

"Sounds good to me John."

"Don't forget to pop by the shack and check my system too John."

"All in hand Bruce. But now its time to get turned in."

All three stood up slowly and wended their weary if slightly tipsy way back to their respective cabins.

Chapter X
Blackmail

It was a pleasant morning to be up on deck for John to make some running repairs. The sea was quiet; as the ship seemed to be rushing her way through it trying to reach harbour before another storm came along.

He looked up at the funnel and saw the black smoke making a long trail in the sky, and judged that the engines were on full power and making the propellers go 'full speed ahead'.

His internal rounds were made in company with Danvers, as was his report to Blayden on the bridge, who was in company with McPhee.

"I've had a look at the bow section, and will get a few strengthening plates welded across it. But realistically captain, you need a new hull. It's either that or the ship gets scrapped." McPhee stated in a clinical manner, which seemed to annoy Blayden.

"What are you talking about? This ship is good for at least another ten years." Blayden snapped, and then dismissed John and Danvers with a thank you and wave of his arm.

"I think McPhee could be wrong 3rd." Danvers whispered, as they left the bridge together.

"Then on the other hand, if that last storm is anything to go by, we might sink before then."

"I thought your name was Grey, not Jonah!" Danvers smiled as the two officers parted company.

"Morning Bruce, Paul!" John greeted, as he breezed into the radio shack to get a cheerful response back from the two radio officers.

"How long to Bermuda Paul? Any late signal diverting us Bruce?"

"No diversion, but we should arrive Hamilton around breakfast time tomorrow. Weather permitting." Larter said evenly as he offered John a cigarette and a light.

John sat in an empty chair to enjoy his cigarette when the 3rd mate popped his head through the door.

"I thought I saw you entering here Grey. I have an item for your attention if you'd care to follow me." 3rd mate Gibson requested politely.

"Sounds like more work for you John!" Southgate smiled, as John left the shack and followed Gibson.

"We have a broken cog on the winding wheel of the starboard aft lifeboat davits." Gibson stated, pointing to the offending item. John inspected the broken part carefully before making his decision.

"You are able to lower the boat which is the main thing, but not able to hoist it for re-shipping. So I'll put it down for repair whilst we're in Bermuda, say the day after tomorrow. Will that do you?"

"Well if you say so, but it goes down in my own report. As long as it gets done by then, as it contravenes the Lloyds shipping and maritime safety rules." Gibson agreed reluctantly.

"Have you found anything else to bring to my attention, such as the three broken bottle screws of the securing wires holding down the for'ard deck cargo?"

"Haven't got that far yet Grey, as I'm working for'ard today, but no doubt it will be done."

"Suggest you get them from your store locker and fit them a.s.a.p. in case we hit another storm and lose the lot. That should make us both even now, yes?"

Gibson nodded his head in agreement then left John who decided to have a sit down at the base of the funnel, looking out to the empty ocean all around the ship.

But his little moment of solitude was short lived when he heard the quick tempo of feet padding across the steel deck. He looked up and saw a group of soldiers coming towards him, jogging along in single file.

"Come and join us 3rd!" Ford invited

"Get some air into your lungs."

"Can't be spared Ben. Anyway, need to conserve my energy fitting up the radio shack with their new a.c.u. Care to join me in that?"

Ford laughed and nodded then said he'd see him in the saloon in about half an hour, before he disappeared down yet another set of ladders.

"Enjoy your jog Ben? You boys must be fit as fiddles!" John conceded, sitting down next to Ford with a cup of tea and lighted cigarette.

"Got to keep in trim for our game John." Ford replied, stubbing out his butt in the almost full ashtray.

"What have you got for the teams today, now that the weather is with us?"

"I'll need the full pack for this one, but only to get organised, then it'll be one team plus you and me." John stated, and then briefly described what was to be done.

"I'll get the men together and meet you on the boat deck, give me ten minutes." Ford said, and left swiftly to get the pack together.

The men worked solidly for two hours before John was satisfied with the installation and test, much to the great delight of Larter and Southgate.

"Our equipment will work much better now, and we'll enjoy a decent temperature to work in as well. Cheers John." Larter said happily, and Southgate echoed the sentiment.

John sent Ford to get McPhee to pass the work and give the team their 'Ten' before they could wrap up for the day.

"It appears that from your 'Queen' and corresponding 'Joker', you've done yet another innovation. Make sure you enter the appropriate alterations to them. In the meantime that's another 'Ten', John." McPhee advised, causing the soldiers to give a cheer.

"All in hand Fergus, and thanks for accommodating me." John replied.

Danvers came out from the back of the bridge to see what the commotion was, but was put at ease when John briefly explained what was going on.

"That's good 3rd. You will be able to install all the others around the ship so that we all can share the same comfort, especially when we get south into much warmer waters."

"Subject to availability, first mate. But it's all down to the good nature of our army friends here. Not forgetting Mr McPhee who supplies the machinery." John added, nodding over to McPhee and the men.

Danvers nodded his agreement then left the group to enjoy a laze on the deck.

"Right Ben, that's it until after we leave Bermuda, if your men are willing."

Ford asked the men directly and got a unanimous agreement from them.

"There's your answer John. Mind you, if that last unit is anything to go by, then you'll have to increase their beer ration."

McPhee laughed at the seemingly outrageous notion of blackmail, but told Ford that he personally would double their rations as long as they remained sober and completed the work, as, under normal circumstances it would have be done during a ship's visit to the ship maintenance yard.

John felt happy that he would be able to complete the ship's conversion from cold weather to tropical weather conditions. He also knew that when it came to reverting back to cold weather conditions again, all he had to do was just switch off the 'a.c.u.' and turn on the heaters again.

The passengers were recovering quickly from their seasickness as they packed the dining hall and eating their lunches with ravenous intent.

John and Lee had finished theirs and were talking 'shop' when Menzies came swiftly up to their table to interrupt their discussion.

"2$^{nd!}$ We're arriving in Bermuda tonight, but I'm supposed to have my promotions board by then, and haven't had the time to complete my task book yet." Menzies said anxiously.

Lee chuckled and turned to John.

"What do you think, 3rd? Do we help this ingrate of a 4th engineer or what?" Lee asked, giving John a sly wink.

"Well that depends on how good he has been." John replied slowly, twigging onto Lee's wind up.

"Aw c'mon 2nd. Please. After all I did help the 3rd with the vent systems, and I did a few jobs for you whilst I was supposed to be on watch." Menzies pleaded.

Lee let Menzies sweat for a moment then agreed that if John would help him get organised, he would start writing out the necessary report forms to give to the chief.

Menzies visibly sagged with relief, and thanked both men by shaking their hands gleefully.

"Aw thanks 2nd, and you 3rd. I'm ready to start now." Menzies said gratefully.

"Hold on a minute 4th. Better get your lunch and make sure you're off watch." Lee advised.

Menzies lowered his head and mumbled that he had the second half of the afternoon and the 1st dogwatch to do.

"Unless you get the acting 3rd to cover him, I'll cover his watch Tansey. But I'll need a swift relief as I've got rounds to do by the end of the last dog." John offered.

"Yes, that's a good idea. You do his watch and the acting 3rd will be your relief, instead of me. That will give me a chance to get Menzies sorted and ready for his board." Lee said slowly, mulling over the possibilities.

"Hey, hang on a minute, Tansey!" John said suddenly.

"How can he do his board when there are no ship-owners or board-members on board to take the board, if you see what I mean?"

Lee and Menzies looked a bit puzzled for a moment, and then Lee gave a big smile, as Menzies was still puzzling on the question.

"That's right! No Board members on board therefore no Board. Simple!" Lee laughed, looking at the still bewildered Menzies.

John laughed and said with a flourish.

"4th! You have no Board until we actually arrive or until just before we sail, if at all. Therefore you'll just have to wait until we do have our lordships as passengers. So consider yourself excused this time round."

Lee concurred with John's statement with a pronounced nod of his head.

Menzies looked at the two officers then slowly grinned, as the penny seemed to have dropped.

"Why that's great. That'll give me the time to catch up. Phew! Thanks to God for that!" he said elatedly, leaving just as quickly as he arrived.

"That as they say is that, and a narrow escape for one very fortunate 4th, John."

"Maybe so, but I'd have much preferred him getting it over with rather than faff about. It'll be bad for his nerves."

"I remember my board for 3rd, like it was only yesterday." Lee said with a far-away look on his face.

"Me too, but I'm looking for my next board for 2nd, if I'll ever get the peace to get it in."

Lee looked at John and said encouragingly.

"Cheer up John. You are almost there already, if what McPhee has said about your work done on board this vessel is anything to go by."

John nodded his agreement and thanked Lee before both men left the dining room to go their own separate ways.

Chapter XI
Nostalgia

It was in the cool of the early morning just as dawn was breaking, when the *Inverlaggan* slipped slowly into the naval dockyard at the northern end of the Bermuda islands, a tiny group of islands some distance from the continent of America.

The ship had arrived much earlier than expected so there was no berthing party to dock it apart from a hastily arranged tug to help get them alongside the dock. Because they had to do it all themselves, it took much longer to have the gangways put into place, much to the annoyance of Blayden, as he condemned in one of his 'fire and brimstone' tirades about the incompetence of the dockyard workers.

McPhee who was on the bridge during the docking, took exception to some of the remarks made. For he had known and experienced before, the long established pairing of captain Blayden and his engineer friend Jones. He had no time for either of them, so kept his silence until it was at a more appropriate time to deliver his own riposte.

John was making his way along the waist deck towards the saloon when he met McPhee about to go ashore with his party.

"Leaving us already Fergus?" John asked in mock horror.

"Morning John. Yes, glad to get off this dangerous bucket. The ship will only be here until 1800 hours before I'll get it shifted down to Hamilton. I'll have your requirements completed before you sail, if that's the word. Have a nice stay." McPhee replied before waving to them then carried his suitcase over the gangway and onto the dockside, to an awaiting car.

"Keep in touch John!" McPhee shouted climbing into the car and was driven away.

'I wonder what's in his mind to upset himself,' he said quietly, but was startled momentarily by a quiet voice behind him.

"Still talking to yourself John?"

"Yes Bruce. This is like old times, or is it an illusion?"

"Each visit will be different, John. Some just as good as the first and some even better that the last. Treat each visit and each place visited as it comes. Our last visit was a good one, but we start afresh again. You with no Happy Day, me without you know who." Larter said philosophically.

"Andy has the saying that nostalgia isn't what it used to be. Seeing that he has the same attitude as you, then I'll do the same and take it from there." John replied with a shrug of his shoulders.

"Going ashore now or later Bruce?"

"Me and Paul will be going ashore about 10' ish, as we've got a meeting with the Marconi agent, but we'll meet up in that hotel of Ben Ford's about 12'ish. Must go now, see you later John!"

"Aye, see you later!" was the response before John resumed his way to the saloon.

"Morning Ben! Ready to go ashore with the lads?"

"Morning John. I've got a few items to see to before that. Probably go ashore around 11ish, as long as the old railway is still running. Understand they had a bad time and might have to close down. Shame, because it is a unique little railway and will be missed by the tourists."

"Are the other passengers staying on board or is the army paying for their board ashore?"

"No. We're staying on board but I understand that there is an open gangway for them to come and go as they please."

"Just as long as everybody remembers that the ship will be moving to the other end of the island later on today. That should be fun for them seeing their ship sailing away without them, or even better, watch and cheer it arriving in Hamilton."

"Now that's a good way to spend a couple of hours. Must go now, so see you later." Ford said, leaving with some of his army pals.

"Hello 3rd, going ashore for a couple of days? Been here before have you?" the steward asked politely, quickly tidying up John's cabin.

"About 11-ish, once I've completed my paper work. Yes, I've got acquaintances ashore. What about you?"

"Yes, I've been here lots of times and just as soon as I've finished here I'm off. Me, my soldier boyfriend, the other three stewards and all the chefs are going to get the provisions for the next part of the voyage, and then we're all going to a beach party. Ooh what fun it will be."

"Don't forget the ship is moving to Hamilton at 18.00hours." John advised.

"Yes I know. That's where we'll have the provisions delivered. No sense carting it from there all the way up to here for us to bring it all back again is there. I mean, it plays havoc with your nail varnish." the steward said with pouting lips and held a hand out to show that his fingers had gaudy red varnish on them.

John just smiled and nodded as his answer, not knowing what else the steward might show him.

The steward finished what he was doing, and with a wave of his hand, he left the cabin, shutting the door behind him.

"Right, that's it all done. Fergus's copies, the captain's, Jones', and my own." John said quietly to himself, re- checking his bundles of papers, before he stowed them in his little lock-up writing desk. *'Now for a good run ashore.'*

"All set John? Where's Larter and what's his name, Southgate?" Ford greeted, when they met on the gangway.

"Bruce and Paul are already ashore. Says to meet us at the hotel."

"Right let's go before we get detailed off for some odd job or another." Ford said hastily, rushing over the gangway, with John in hot pursuit.

They walked swiftly through the dockyard and through the main gates to the little railway station where a small steam engine coupled to several gaudily painted carriages were waiting.

John looked at them and remembered them from his last visit, but was distressed to see the state of the little engine.

"It's seen better days Ben. Can't the railway do something to spruce it up?" John asked, watching the little engine labouring hard to pull the now, very full carriages.

"It's the last of its kind, and they can't get the parts. We've offered to make them up home, but it's not just the engine, as you can see from the tracks."

John looked at the engine puffing away and then at the tracks to see what he was supposed to look at, but said he wasn't sure what he was looking for.

"Simple John. The space for the train is getting narrower, and the passing place has been taken away. Look at this tunnel we're going through, it's got a dirty great house sitting on the top of it."

"I see what you mean. A gradual encroachment, as if strangling it to death. Maybe the politicians have decided its fate long before now and are allowing it to die in its own way." John observed.

Ford did not answer, merely nodded as both men sat down on the hard wooden seats.

It wasn't long before the little train arrived at the other end, for everybody to get off, and let the impatient boarders get on.

They walked along the very spot that the 'Brooklea' had been some years ago. They went up some steep steps that John had recognised as the very ones the stokers performed on, before turning left just in front of a neatly kept church. Down a little side road to the very same hotel he had stayed in with his engineer friend Happy Day.

He felt a thrill of excitement of what the day might have in store for them, but with a tinge of something that he put down as, not being quite the same. Nostalgia.

The two men entered the hotel where Ford had a happy re-union with his relative before she was re-introduced to John.

Everybody was happy to see each other again, and after the mundane business of checking into the hotel and getting settled into the room, all was resumed again.

Larter and Southgate joined them shortly afterwards, and a party was being held in the lounge.

"Remember the party we had John? A good night was had by all, and because of it, we have had some of the original guests re-booked with us since." Mrs Thompson revealed.

"As a matter of fact, John. Thanks to the events on that day and your initial donation, the local rotary club has made it into an annual affair. In fact, it's now turned into a full blown carnival for this year." she added excitedly.

"Sounds good, but what day do they hold it Deborah?" Larter asked.

"Not on the same day as you would think, but held in May during the peak tourist season. But if you'd like to speak to the chief organiser of the carnival, then he should be arriving shortly for the committee meeting held here every month." she advised then left to attend new arrivals.

The cocktails were flowing freely when the chief organiser arrived to meet them, and John was surprised to find it was none other than the police inspector who demanded that the fines be paid in Bermuda pounds.

The memories started to flood back into John's mind, and he felt that tingling sensation again.

"Hello inspector. No stokers around this time, so not guilty M'Lud." John joked, and shook the inspector's hand.

"Let's see. You're engineer Grey. Where is engineer Day, or are you on another ship?"

"Yes, I'm John Grey. My colleague Henry Day is in another part of the ocean no doubt. How is it you're encouraging such mayhem on the streets of Bermuda these days?"

"Actually, Grey. It was because of the carnival atmosphere and street party that evening that everybody enjoyed, that we decided embrace it and have one big one, using the same, shall we say, mayhem, as the main theme." the inspector said, drinking down yet another cocktail.

Ford and Southgate looked a bit confused, but Mrs Thompson gave them a brief account of what had taken place that day, the street party and the one in the hotel.

Ford nodded, and said with delight

"Oh, that party, yes I've heard about that. So you two were involved in it. Glad I invited you here then."

John looked at Larter, smiled and said softly

"What's that about nostalgia Bruce?"

The inspector stated that he had a lot still to organise and must leave, and was disappointed that John and Larter were not able to stay for the carnival. But he promised that he would send them a souvenir of the event as and when ready.

The little party went on into the afternoon until finally everybody decided to have a little siesta, before the main event of a barbeque some time in the evening.

"Wake up John, the ship is alongside in Hamilton now and we are required on board straight away." Larter said, shaking John firmly but gently awake.

John woke with a start and asked the time and if they were too late for the barbeque.

"Forget that John, we're required on board, and the *Waterlea* is due alongside us."

"The *Waterlea?* What's that got to do with us Bruce? We're inboard of her, so it means that she will sail before us. Besides what does Blayden want at this time of night?"

"I can't tell you why we're to report on board, but Andy is on the *Waterlea.*"

John dressed himself quickly, then gathered his things together and threw them into his overnight case.

"I take it we're not coming back. If that's the case what about Ford and the others still ashore?"

"The difference being is that they're passengers John, not us." Larter said with disappointment.

"Well something is up for us to miss out on two good runs ashore Bruce, and it better be good."

They met Southgate waiting in the foyer for them as Mrs Thompson appeared.

"I thought you were booked for two nights, what's happened for you to leave suddenly?" she asked with concern.

"Crew recall that's all. Tell Ben that we've gone back and hope to see him tomorrow. And offer our apologies for our absence tonight." John responded diplomatically.

"Yes, I'll tell him, but it's a pity you have to leave so soon and I'm afraid I will have to re-let your rooms now."

"That's the way of it, but hopefully you can get some takers from the other ship of our line that is due to dock soon. I'll spread the word if I can." Larter stated sympathetically as the three officers left the building.

They arrived on board and were ushered to the saloon where a posse of ship-owners were ensconced at a large table, surrounded by most of the crew who managed to get back quickly enough.

Lee beckoned them over to some empty seats beside him.

"Sit here gentlemen, and I'll get the steward to serve your drinks." he said quietly and settled down into their chairs, with a large drink that was thrust into their hands by a steward.

The whispering and chatting came to a halt when Belverley stood up to address the crew.

"Thank you all for attending. I have some important news that affects both the *Inverlaggan* and the *Waterlea* when it comes alongside. In fact, every vessel within our consortium, but one cannot be everywhere at once." Belverley commenced in his customary polished oratory manner then went on to explain in great detail what it was.

It was nearly an hour that passed before he finished, but he asked for and replied to any questions or observations from his audience for another while, before he stated that his duty had been done.

"Captain Blayden will expand on what I've told you, but for now, enjoy the rest of your visit here, as you've got one large voyage in front of you." Belverley concluded, gathering up his ream of papers, stuffed them into his briefcase, and left with his group of ship owners.

The saloon was quiet as the crew were still taking in what had been said, then everybody started to leave in dribs and drabs.

"John, you will not be required until we sail, but make sure you've got everything you need from the dockyard. I also suggest that you get in touch with the *Waterlea's* 3rd to put you wise on a few things. That way you'll be kept out of 'Spanners' way. Have a good visit while you can." Lee advised then left.

Larter gave Southgate a set of instructions, which dispatched him post haste out of the saloon.

"Then there were two Bruce!"

"Not for long John. We've just got time to catch Andy before he shoots ashore. Leave your bag here; the steward will stow them for us. C'mon lets go!" Larter said eagerly, and grabbing their caps they left in a hurry.

"Hello you old Scotch egg! What's a fine looking bosun doing lolling around the gangway?" John said softly in the ear of his friend Andy Sinclair, who had his back to them at the time.

Sinclair spun round to see whom it was that crept up on him.

"John! And you Bruce, you old Scouser!" Sinclair said with surprise and full of delight.

"You two are a sight for sore eyes. How's about a good drink in the saloon, now that the passengers have disembarked." Sinclair added, shaking hands with both of them.

All three men were happy and delighted to meet up again, as they knew that their little band of brotherhood would be enriched yet again. They trooped into the *Waterlea's* saloon where they found a few officers and a few passengers who were enjoying themselves with perhaps one more drink before leaving the ship.

For hours the three close friends swapped stories and personal accounts of what each had got up to during their separations, until it was time for the steward to close the bar.

"Bar closing in ten minutes." the steward announced in a loud voice to nobody in particular.

"Do us a favour steward. Would you fix us up with a few sarnies, we're starving." Larter asked politely.

The steward nodded his head and left but came back shortly with a plate of food for them.

"Cheers steward. Just one more drink then you can lock up." Sinclair said gratefully, taking the laden plate off the man.

"I've got a crate in my shack that's cooling very nicely, and it should be just about ready for sampling." Whispered Larter, whilst stroking the side of his nose and winking at his two friends.

Their little reunion lasted into the early hours of the morning when all three decided it was time to hit the sack, preferably very gently. For they all had a hectic day ahead of them.

Chapter XII
A Party

John found the *Waterlea's* senior 3rd engineer conducting his rounds, and spent a good hour discussing the various items that he had written down as his agenda.

"It seems Grey, you certainly have an inquisitive mind as you've almost come to the end of my knowledge, that's for sure."

"I thank you for your help Brown. Maybe we'll have a drink ashore before you sail, but I've got several items to chase up with the dockyard first. See you say at about 13.00 hours on our gangway?"

Brown chuckled and told him that the ship was sailing in about three hours time, but that he would make it another time.

John held out his hand and shook Brown's before he thanked him again and left.

On his way over the *Waterlea* gangway that bridged the gap between the two ships, he was fortunate to see Sinclair going over the *Inverlaggan* gangway, and ran after him.

He managed to attract Sinclair's attention before Sinclair was about to climb into a waiting taxi.

"What's up John?" Sinclair asked then asked the driver of the taxi to wait.

"You're sailing in about three hours, yet you're going ashore with a suitcase in your hand?" John asked anxiously.

"Glad you miss me John, as I do you. But not to panic as I'm only going ashore for the night."

"For the night, and your ship is sailing by 11.00 hours? That means you're joining another ship, Andy. One of ours?"

"Yes, you can say that. It's the 'Mad Monk's' floating museum John. Yours, I believe!" Sinclair teased, then quickly explained why.

John was delighted to hear that Sinclair was joining, but told him to go to the hotel and look up Ford who was staying there, and who would see him fixed up until Larter and he arrived later.

Sinclair smiled and repeated one of his very first statements he ever made to John.

"Ye're a canny man John Grey!" he shouted as the taxi roared off.

The rest of the day for the crew was split into hard work in the morning, and after the *Waterlea* sailed, the afternoon enjoying the delights of Bermuda before it was their turn to sail away.

John managed to have a quick visit to the dockyard and saw McPhee to finalise his paper work.

The meeting went well as usual and broke up in the usual flourish before John finally had the chance to meet up with his two best friends and others waiting at the hotel.

"There you are John! Thought you swapped with the *Waterlea's* 3rd, for a holiday." Larter cheered as John arrived into the company of Ford and several of his soldiers from the 'pack', who in turn clapped and cheered at his appearance.

"Looks like a good party is about." Ford inferred quietly, giving John a large beer to slake his thirst.

Mrs Thompson was the perfect host, as she got the men mingling with her other 'paying' guests, who were delighted to meet these brave men that were off to yet another war.

Yet again the party mood was quick to take hold and went with a swing into the early morning, and where there were more sleeping bodies around than those standing up.

"Looks like we're the 4 musketeers John." Ford said proudly, looking around the lounge and saw bodies draped in all shapes over or under the furniture, all drunk and all fast asleep.

"Yes, but three of us has to go back on board before you lot return. So see you sometime later tomorrow Ben. Thank Deborah for a good evening, and tell her that we hope to see her again some day. God willing." John said softly so as not to waken anybody.

Ford returned the sentiment and waved to them as they stepped over the prostrate bodies and out of the lounge into the main foyer, before shutting the main door quietly behind them and making their way back to the ship.

95

"That was one hello and goodbye party Bruce, can you think of one better?" Sinclair asked when the friends walked slowly and carefully down the steep steps leading to the quayside.

"Can't say I can. Except maybe the last time we were here, what about you John?"

"Same here." John agreed, and all three falling into silence for a while until they walked over the ships gangway.

"Well, its goodnight from me. See you later." Sinclair sighed, giving a mock salute to his friends.

"Yes, see you Andy. Usual place but don't know when." Larter and John said in unison before they tramped wearily to their respective cabins to catch what was left of the night, or even early morning.

Chapter XIII
Egg And Humble Pie

The pilot launch sped away from the safety of the towering hull of the *Inverlaggan* as it bounced over the waves and back to harbour, whilst the ship turned slowly around and headed due south again for another 4,000 mile voyage.

John was inside the bow storage space with Danvers inspecting the workmanship of the Bermuda dockyard mateys.

"Looks good to me first mate, but we won't know until we meet the next storm."

"That will be sooner than you think 3rd. We're fast approaching 'Hurricane Alley' as the Yanks have dubbed this part of the ocean. But let's hope we skirt around it by using the 60 w longitude."

John had heard this expression several times and knew exactly where he meant.

"If we can sneak down this alley and get into the Carib before the storms spots us, then we might get away with it." John said jokingly, but got a disapproving look from Danvers.

"Then of course there's the Sargasso Sea. A very foggy and dangerous place to get lost in. Hope this bow can stand another good belting, otherwise we'll all be rowing home instead of sailing home." John teased again, but a loud sigh and a grunting noise from Danvers, told him that Danvers wasn't in the mood for a bit of light-hearted banter.

Danvers continued the rest of his part of the rounds in silence, only to state that he was going onto the bridge to make his own report.

"Last one onto the bridge buys the beer." John said with a large grin and charged past Danvers to get first up the ladder. His brief stay in Bermuda had charged his batteries but obviously not the first mate's.

"Bow section and all upper deck machinery handed over to the first mate, captain!" John reported, and watched Blayden 'walking' his dividers across the sea chart, plotting his next course.

"Very well 3rd. You can start the second phase of your rolling refurbishment as soon as you like. Preferably after lunch, so leave the bridge now." Blayden mumbled, then turned to Danvers and ordered lifeboat drill within the hour.

John went out onto the boat deck to re-check the repaired lifeboat davit, when he came upon the 3rd Mate Gibson doing his own rounds.

"You've done a good job there, lets' hope we don't have to use it. A deckhand found another fault, but that's on the captain's launch. Come and I'll show you." Gibson invited

John followed him and was shown the problem, and found anger rising from within him.

"It seems to me Gibson, that someone somewhere is playing games either on me, on you, or even on both of us. I shipped a new shaft and prop on this launch only the other day. Unless it's been used to drive down the cobbled streets of Bermuda, I'd say somebody has deliberately broken it. Unless we have one in our engineers stores, I shall have to make a new one providing I can get the right metal." John said angrily.

"And before anything else happens, I can state quite categorically that all machinery, including all hand operated ones on this and in every deck of this ship, are working perfectly. I'm telling you that 3rd, because I keep a good maintenance schedule and a record of each inspection or repair done. I suggest that you put this into your report and notify Danvers at least, about this damage. That to me is tantamount to sabotage, Gibson. I don't want to be held responsible for it should this launch be required at any time prior to me fixing it. Do you get my drift?"

Gibson nodded his agreement then scribbled notes into his rounds report book before departing from John's obvious annoyance.

John's anger was neither volatile nor quick, and once he got angry and got what he had to say off his chest, he would return to his normal quiet self again.

"Morning Bruce, Paul!" John said politely, stepping into the radio shack.

"What's that new radar like Paul, can we see further than our noses now?"

"It'll do, but not as good as the one on the *Waterlea*. That one is a beauty because you can see twice as far as this one, and it gives a 360-degree scan. I reckon it must be the type the RN uses." Southgate replied.

"As long as it tells us the difference between a cloud, an iceberg and a ship, I'm not caring." Larter said with a smile.

"By the look of you Bruce, you're about to crack open that safe you're fiddling with."

"Got to match our aerial to the new frequencies we were given. Be with you in a minute." Larter replied, nodding to an empty chair for John to sit in.

John sat down and offered a cigarette to each of them before lighting one up for himself.

"What's our next port of call Paul! Barbados, Grenada, Tobago?"

"Judging by our chart, we'll go south from the 67 degree West longitude over to the 60 degree West longitude. The skipper will head for Barbados and Tobago then turn left onto the 57 degree West longitude. Then along the coast of Venezuela, before going down to the 7degree North until we arrive at Georgetown. See here John." Southgate said, tracing the ships' course over the 3,000mile distance from Bermuda to Georgetown British Guiana.

"Presumably non-stop, or maybe a quick run ashore in Barbados?"

"Yes non-stop, but doubt a run ashore anywhere other than Georgetown considering we're about three days behind schedule."

"Give or take a few hours, and at optimum speed per consumption, I reckon it should take us ten days. Mind you if we meet any more nasty storms like the ones we've just been through then add another day or so." John said almost automatically, scanning his memory on fuel over speed ratios.

"Anyway, if we're supposed to be accompanied by the troopship when we arrive in B.G. where are we meeting up with it, assuming of course it's going to be in some harbour or other?"

"We'll arrive before them as they've got two ports of call to make prior to arriving B.G." Larter interjected.

"Some people get all the luck." John said glumly.

"Never mind John, we'll have an extra day or so in Georgetown to have a good run ashore and I know a few good places for us to visit." Southgate said cheerfully, pointing to a seemingly uninterrupted green patch of land on the map that stated 'Rain forest'.

"Oh well, whatever. We've got that big expanse of ocean to cover first. Anyway, it appears that you both are busy just now, so I'll mosey on and leave you both in peace. Thanks for the info, as now I can plan my refurbishment and other maintenance schedules." John offered, and shut the radio shack door behind him, stepping out onto the boat deck again.

For a few days the *Inverlaggan* crept around the dangerous so-called 'Hurricane Alley' and headed into the gradually warmer waters of the central Atlantic. The days became longer and warmer for the passengers to spend more time on the upper deck, which the children seemed to love.

There were games organised for the children during the day, and evening entertainment for the adult passengers, whilst the crew enjoyed a more lazy time in doing their jobs on board.

John even got the junior deck officers to rig some canvas awnings onto the after cargo deck so that he could pump water into it for the children to swim around in a make shift swimming pool. This was the magnet that drew and kept most of the passengers in the one place instead of being found in places that the crew did not want them to be in.

It was also the time for the officers to change into their 'whites' as the uniform for the tropics, and other such warm places. The passengers also changed from heavy clothing to much lighter and more colourful clothing, giving the ship the look of not so much a tramp steamer, but a good passenger cargo vessel.

As the ship sailed downwards towards the equator, and the temperature rising higher each day, it became more stuffy and intolerable between decks. The passengers wished John would hurry up and finish A.C.U. installation.

"How much longer will it take your team to complete the work 3rd?" Blayden asked, as John completed his early morning deck rounds and made his report.

"The teams are working well captain, and everything is going to my projected plan as approved by Mr McPhee. So I'd say and with luck, tomorrow afternoon. That is if you and the chief engineer are satisfied and pass the work first."

"Judging by what I've seen and the effectiveness of what machinery you have installed, there would be no problem in passing the work. Report to me as soon as you've finished." Blayden stated, dismissing John from the bridge.

John went back to his teams that were now sweating profusely as they placed yet another heavy a.c.u. into place.

"Well done men. Now that one is in place, we've only got two more to do now." John said encouragingly, and set about testing and inspecting the machine.

The men sat around having a breather and a smoke whilst Ford and John gave the unit a good robust testing.

"That will cheer the passengers up Ben. Give it a few hours and we'll be able to get ice cubes from it to put into our drinks." John said with a large smile on his face.

"Speaking of which John. We'll have to rig one or two up in the holds as the smell from the vehicles is getting, shall we say, a bit rich. Not only that, we'll have to reduce the output to the men's accommodation."

"Oh why? Too cold for them now Ben?"

"No John it's not that. It's just that we need to get accustomed to working and handling the vehicles in hot climates.

We can't bring your fancy fridges with us when we go up jungle, or in our workshops back at camp. The accommodation will help us get acclimatised quicker for when we do arrive in B.G., AND the men can always stay on the boat deck and sleep up there during the nights if they want to. But for that, permission needs to be arranged between the major and your captain." Ford explained.

John nodded in agreement and stated that it was a good idea, then discussed the problem with the smell, but agreeing to sit down and work out a plan of action once the last unit was tested and in working order.

The moment came when John reported to Blayden that all was completed, so that he could do his inspection.

Blayden and Jones conducted a thorough inspection, testing units at random, before both men agreed that it was a job well done. Blayden had already told John that the passengers were now thanking him for their nicely cooled cabins, and indeed the vast improvement to the entire accommodation areas of the ship.

The grudging praise from Jones was for John, music to his ears, and felt elated that Jones must have felt that he had the proverbial egg all over his face, and the large slice of humble pie he had to eat.

"Now 3rd, don't get too cocky for what I've said. I've still got my beady eye on you." Jones said grudgingly, leaving John to go and spread the good news to the 'pack'.

"I'll get Bruce to signal McPhee to authorise your men's reward, as you, shall we say, requested. Double beer rations I believe, Ben?"

Ford turned to the men and told them the news and announced double rations of beer, but warned of drunkenness. The men cheered the news about the inspection and even louder when the extra beer was mentioned, then quickly and methodically cleared everything away.

"Any more 'Queens' or 'Jokers' about number 'Six'?" Ford asked over the noise, but got some ribald remarks and lewd gestures from the very happy men.

Ford just smiled, shook his head and looked over to John, who was grinning like a Cheshire cat, feeling just as happy as the men.

"Number 'One', here is a chit to take to the steward for your extra ration just for today. Tomorrow you'll be able to draw it yourselves as and when." John said to the nominated soldier, who took it eagerly and went away to get their dues.

"Right then Ben. Let's have a look at your smelly problem. But I suspect you'll have to drain all your vehicles and replace it with lighter oil. Maybe you've got some sort of coolant in your radiators, so they would have to be drained down and replaced with ordinary tap water."

"We've done the rads, but the change of oil will be difficult, even from where I'm standing."

Both men clambered down through the maze of access tunnels to see what could be done, and emerged on the upper deck some half an hour later.

John looked at his watch, checking his time.

"It's the appointed hour, as I have to conduct my rounds now. Care to join me Ben?"

"I have to see the major about the men sleeping on deck, so on this occasion I'll have to refuse."

"Never mind, we'll tackle this problem in my cabin after dinner, if you wish."

"Sounds good to me, so see you about 20.00 hours" Ford agreed as both men went their separate ways.

John was in his cabin preparing for Ford's visit, when Lee poked his head through the cabin doorway.

"Hello John, understand you made 'Spanners' day for him by making him eat humble pie. It takes a good one to do that, even though I was the last one to do so on our last voyage."

"I don't know about that, but even a junior engineer could have done it. After all, those units are only a fridge disguised up a bit, because they do the same and operate in the same way." John replied modestly, then waved him in to sit down.

"Can't stop just now John, I've got the 1ˢᵗ watch. Might see you later though, but congratulations again to you. I'll buy you a drink to celebrate, but must dash." Lee said, disappearing quickly out of sight.

It was a knock on his cabin door made by Ford that attracted his attention again.

"Shut the door and c'mon in Ben. Here, have a nice drop of Irish whiskey to get you going." John greeted, offering Ford a large tumbler full of drink.

"Now where we, Ben. Last off it was the oil change and the difficulty in getting to the oil sumps." John opened, and both men discussed thoughts, ideas and possibilities, before they finalised their plan.

"That seems to be about it Ben, unless you have anything else to drum up?"

"I'll get the men organised tomorrow morning and ready to start. By the way, your captain gave the major his permission for the men to sleep up on deck, as his own reward to the men for helping you."

"Well, that was kind of him. The other thing is, here's McPhee's signal back for the authorisation. The captain will be highly pleased considering that he's a teetotaller and a bible thumper of the first water."

Ford laughed at the expression, took the signal and suggested that they join the rest of the passengers in the saloon to round off the evening. Which John duly accepted and left his cabin.

Chapter XIV
Watches

The ship was moving effortlessly through the calm ocean, swaying and rocking gently when she rode over the undulating swell. Porpoises were playing hide and seek and racing ahead of her as she carved a creamy wake through the cobalt blue waters.

Her crew were vigilant and quietly doing their work while her passengers still slumbered in their bunks, with the radar dish swishing slowly round like a little clockwork key turning in a toy, but keeping its invisible eye very observant to any perils that might come her way.

Even her funnel was almost bereft of the usual thick black ribbon of smoke that twins up with the wake to mark the place on the ocean from whence she came, and can even be seen way over the horizon.

'Best time of the day, and yet another lovely morning ahead of us' John thought, sitting on the foc'sle capstan to enjoy his pre-breakfast cigarette. He watched the bright orange globe of the sun finally arise out of the sea to take its place in the sky, before he moved from his temporary seat.

"Rounds completed, no problems to report." John said quietly to Blayden, who was draped over the chart table calculating his ship's position.

"Very well 3rd." Blayden said almost robotically and nodded his head as he continued his own task.

"We've made good progress on this leg of the course. Lets hope the next leg is just as good." he said absentmindedly, before ordering a change of course to the duty helmsman.

John went to the bridge wing and looked aft to see the neat creamy curve of the wake being marked out as the ship changed its course once more. He imagined that it was the ship's way of marking the chart and the sea to rub it out once the ship had gone.

"You need me for something else captain?" John reminded Blayden, who looked up with surprise.

"Oh no. You carry on 3rd." Blayden replied, dismissing John, who walked out the back of the bridge to visit two more of his friends.

"Morning Bruce, on your own this morning?"

"Hello John! Yes, Paul had a long schedule and has just gone to breakfast. Had yours yet?"

"On my way Bruce, coming?"

"I'll see you later, I've got some signals to send off first." Larter replied, switching on his powerful transmitter and searching for a suitable receiving station.

John nodded and smiled to his friend and left to satisfy his hunger.

"Morning 3rd, same as usual?" The steward asked politely then started to hum quietly to himself again as he waited for John's reply, which was quickly given for the steward to leave.

He dined alone at the large table, as he was the first ship's officer to arrive. Soon the other officers started to arrive as their duties allowed.

"Just the man I want to see. I need a word in your ear Grey." Jones said and sat down wearily next to John, who was surprised by Jones sudden appearance and steeled himself for perhaps another verbal onslaught.

"Morning chief, what can I do for you?"

"The salt water evaporator and distiller has packed up since this morning and I need a new valve made for the brine ejector, apart from the evap needing a good descaling." Jones stated and went on to tell John what he wanted doing.

"It's your call chief." John stated evenly, but offered some of his own options.

Jones was taken aback with John's reply, then took a few moments to give his own.

"Get yourself sorted and available as you will be taking over from the acting 3rd and do the afternoon watch. He will make the part, then if he and I have not finished the task by the time he goes back on watch, you will do his last dogwatch. That way you can get your own work seen to as well." Jones commanded in a booming voice.

"I see no problem with that chief. What's wrong with the evaps anyway?"

Jones explained in engineering terms what was what, and what needed to be done. John nodded his head and offered his help instead of keeping watch. But Jones declined the offer by stating the lack of qualified officers to take charge in the engine room.

"You know that army sergeant, Ford who was working with me? Well he's a qualified marine engineer. If you don't have any objections to him coming down with me for a spell, then you could have the use of a couple of the junior engineers to help you. What do you say chief?"

Jones gave John his now famous sideways look for a moment before he replied.

"A qualified marine engineer did you say. Well if that's the case then I'll accept your offer. But mind you, I'm only in the next compartment so I'll be able to keep…"

"Your beady eye on me!" John said to complete Jones' now equally famous saying.

"I'll be down during your watch to see if all is well. If not, then look out 3rd." Jones said gruffly, leaving John in a cloud of smoke.

That was one ungrateful chief, and typical of his kind. Still, extra engine room hours won't go amiss, especially on this ancient tub.' he mused, wandering back to his cabin.

The afternoon watch in the engine room was an easy one for John, as he had met most of the antiquated machinery during his engineering apprenticeship.

The duty stokers on watch had not seen John perform in the engine room and were not familiar with him, so they were dubious to act on his orders. Instead, they acted on the orders of the duty petty officer. But after a short while when they observed John carrying out his prescribed duties as the engineer officer, they knew that he knew his machinery, checks and procedures, so they relaxed and treated him just as they would their own duty watch officer, with respect.

During the watch, and as everything was fairly quiet task-wise, John got two stokers to clean up all the ladders and some of the deck plating that had grease and oil smeared over it, and to give the engine room a good tidy up. He pointed out several hazards around the engine room he found, and gave them all a little lecture on how to stay safe and healthy whilst in the compartment. Even the electricians had a lecture on their sloppy and careless attitudes, much to the embarrassment of the electrical officer who was there at the time.

"If you are so concerned 4th, then speak to the 2nd as your instructor, or even the chief if you have the nerve. But I feel sure that they would agree with what I have said and have done here. For all the items that I've mentioned, you would do well to take note, especially when it comes to that subject during your promotion board." John advised sternly, concluding the verbal exchange.

Jones clattered down the ladder and landed next to John as he was making one of his checks, then stood looking around at the now fairly clean engine room.

"You certainly didn't take long to settle in Grey." Jones said loudly into John's ear so that he could hear over the noise.

"Glad to be of service chief. Got the valve made yet?" John enquired as if to change the subject.

"Not yet, but I've got a team of stokers finishing off the clean down. You should see the debris they removed, at least three months worth, instead of a week." Jones said almost civilly.

John didn't correct him by saying it should be done daily, instead he asked a couple more questions and was surprised by the almost human response he got back, instead of the usual snarl.

"We had the same problem on my last ship, but I cured it good and proper by using a method that my grandfather used to use. Maybe when you flash it up again, I shall show you, chief."

"It obviously works, so why not 3rd." Jones agreed, as he turned to meet the acting 3rd coming down the ladder carrying his newly made valve, then both left to go into the evap room.

'What a surprise. The chief being nice to me. Perhaps he liked the new décor or something.' he thought, as he made yet another inspection.

The watch came to an end with the hand-over to Menzies, his relief, whilst the stokers also changed over.

Menzies echoed the surprise of the stokers when they arrived to find a clean looking engine room, and for a bit of fun, made to go back up the ladder saying that they came to the wrong engine room let alone the wrong ship. The banter was good-natured as was John's turn over, and he left in good spirits with the knowledge that he had kept his engine-room skills, even though it was some time since he had kept a watch down there..

He arrived into his cabin, removed his overalls and cleaned himself up before he heard a knock at his cabin door.

"Hello 3rd, enjoyed yourself down that nice hole?" the steward asked suggestively, emphasising the last two words.

"Hello steward. Yes thanks, I might just do it again later on if the evaporator doesn't get fixed."

"Oh so that's the matter. And here's me thinking I've swallowed something I shouldn't, for there's an unpleasant taste in it. Come to think of it, it was the glass of water I had with my biscuit. Anyway, here's your tea, hope you enjoy it." he remarked, putting the tray down onto the small table.

"Thanks steward. I'm going to get my head down for a while and I'm due for the last dogwatch. So please give me a knock around 17.30 hours. I'll have dinner when I come off watch." John said, scoffing his rock cake and drinking his tea down in great gulps.

The steward nodded, then took the tray and left the cabin, shutting the door behind him.

The last dogwatch was only a 2-hour one, which seemed to fly for John, and before he knew it, Lee came down and relieved him, with the appropriate turn over.

"You still remember your duties then John. That's good considering you've been the outside engineer for some time now. By the end of this voyage you should be able to apply for 2nd, providing of course that doesn't spoil it for you." Lee said pleasantly.

"Well according to him, I'll only be promoted to acting 4th. Still, at least it's a promotion, either way Tansey." John said philosophically.

Lee merely agreed with his sentiment then left to conduct his own inspections and observations, as John clambered up the now very clean ladder and into the air lock chamber, before finally making his way to his cabin, only to find Jones waiting for him.

"You don't have to do your evening rounds today Grey, as I've already had them done for you. But don't think I've gone soft on you, because as you've done a good turn for me, so I did one for you in return. Now we are evens again so I'll see you tomorrow as normal."

"Thank you chief. I enjoyed my watches and was glad to help." John replied to the departing chief.

"Yes, well. We'll leave it at that. Good night 3rd" Jones said wearily and left.

Chapter XV
Overweight

"**H**ello Andy, haven't seen much of you since we left Bermuda, how are you doing!" John asked, when he arrived onto the bridge to see Sinclair standing large as life, in front of the large spoked steering wheel.

"Hello John. We must have been in different watches or whatever, but I'm okay. I don't suppose you knew it but the last bosun had a nervous breakdown that's why I took over. Be that as it may, most of the sailors are still loyal to him and are proving a pain in the neck when I want something done." Sinclair said glumly.

"That sounds bad Andy. Maybe you need some sort of proof or a demonstration to show them that you're probably much better at the job than your predecessor. I faced that too, only yesterday when I had to cover a couple of watches in the engine room. Now all is well on both sides." John replied sympathetically.

"Port 15. Steer 095!" a loud voice shouted from the back of the bridge.

Sinclair repeated the orders then reported his change of course when done so.

"That's a big change of course Andy?"

"Yes, we've nearly run out of sea room ahead of us. If we kept on going we would have bumped into Venezuela. I expect the skipper wants to sight land for a while to find out just where we are on the map. He'd been navigating by sun and star sights since we left Bermuda, and will have a reasonable idea what part of the Venezuelan coast we will reach. We'll skirt around the coastline until we reach B.G. But there's one thing I'm worried about and hope the skipper has taken it into account. Otherwise we might just end up swimming to Georgetown."

John looked closely at his friend to see if he could gain any clues from Sinclair's poker faced expression. But gave up when there was no follow up statement, and changed the subject.

"Been to B.G. before Andy?"

"Twice for a cargo change, and once for a run ashore during my time in the R.N. There used to be a naval base there but there's not much to see except for a lot of jungle. Mind you, the streets are almost literally paved in gold, diamonds and other precious stones. That's why our shipping line has the franchise from the government to bring it back to Blighty. Lots of back handers and the like, if you get my drift John."

"I can understand sending a Lea ship, but would they send a ship such as this one to collect it all, Andy? "

"You've got a point there. Maybe a few crates of the stuff hidden in amongst the rest of the general cargo, but I suspect we'll only be carrying general cargo such as sugar, rice, maybe a few thousand tons of copper ore, or bauxite and the usual deck cargo of hardwood timber. Who knows with this shipping line, as they always seem to swap cargo between ships, at the drop of a hat."

"Well, as long as I get to know what cargo is coming on board, to be able to have it stowed correctly, then I'll take what comes along."

Their conversation lasted a few more minutes before Larter arrived onto the bridge.

"Hello you two. Enjoying a quiet evening on the bridge instead of the noise of the saloon?"

"Something like that Bruce, although Andy here has his hands full at the moment." John replied.

Larter smiled and left just as quickly as he arrived, stating that he needed a quick radar bearing.

"It seems that Bruce is thinking the same as me. I think you'd better stay here with me John, as the skipper will be on the bridge very soon to take charge of the situation when it occurs." Sinclair stated enigmatically.

"Give me a clue and I'll probably work it out Andy."

"Just think of fresh water then look at our position on the chart, then follow it along the coast line."

John did so and spotted the area marked dangerous, then thought of the implications.

"We should be okay Andy, as we're only three quarters loaded. Anyway, I expect Blayden would skirt around it just like he did the Hurricane alley and the islands of the Caribbean."

The two friends said nothing more, but just stayed in each other's company until Sinclair got relieved off the wheel, for them to leave the bridge.

"According to Bruce, we'll be in Georgetown for a couple of days before we take the outgoing army unit back to Gibraltar. Although I really can't understand why we can't take them to, say Colombo via the Cape. In fact right up to Singapore or even Hong Kong."

"This ship is not war-zone equipped, John. But then, apart from a warship, which one is?"

John asked then shook his head and added that the purser hated handing out extra pay, let alone war-zone payments too. Both agreed with that statement and parted company when they left the bridge.

John heard the S.O.S. alarm buzzer go when he passed the radio shack, and was nearly bowled over by Southgate who was rushing in, so John followed quietly to observe his friends at work.

Larter was busy writing down the details of the S.O.S. calls, and asked Southgate to check on their own sea-chart the positions of those ships that were in difficulty. Then told John that whilst they were able to listen to and record the calls, they dared not answer just in case the ship in distress was too far away. Southgate stated that they were out of radar range and if the ship's position was correct, they were only about two hours steaming away. Larter told him to go and tell the captain and advised John to get a life jacket from somewhere, as he would probably be required on deck.

John looked at the sea-chart and told Larter what Sinclair had to say about the area to where those ships seem to be.

"Thanks for the warning John. It looks as if we'll all be needing life jackets if Blayden takes us too close. I've seen many an unwary ship sink like a stone within minutes and sometimes without warning."

John made a few calculations on a scrap piece of paper, and stated that they may be on the weight limit, and probably Blayden would not attempt his ship in rescuing those unfortunate ones.

"If you feel the ship give a massive lurch downwards from the bow, or even drop from under you then you know we've joined them." Larter stated, listening to the now silent radio.

"Hmm. Not a peep from them now so it looks as if they've both sunk John. Lets hope there's some survivors, but in these cases that's a rare occasion as the ship goes straight down like a lift in a high rise hotel." Larter said sombrely, as Southgate came rushing through the door.

"Blayden will not be entering that area saying that the ship is too heavy for it." he stated hurriedly.

"That is strictly academic now Paul. I've not heard from them since you left, so they've probably sunk by now, just like those fishermen off Scotland." Larter replied, closing the logbook and stowing it neatly away.

"So what's the score on that then John?" Southgate asked grim faced, looking at the sea chart again.

"It's a simple case of being overweight, Paul. If a ship gets loaded in a salt-water area, which is a lot denser than fresh water, and enters a fresh water area such as a river, or its outflow area such as the Orinoco, or the Amazon ahead of them, it sinks to that level for fresh water. Too much weight and the ship would go under due to not enough free board. Depending on the river outflow would determine how far out to sea a ship would have to go to avoid it. The Orinoco has about a 30mile outflow, whereas the Amazon would be around the 300mile mark. That type of rule also applies to any ship going down to the Southern Hemisphere, due to the fact of a heavier gravity. Ships coming from the other way always arrive lighter because of it." John explained, which was confirmed by Larter's stories about some of the ships that he'd seen sink in similar circumstances.

All three knew that this type of tragedy was part of the seafarers life, and it was wise to not dwell on it, but heard and listened to the booming voice of Blayden sermonising on the bridge for the lives of all those people lost on the two ships. For all those in peril on the sea, as the seafarers hymn goes.

Chapter XVI
Lazy Joe's

The smell of the land was in the air, and everybody on board were getting happier at the prospect of walking on solid ground once more and were busy preparing themselves for it.

From day one, John always stood on the foc'sle when entering or leaving harbour and this time was no exception, as the ship manoeuvred itself inside the wooden jetties that formed the harbour of Georgetown British Guiana.

It was in the cool of the morning, which he enjoyed, looking at the collection of houses scattered around in among the tall trees, and the other ships already in harbour.

The ship slid alongside the jetty to where the berthing party was waiting to secure her alongside, and have the two gangways positioned onto her.

He felt a little bump from under his feet, which told him that the ship had finally arrived alongside and for the crew to relax, and the engines shut down.

Once the gangways were ready, the usual stream of people came on board as Blayden waited at one gangway to meet them. They would be the 'chain gang' of the local dignitaries, the health and customs officers, and anybody else with business on board. For it was they who allowed people off the ship once the diplomacy and procedures had been sorted and conducted.

British Guiana (Land of the many waters) is one of three small states on the northern coast of South America and sandwiched between Venezuela and Brazil.

It is only 7 degrees north of the equator with 85 percent of the land covered in dense forest that forms part of the rain forests of the world.

Georgetown is its capital and is run by the British Governor and the High Commission but under orders from Great Britain.

It is a valuable piece of real estate where gold, diamonds,

silver and copper are mined extensively and shipped to the United Kingdom. It also produces sugar and rice for export, and an abundance of hardwoods and other timber from the forest. There are few proper roads outside the capital mostly compacted earthen ones, but there is an extensive rail network that is used by the various mines dotted around the country.

This was the new temporary home for the *Inverlaggan* and her crew, until she sailed again.

The passengers were disembarked and loaded into several coaches that took them away leaving a group of soldiers as a working party to organise the off-loading of their weapons and armoury.

John was on the after cargo-loading hatch talking to Ford, but watching the dock cranes as they quickly lifted the cargo of vehicles out of the hold and depositing them onto a long string of empty railway wagons on the jetty.

"Well Ben. Here we are, all safe and sound. I suppose you'll be busy for a few days sorting everything out." John said quietly, observing his temporary decks being stripped away to uncover yet another layer of equipment.

"Yes John, something like that. I've had a chat with my opposite number from the depot and told me that there is a shortage of various parts and equipment to work with. I didn't tell him that we've brought everything with us, including the proverbial kitchen sink." Ford said cheerfully.

"Sorry to see you go Ben, pity you couldn't stay on board. You and your lads did me proud over the last few days. I hope that we get the chance to bring you boys back home again when the time comes."

"The feeling is mutual John, but the army needs me more. Still, maybe one day if your ship visits my neck of the Canadian woodlands we will have a good party then." Ford enthused cheerfully, holding out his hand and shook John's.

"Yes Ben. Goodbye and good luck. Tell the men I wish them well." John replied solemnly and left Ford to his tasks.

"John, there you are. I've been looking everywhere for you. We have another evap failure, so could you get ashore and organise a hosepipe connection for us." Lee asked, arriving inside John's cabin.

"Certainly Tansey. But I'll do that on my way ashore." John replied, donning his freshly laundered tropical gear.

"Going anywhere nice? Or just a sight see around the place?"

"It's a mystery trip for me but not for the bosun and radio officer Larter. As they've been here before, so they've invited me to join them. Somewhere up the jungle I believe. What about yourself Tansey?"

"I stayed here for a while shortly after the war as my ship was sunk just off the coast north of here. Stupid skipper had too much cargo on board. I was on deck at the time and managed to hang onto a Carley raft, until a passing R.N. warship picked me up, two days later. I was the sole survivor and I stayed in that tall red painted building over there on the hillside.

That is the local 'Ritz' hotel, and if you look down to the other end of the avenue type of street where an even bigger building is, that's the governors residence. Over there in another clearance is the hospital, and school. You can see the church spire from here too.

This is British territory so we have British bobbies and the red GPO phone boxes, English is the official language and we get the Blighty newspapers that come in every two or three days by the BOAC clippers." Lee said, pointing out to the buildings from John's cabin porthole.

"Thanks for the impromptu guide Tansey. I'll get that water hose jacked up for you. See you ashore, maybe in that hotel." John said cheerfully, and shutting his cabin door went to wait at the gangway for his two friends.

"We can't go up jungle to see the famous Kaieteur water falls, as we've been restricted to the town. So we may as well make ourselves comfortable in the local hotel and take it from there." Larter announced.

"That's the best place to start from I suppose Bruce. I've got a fresh water supply for the ship to organise before we leave the jetty anyway."

"I know just the man to get it too. Follow me." Sinclair advised, for all three to walk steadily towards a large shed further down the docks.

They arrived at the warehouse and strode out of the warm sunlight into the cavernous depths of the cold and dimly lit place, to be met by a large man smoking a big fat cigar.

"Can I help you?" the man asked crossly.

"Hello Taffy, you old scoundrel! You still here playing havoc?" Sinclair said with delight, holding out a hand to the man.

"Well if it ain't the flaming 'Haggis Yaffler'. How the hell are you Andy?" came the equally delighted reply.

Once the introductions were made and the reason for their visit, the Welshman had four local workers set up the water hoses for the ship.

John was told that although there was plenty of water all around the place, it had to be treated in case of all sorts of diseases.

"My grandfather used to have Blumstone and grit in a mix and put into the water filters." John revealed.

"Never heard of that, but we've got plenty of both. Tell me the mix and we'll give it a try on this header tank." Taffy stated, and sent yet another team of men away to get the items.

It did not take long for the mix to be added and a sample taken for the Welshman to give his verdict.

"There's a lovely brew, isn't it!. The finest fresh water I've tasted in years it is. The hospital will be pleased with that when it gets pumped up to them." he said assertively, wiping his chin with a huge bare forearm, covered in tattoos.

"I'm hoping you can fix me up with about half a ton each of Blumstone and grit. We'll be able to put it into our own header tank, just as soon as our evaps are fixed." John asked with a smile, and felt pleased and surprised that his Grandfather's magic potion worked as well as it did.

"You have just given me an idea that will make me lots of money. For that, you can have the first ton off me, but anybody else will have to buy it from now on." Taffy declared, patting John's shoulder with his large shovel like hands.

"I'll have it stowed on board just before we sail if that's all right with you Taffy."

The Welshman nodded, then all four men walked back into the open air again to warm themselves up again.

"Now that you're here for a day or so, call by and see the missus and me." Taffy offered and described where to find his house, before the three friends left him to his work.

The hotel was a typical colonial style one with high ceilings and overhead electric fans to keep the place cool. Everywhere was spacious and clean, with a highly polished floor covered with rattan mats, and cane furniture that had large cushions in abundance everywhere for the comfort of the guests.

The three friends arrived into the spacious foyer and after checking in at the reception they made their way into the posh looking bar that had quite a few elegantly dressed women and their nattily dressed men-folk sitting around with various coloured drinks in front of them.

"This is going to be a good run ashore Andy. What do you say Bruce?" John whispered, looking around the hotel lounge.

"Just be careful what you say and to whom. Most of these people are rich beyond most people you meet in a bar. They're gold and diamond mine owners. One wrong word or false move and they'll ruin you." Larter whispered, as Sinclair nodded in agreement.

"Well we're only here for the beer, so what's your pleasure gentlemen." John asked his friends, then after a snooty looking barman served them they went and sat in empty chairs by a round glass-topped table.

"Pass the cigars Bruce." Sinclair asked with a grin and got one for his cheek, as Larter handed each a big fat cigar, which they promptly lit and started to relax.

The other occupants in the lounge were giving the friends some looks, from the 'look at what the cat brought in' to, 'how dare these peasants come into our place and try to show off'. But the friends took no notice nor did they care. The others gave up in the end and just ignored them as if to pretend they weren't here.

Lee came walking into the lounge and greeted them cheerfully, then after getting his drink from the bar, he too sat with them. Such was the snootiness that the others got waited upon, whereas the now four friends had to get their own.

"I used to know the proprietor of this place. He went bankrupt because his so-called patrons, just like the set we've got here today, ran up too many hefty bar or hotel bills. When he asked them for payment, despite their vast wealth in gold and diamonds they didn't bother, but went elsewhere instead." Lee said in a loud voice, which seemed to reverberate all over the lounge.

There was an ice-cold silence, which descended over the lounge, where even the noise of the overhead fans seemed to stop. The silence was eventually broken when Taffy came in and made his way over to the table.

"I see you lot are getting along famously with our local residents." he said sarcastically, looking around the room at the angry faces of the others.

"Hello Taffy, did you pump that new water supply up to the hospital?" John asked with unconcern about the onlookers.

"Yes, but I ran a test on it before hand. The Doc up there agrees that it's pure nectar, and worth its weight in the old proverbial. Thanks for the recipe John, the beer is on me, but we'll go somewhere somewhat cheaper than this dump before we go for a decent bit of grub. The missus is making a roast dinner for us." Taffy said, emphasising the words this dump and roast dinner.

121

The friends followed the Welshman out of the hotel and down the slight slope of the driveway until they found a jeep waiting for them.

"Climb aboard and hold tight. Driver, take us to Lazy Joes' place." Taffy ordered, as the jeep sped along the tarmac road, which gave way to the compacted earthen one.

John noticed that the capitol was somehow split into three parts. The rich, or upper class occupying the city centre, the mine officials and other middle class families around that, with the labourers and other menials on the outside and living in shanty villages.

The jeep stopped in a cloud of dust at a clearance in the trees, where there was a large stone-built building lit up like a Christmas tree, with plenty of music and laughter coming from it.

They got out of the jeep and climbing up the flower festooned stone steps entered the cool interior of a large foyer, where there were servants scurrying about carrying drink laden trays.

"Do you remember this place 'Haggis'?" Taffy asked with a large grin on his face.

"Do I? He's asking me if I knew my Granny." Sinclair said boastfully.

"And I do. I should have a bench out in the grounds somewhere with my name on it." Lee stated with equal pleasure.

"Well don't just stand there, come over to the bar and we'll get ourselves a good flagon of the best ale ever to be sold in B.G." Taffy ordered.

A large, bosomy woman, gaudily painted almost like a parrot came over and sat on Taffy's lap.

"Who have you brought for me today Taffy. They look as if they need cheering up." She cackled then clapped her hands.

"I'll have my best girls to see to your needs, just as long as you pay up. If you don't then they'll cut your balls off quicker than you can bat an eye." she said ominously, for four young, almost naked, girls arrived at the table, laughing and giggling as they set down a tray of drinks for the friends.

"Just leave the drinks girls, we'll come back to you later. Now off you go." Taffy ordered then playfully slapped their bottoms as they left the table.

"Thanks for that Taffy, I'm not into women at the moment as I've got too many things on my hands." Lee said gratefully, but was met with a hearty laugh from the others.

That started the mood off for them to drink and enjoy the ambience of the place for a while before the Welshman announced that it was time to take another hike back to town and meet the missus.

The evening at Taffy's home went well as everybody enjoyed themselves enormously. But with their stomachs full of home cooking, and their thirst slaked, it was time for them to return to the ship. The jeep arrived and took them back along the now very quiet and almost empty roads towards the dockyard.

There was a crack and the sound of glass shattering, forcing the driver to swerve the vehicle almost off the road, then slumped over his steering wheel. That was followed by several more cracks and pings around them.

"Bloody hell! We've been ambushed. Get out of the jeep and into the ditch, quick!" Sinclair whispered, for the friends to clamber out of the vehicle, dragging the driver with them.

"He's dead, so leave him." Lee also whispered, and pointed to a narrow gully that led between two houses.

"We can get help from one of these people inside…" Larter started to say but was interrupted by Lee.

"Not likely, they don't want to be involved." Lee said, as more bullets flew around them and into the now burning vehicle.

"What happened to cause this Tansey?" John asked, hiding behind a large log.

"It's the local bandits. They must have thought we were para-military, because the army garrison here have been on their case for some time now, at least since I left nearly eight years ago." Lee whispered, as the friends crept through the gully to the back of the houses.

Larter pointed to a truck that was parked under some trees, and beckoned the friends to follow him to it.

Lee and John checked it over and gave Larter the nod to hot-wire the engine to get it started. The vehicle roared into life and for the friends to clamber into it before it sped away.

Sinclair was wrestling with the steering wheel, driving the vehicle full speed over bumps and potholes, until they finally arrived into the lighted streets of the city centre where they slowed down then eventually stopped.

"Take it back to the ship and leave it by one of the dockyard cranes along the jetty. Nobody will know it's us that borrowed it." Lee ordered, as Sinclair swerved the truck violently to the right and roared through the open gate of the dock complex, before skidding to a halt at the side of a large warehouse.

"I think it's best to leave it here and stroll around the other side to the gangway." Sinclair stated, shutting off the engine and jumping out, followed quickly by the others.

The friends arrived back on board ship just in time to see army scout-cars arrive alongside the truck, with their cannons pointing to it.

"Bloody hell. We've got back just in the nick of time, or those men would have blown us to pieces with their cannons." Sinclair said with relief, as they stood and watched the soldiers search the area for the missing occupants of the truck.

They finally observed one of the soldiers climb into the truck and drive it away, sandwiched between two scout-cars.

"Those boys didn't waste any time. To think that those armoured vehicles were part of our cargo until this morning." John said quietly to his friends, as they ambled along the deck, unaffected by the scene and entered the saloon. But as they found the place empty and the bar shut, they decided it was time to get turned in, to close what was one very eventful day ashore, by any standards.

Chapter XVII
Good News

It was the deep-throated sound of a ship's horn that woke John out of his sleep.

He climbed out of his bed, drew the little curtains back from his porthole and looked out, only to shield his eyes against the bright sunlight streaming into his face.

He heard and saw a military band playing as they marched along, and after opening his porthole and sticking his head out, he observed that it was the troop-ship had finally arrived.

'Judging by the state of her, she has most of her hull paint stripped right off so she must have been clobbered by some rough weather.' he mused, dressing quickly and making his way up onto the foc'sle to get a better look.

He looked at his watch, which told him it was past breakfast time and realised that the steward had not given him his usual early call.

He sat on the capstan smoking a cigarette when Larter arrived next to him, also to get a good view.

"What a wasted voyage John. But judging by those cheering passengers and the state of the ship, they're glad to arrive alongside." Larter said quietly, watching the army parading up and down the dockside, whilst the ship was being tied up.

"What do you mean, a wasted voyage Bruce?"

Larter handed John a piece of paper.

"This signal has just this minute arrived. My opposite number on the troop-ship, just like me, hasn't had time to show his skipper it yet." he said excitedly, as John read the signal:

'At 1100 hours GMT. The Prime minister has announced from Downing Street, that a ceasefire out in the Orient has been achieved and that all hostilities will cease forthwith. All current troop movements will cease as of tomorrow and a gradual withdrawal from the war- zone will be conducted by the end of the week. Further bulletins will be issued as they come through. God Save the Queen.'

"Well thank god for that, no more stupid killing." John said sombrely, then realised what he had just read.

"But that's just great Bruce. We'll get to take our passengers back to Canada and have that run ashore after all. Maybe we can be sent up into the lakes in time for the season again." John said with delight.

"Why yes. You're right there John. Our ship is the only one equipped to take them back." Larter replied with the same enthusiasm, but he too changed his mood.

"Hah! We should be so lucky John. If Belverley and his cronies have anything to do with it, we'll be going the other way, swapping cargoes at sea even, if he had his way." Larter said glumly, which did not dent John's optimism.

"Don't be like that Bruce. Judging by last night's run ashore, we've been run out of town with bullets flying our way. You know it and so do I that this is no place for tanks and armoured vehicles, only infantry and maybe those Ghurkhas or whatever they're called."

Larter merely nodded then gave John another piece of news.

"Belverley and his gang are arriving by plane this afternoon, and will be reviewing our next cargo. So we've to remain unladen until then. In other words, it looks like we're back to the mixed cargo and timber again. Anyway John, I must go and find the mad monk, before he climbs into his pulpit again to have the commandments thrown at us, you watch." Larter chuckled, leaving quickly to spread the news.

The army band had just finished playing and there was a moment of silence just as Blayden began broadcasting over the *Inverlaggan's* tannoy system.

For some reason everybody stopped what they were doing at the time, and a hushed silence befell the place.

Blayden read out the signal clearly to the hushed audience. It must have taken everybody a full minute to register what he announced, but it was swiftly followed by the roar of cheers, as delighted people started to dance when the band finally struck up again to celebrate the good news. The strains of the famous sound of 'Glen Miller' music filled the jetty and even echoed throughout the troopship and the *Inverlaggan,* as John strolled back to his cabin feeling just as elated as those disembarked troops.

'More lives saved thank goodness.' he muttered to himself, when Lee met him in the cabin flats.

"Amen to that John. Now to the business of yesterday, and our friend Taffy Jones." Lee said calmly, and explained to John what he was required to do.

"We'll have to render it down into smaller quantities stowed around the evap room Tansey, but the first half can be loaded straight into the header tanks, providing you place an external filter over the drain valve. That way we can re-use the mix until it starts to sludge, then we ditch it overboard. One thing though. Does 'Spanners' know about this?"

"Yes, but only you know the true mix, John. That should keep him guessing until we arrive back in Belfast."

Both engineers talked shop for a while before their conversation touched the shooting last night.

"Taffy phoned Andy this morning asking where his jeep was. When he was told what happened, he was most concerned. But Andy and I smell a rat, and I think its something to do with me and the statement I made in that hotel yesterday."

John was taken aback at this statement, but said that he would do anything to help them, even to enlist help from Ford and his army pals.

Lee deemed that a good idea and suggested that they all meet up in Taffy's warehouse and try to flush out those responsible, but with Ford and his troops standing by. All this had to be done before the ship was loaded up again. Larter had just joined them and was quickly told of the conversation and what they were planning.

"Just as well we've got a few hours to play with before we meet our ship owners, Taffy. So we'd better get our army boys down here on the double, but discreetly hidden for when we make our move." John ventured, as the men hatched their plan.

Taffy's new jeep roared into life and moved sedately down the roads to their target, which was arrived at in safety.

The men sauntered into the hotel foyer and went straight into the lounge where they saw a collection of expensively dressed men sitting around a table.

"I understand one of you so-called gentlemen wishes for my demise, and that you had my driver shot and my vehicle destroyed." Taffy yelled, entering the bar and approaching the men.

Two of the men went as white as a sheet at the sight of the five men standing before them as large as life.

Lee spotted them and singled them out calling them by name, with Taffy also recognising those named.

"Fancy you still being around! And here's me thinking the governor had you shot. Still fiddling the tax books are we Hughes?" Lee accused, and grabbing the man by his lapels dragged him right out of his chair. Taffy did the same to the second one with similar vehemence.

Two of the other men squealed and shying away as Larter and Sinclair advanced towards them, who tried to escape but John barred their exit.

"Quick get the police." one of them shouted to an astonished waiter.

"Don't just stand there, get the police or you'll find yourself down a mine without a ladder." he wailed, but the waiter just stood there almost petrified.

"And as for you Lomax. You've had it in for me for some time now, ever since I had your utilities shut down on your mining operations. You lot really must learn to pay your bills instead of bankrupting everybody." Taffy said to his captive.

Lee asked a few questions and got his answers with the help of a few slaps and some arm twisting before he was satisfied, and did Taffy, who threw his captive into his chair like a rag doll.

As he turned, Larter warned Taffy that the man was pulling a gun on him, but before he had time to pull the trigger Taffy had grabbed hold of a knife from a nearby table and threw it, which struck hard into the middle of the man's stomach.

Larter leaned over the victim, withdrew the knife and gave it back to Taffy.

The man screamed and held his stomach and started to cough up blood.

"I'll get you for this. You're all dead. My boys will burn you out and string the lot of you up." he avowed haltingly.

"You are in no position to get anybody. I know where your boys hang out and that's where the governor will put an end to all this gangland hooliganism." Lee said menacingly, then gave his signal to Ford and his men.

"You have witnessed all that was said, and what took place, officer. Place them under arrest pending governors assizes." John stated, standing aside to let the fully armed soldiers come into the room and grab the group of men before they were dragged out to a waiting lorry.

"Thank you for your help in catching these men, maybe we'll have some peace now. The outgoing regiment will be pleased, as they've been a thorn in the side of our boys for quite a time. The irony of it all is that its been caused by just a few men with enough wealth to hire their own army. Men supposed to be loyal to your new Queen and our Commonwealth." Ford said with a smile, and watched the last of the soldiers file out of the lounge.

"If ever you need a few helping hands again, just ask for me, John. Must go now." Ford said gently, shaking John's hand then the rest of the friends' hands before he also left.

"There you are Taffy, a grateful soldier on your doorstep. Treat him good for us won't you." John said, turning to Taffy.

"He seems a good one. Yes, I'll do just that..." Taffy began but was interrupted by John.

"Don't even think of Lazy Joes'." he said with a grin.

"What me? Never!" Taffy said in mock surprise, as all the friends trooped out of the building and went back to the ship.

"Thanks for everything Taffy. Try and see us before we sail." Sinclair said on behalf of the others, who nodded their heads in approval.

"Will do just that." Was the reply as Taffy sped off in his jeep. Lee looked at his watch and stated that they were just in time for early lunch before the 'gang' visited them again.

Chapter XVIII
An Oddball

"**S**ettle down gentlemen." Lord Invergarron invited, as his co-partners were getting ready to deliver their next task for the ship.

"Good morning to you all. No doubt you've heard the good news about the cease-fire out in the Orient. Not only is that good news, but it also means that you will now take on a much different cargo and a different destination to reach. That is providing all stays equal, and we are not forced to change our mind mid-channel, so to speak." Belverely said heartily then commenced his speech.

He described and explained in great detail why he was down in this part of the world and what he wanted them to do.

His usual impeccable oration lasted for an hour, before he handed the proceedings to Blayden.

He in turn echoed the thoughts of Belverley, Invergarron and the others of the entourage, and gave the crew his own version as to what he required from them.

The proceedings came to an end for the ship owners to file out of the saloon, leaving the officers and men scratching their heads as to which direction they were sailing next, but most importantly, when they would be able to return home again.

John was called away to see Jones, who was standing in a group with lesser company managers.

"That decking arrangement you augmented was a success engineer Grey. It's just as well your chief spotted the changes necessary to accommodate the extra, shall we say, passengers." one of them stated.

"It's just as well we've got a good chief engineer then." John replied, thinking he was being sarcastic, but Jones took the reply in quite the opposite manner.

"Nice of you to say so 3rd." Jones said pleasantly, then turned to the men and described his new mix for making good fresh water, suitable for any passenger liner.

John did not wait to be dismissed, but left the group anyway, who were very surprised at John leaving without their permission, but let him go anyway, preferring to listen to Jones' newest invention.

John arrived back into the fold of his friends and enjoyed a couple of drinks with them before he had to supervise the loading of the cargo with Walters the 2nd mate.

"We have a whole range of building material to load, including sand, but that will be in bags. What we need to do, is to devise a load pattern so that the ship is stable and the cargo safe." Walters explained, pointing to the train of wagons loaded with goods that was arriving alongside the ship.

John thought for a moment then asked what other cargo is being loaded, before he made his decision.

"The ship has to be trimmed just right, just like a balanced see-saw 2nd." John stated then went on to explain just how it was to be done. Walters nodded his head from time to time, in agreement with what was said, before he was left to his task.

"I'll be up on the boat deck if you need me 2nd." John called, walking for'ard and making his way up to the bridge then onto the boat deck..

"Hello John, looks as if we've got a nice round trip as a floating builders merchant, right down the middle of the Atlantic." Southgate volunteered, meeting John on the boat deck.

"That's what's bothering me. This old crate is okay for the Canadian lakes where it belongs, not in the middle of a ruddy great ocean."

"All we'll be doing is island hopping, John, so it's not so bad after all."

"It's not the islands I'm bothered about, it's the lumpy wet bits in the middle."

Southgate chuckled and told John not to be such a worrier, saying that they'd be mostly in the calm warm areas found in the middle.

John smiled at the thought of Neptune visiting them again, shrugged his shoulders and left Southgate packing away his flags neatly into his signal locker.

* * *

It was nearly dark when John had finished working on the ship's whistle and foghorn before he decided to wrap it up for the day.

He entered his cabin, stripped off and had a cool shower before donning his evening wear, suitable for the saloon, and was surprised to find that it was almost full with passengers again.

"It never ceases to amaze me where all these passengers keep coming from Bruce." John stated, looking around the crowded compartment.

"These are the relief scientists bound for Tristan da Cunha, who will replace those that will be going onto Gough Island. They are in no rush to get there as they have other scientific work to do on the way. But we've got a detour to the Ascensions first. Special cargo and all that, at least that is the plan." Larter said with a smile, offering John a cigarette.

"Then what of any replacement cargo?" John asked, then hesitated.

"I know, transferred!" he added.

"Now you're getting the picture of how this company works. You are paid less each time there is a change of cargo, due to the incomplete voyage. Lowther arrived in person to give us our danger money for the ammo we had on board, but he took some of it back because all the ammo got off-loaded and not kept for the military base on Ascension. That deduction will pay for their flight back to Barbados or wherever he decides to go to next."

"That is downright disgusting Bruce. We're being robbed left, right, and centre."

"That's only the half of it John, but I don't want to bore you. Come, let's have a drink." Larter offered, quickly changing the subject.

The friends chatted and discussed their recent run ashore for a while before they were joined by Southgate, and shortly after, Sinclair.

"That state of play was almost like Barbados, but in reverse, Andy." Larter stated.

"Aye indeed, that was just what I thought. But at least it wasn't John's fault this time." Sinclair said philosophically as Taffy arrived to join them.

"All set for your swim around the 'oggin' then lads, is it?" Taffy asked amiably.

"Just about. We're sailing about six in the morning, although I don't know why, because there's hardly any tide here to bother about." Sinclair opined.

"That's when the dockyard workers start up! They won't start before sun-up for fear of the big 'Ju-Ju' spirits take them away and throw them down some pit or other." Lee said knowingly.

"Speaking of pits. Did Ben Ford get those bandits that attacked us last night, Taffy?" John asked, contributing to the conversation.

"The army had a big purge, all day it was, and rounded up several more seedy characters such as those in the hotel, and shot several of the nasty ones whilst they were at it. Getting their own back, so to speak. But as the man said, its peace in our time now, isn't it!" Taffy grinned.

Their conversation was cut short with the tannoy announcement that all visitors had to leave the ship, and all passengers to ensure all their excess baggage was properly stowed in the baggage room.

"Well lads. It's been nice knowing you all. And nice to see you again you old Scotch egg! Come back again some time, you know where to find me. There's nice it'll be!" Taffy said affectionately, shaking each friend warmly by the hand, before Sinclair and Lee escorted him go the gangway.

It wasn't long after the two came back, before it was time for the passengers to get turned in, and the crew to get an early night's sleep before the start of yet another roller coaster of a ride.

The ship slipped quietly out of Georgetown harbour and headed once more into the vast empty spaces of the central zone of the Atlantic, for yet another long haul to other out-of-the-way places that you wouldn't dream of going to, on any ordinary voyage.

John was satisfied that his end of the inspection round was okay, as both he and Danvers made their report to Blayden.

"Bosun, steer 125, and tell the engine room to make revs for 15 knots. Secure from harbour duties and set up a passage watch. Next stop Ascension Islands. First mate, conduct lifeboat drills in three hours, say 11.00 hours. But if anybody wants me, I'll be in my day cabin." Blayden commanded, taking his last visual land bearing and marking his sea-chart accordingly. He listened to the two reports and was satisfied with them before he dismissed them.

"How long will it take us to Capetown first mate?" John asked politely.

"It depends on several factors such as our speed, how long we stay in port and most importantly, the weather. But if I remember the last time I did such a voyage, it took us about five weeks. Mind you we had about one week stoppage time in harbour."

"From Capetown to Belfast would add about another four weeks. That is some sea time we'll have done by the time we get home again, first mate. Oh well, let's hope we have a straight voyage home, and not turn right into the Med or somewhere." John said philosophically, as they parted company on the bridge, with John staying to speak to Sinclair.

"Hello Andy. What have you got in store for this leg of the voyage?

"Morning John! Providing the skipper keeps us seaward side of the Amazon, nothing much."

"I spoke to Walters this morning during his rounds. He's rigging up a second pool on the foc'sle for the lads, and wants me to rig the pumps for it. So you might be able to sunbathe and generally take the sea air when off watch."

Sinclair laughed at the expression, 'taking the sea air', but agreed it was a good gesture by Walters.

"How are you getting on with the men now, Andy?"

"Getting there slowly. Just one or two die-hards left, but they're not worth bothering about, as I'm in charge, not them. Anyway what will you be doing?"

"Usual maintenance checks and rounds, now that I've sorted out the ventilation. But I have a theory and a plan that I would like to test out, and need your help in the matter. But only you, nobody else, that is if you're willing to do so Andy."

"Certainly John, anything to keep myself busy. What is it?"

"I have some calculations and work to do first, but once you're involved you'll like it, eventually." John said with a smile..

"Oh aye! What scheme are you plotting this time, as if I didn't know already." Sinclair grinned.

"I've got to do this in a covert manner, and as I've said, only you will be involved. Give me until the day after tomorrow, and I'll come and give you the nod."

"Can you give me a clue in case I get detailed off with yet another hair brained task, Danvers always seems to come up with. Last time it was re-rigging the after cargo derrick booms."

"Let's put it this way. You'll be on the bridge doing what you're doing now, only with no hands. Andy."

Sinclair looked out to sea in front of the ship for a moment, then at the course he was steering, until he smiled broadly.

"Why you crafty devil. You don't mean what I think you mean, when you mentioned it on the *Brook*?"

John chuckled and nodded his head slowly.

"The very same. I was trying to get it organised on the way down to B.G. but had my hands full at the time, so now's my chance before 'Spanners' has other ideas for me."

"You can count me in John. I'll arrange to be the relief for the duty helmsman when you're ready."

"Thanks Andy. See you then." John smiled then left for his cabin.

* * *

"Do you hear there, this is the first mate speaking." Danvers announced over the tannoy, announcing to the passengers of the imminent lifeboat drill, and for the duty upper deck crew to muster on the boat deck, with the 3rd engineer in attendance.

John was busy in his cabin doing his maintenance logs and trying to sort out his new plan, when the steward minced in and announced that he was required on the boat-deck straight away

"What ever for steward?" John asked absentmindedly.

"Only lifeboat drill 3rd. Still it's a lovely day for it, and I might go up and have a look at what goes on, just for a bit of fun." the steward lisped.

"I wouldn't if I was you steward, you might get detailed off as part of the demonstration team. Think of what that might do to your hairstyle." John said with a grin.

"Oh yes you're right, must think of my perm. It took Flossie ages to get it right. And here's me thinking you didn't care about Julie, you naughty man you!" the steward said, and gently but playfully punched John's shoulder, as John stood up to leave.

"But I like you!"

"Well at least that is a favour repaid. Kindly leave my papers where they are, as I'll be back to them in about 15 minutes. Maybe a nice cup of coffee when I come back?"

"Brazilian, Rhodesian or Turkish?" the steward tempted.

"Whatever is the flavour of the day, but make it a large one."

"Ohhh, I like large flavoured ones too." the steward said suggestively using a double meaning.

John just shook his head gently and gave a little smile as he finally left the cabin.

'He's such an oddball and too much for me, so mustn't encourage him' he sighed, arriving onto the boat-deck.

"The swivel mechanism on the port for'ard davit appears not to work, Grey. Just as well the first mate chose the starboard side." Gibson whispered to him as Danvers was explaining to the passengers what would happen in an emergency.

"This is the third such incident that has happened here, Gibson. I shall need you to accompany me and speak to Danvers after this drill. It's about time we sorted out whatever it is that is going on." John said, taking a closer look at the offending mechanism.

"See here. It's a piece of rope stuck in the gears, and by the look of it, it's not the type that is used to lash the lifeboat with. See what you think?"

Gibson took the piece of rope and examined it carefully then stated that it belonged to the cordage that is always kept on the lifeboat.

"This is a length of rope that is used to tie the craft up when it is moored or being hauled ashore. It is part of the emergency equipment and emergency rations always kept on the craft. Better see what else is amiss." Gibson stated, climbing up and into the lifeboat.

Whilst John waited for Gibson to climb back down again, he worked the mechanism until it was turning free again, and under the straying eyes of some of the passengers who were supposed to be paying attention to Danvers and the 4th Mate.

Gibson clambered down and saw that John had a finger over his lips to signal him to keep quiet.

"We will discuss this on the bridge." John whispered, as the two officers left the deck and went into the bridge, where they found Blayden working at his sea-chart.

"Aren't you two supposed to be helping the first mate, or has the boat drill finished now?" Blayden snapped.

"Yes captain. The first mate will be here in a minute, once he's disentangled himself from the inquisitive passengers. You know what these scientists are like, they keep you talking for ages." Gibson said swiftly and gave John a quick sideways glance.

"Very well. Wait on the other side of the bridge, and be quiet about it." Blayden conceded then went back to his navigational chores.

Fortunately for them, Danvers arrived on the bridge on the same side as them, as Gibson spoke to him.

"I have a problem with one of the life-boats that I need your opinion about, first mate." Gibson said firmly, and beckoned Danvers to follow him back out and onto the boat deck again. John followed behind them until they found a suitable spot to talk.

"What is it 3rd mate. One more of your hair-brained ideas again?" Danvers moaned, but shut up as soon as Gibson, with the input from John, explained what they found.

Danvers was horrified at the prospect of possible sabotage or theft on board.

"Get all deck hands mustered up here now. That includes the two junior deck officers. Then have each boat checked over. I want an inventory made for each one." Danvers said angrily then turned to John.

"You can go now 3rd. This is a sailors job now, and thanks for nothing."

John shrugged his shoulders and left the irate first mate shouting at the hapless deck officers.

'Ungrateful swine. That's the last time I'll help any of them.' he muttered, and went swiftly back down into his cabin to find a cup of coffee steaming away on top of a pile of his books.

'At least the steward appreciates help when It's' needed, despite his' poofter' ways,' he thought to himself, drinking down the welcoming beverage.

Chapter XIX
Swimsuits

The second pool was welcomed with delight and proved to be very popular with the crew, as both pools turned the ship into almost a real liner, as opposed to a passenger-carrying cargo ship.

Everybody made good use of the lazy days by sunbathing or splashing around in the cool seawater of the pools. The tannoy system had popular music blaring from it, with the stewards strolling around serving equally cool drinks of all colours and alcoholic flavours.

Even Blayden was seeing the wisdom of this, despite his loathing for the demon drink, as the ship steamed further into the middle of the Atlantic and towards the dotted line on the water that marked the Equator. He knew that this was the best part of the ocean, where the water would behave itself and beguile the humans into a false sense of well being before the rude awakening of tempests awaiting them as they sailed further down into the cold and murkier waters.

But for now, everybody was enjoying a brief visit from the King of the deep.

Neptune sat on his throne, whilst his little helpers scoured the ship for those un-initiated landlubbers that dared to sail without his permission, and brought them to face him. Nobody was excused or let off and had to face Neptune's court, where all the heinous crimes the landlubber did or did not do was read out, with much booing and jeering from the other helpers.

Once the person had been pronounced guilty, as always, and received their various outrageous and dastardly punishment, they were allowed to proceed over the dotted line, as his new helpers. This was, and still is a silly but very funny and hilarious ritual that gets conducted on every ship that crosses the equator, and is called 'Crossing the line' ceremony.

"Are you ready Andy?" John asked, pushing a button and pulling a lever, then asked Andy to watch the ships 'head'.

Sinclair stood by the large wooden spoked steering wheel, and watched closely as the ship kept its course, without his guidance. He stood watching this plan of John's working for a while, and even sat down in a chair next to the wheel smoking a cigarette, before he was satisfied with what he saw.

"So all I do is set the course, put the helm into this automatic steering device and sit back, John."

"Yes. It will keep the ship on course almost as good as you Andy. At the moment the sea is calm and benign, so I'd need another test when it gets a bit lumpy. Maybe I'll have to make a few adjustments to the deviation angles to which the rudder will move between to maintain course."

Sinclair stared at the wheel again, watching it move on its own, keeping the steady course the ship was maintaining, before he put a long arm around John and hugged him gently.

"You have certainly kept your word John, and here's me thinking you were joking at the time. Well done. Wait until Bruce hears about this, he will be chuffed just as much as you no doubt." Sinclair said with delight at the new invention his friend had made.

"Hear about what, Andy? What are you two plotting this time?" Larter asked, appearing suddenly onto the bridge with a signal pad in his hand.

Sinclair showed Larter just what was happening and how it worked until he too was exclaiming his delight and congratulating John for his inventiveness.

"Keep it under your hats for now, until I get my plans ashore and posted off to McPhee. You will have to keep them for me Bruce, as the chief has very sharp eyes and is always poking his nose into my cabin when I'm not there. Andy, only you know of the set up and the new additions to the steering controls, so it will only be you that will operate it. Any awkward or inquisitive questions about the new features just tell them its only temporary to help the steering gear. That is the truth, but they won't know it nor take it any further."

Sinclair heard Blayden and Danvers talking when they approached the bridge, and quickly disengaged the automatic steering device. John and Larter were pretending to look out of the bridge windows so as not to be conspicuous, with Sinclair swiftly reverting to his hand steerage.

Blayden and Danvers paid no attention to the 3 friends, instead they crossed through the bridge and into Blayden's night cabin at the back of the bridge, talking as they went

"Phew, that was close Andy. The ceremony must be over now, so we can expect your duty helmsman along any moment now." John whispered, with a sigh of relief.

"All in good hands now John. See you again when we have a drop of roughers." Sinclair replied with a nod.

"When you do your evening rounds, I'll be on watch, so give me your plans then and not Paul. That way, and no offence to Paul, there is only the three of us in the know. 'Spanners' is a different kettle of fish so you'll have to devise some bogus plan or other to satisfy him if he happens to spot the new gear attached to the steering column or wherever you have it connected up to. So be warned my friend." Larter advised, as they walked off the bridge and along to the radio shack.

"Yes Bruce, that's a good idea, and I agree with you about Paul." John agreed, then changed the subject and told him about the lifeboats.

"I saw a sailor and a stoker up on the deck when we arrived in Georgetown, but I was too busy to check up on them. Probably pinching rope to flog ashore, and it got caught in the winding gear so they cut it loose."

"Well let's hope so. I'll be able to tell you later on, when I've met up with the 3rd mate on his rounds later. Must go now Bruce, see you later, if not then in the saloon after dinner."

"Aye, see you then." Larter replied, as John shut the door behind him and made his way back to his cabin.

"Here are the plans and drawings Bruce." John said, handing Larter a large brown envelope.

"I'll get it wrapped up in one of my mailbags, sealed, and marked for onward delivery to McPhee. But he's still in Bermuda, so it might take a few weeks before he gets it." Larter advised then asked about the lifeboat problem. John told him what Gibson had said, which was mostly what Larter had stated.

"There you are. Just as long as everything is as it should be in those boats, then all will be well. Else somebody is in for the high jump, should we have to use them in the first place."

"I must report my rounds soon Bruce, and by the way, here's your lighter back. I found it behind a stack of ashtrays in the saloon." John said, handing the lighter over.

"Speaking of which, how are you getting along with the passengers? Only I seem to have collected one of them, and she's right stunner with or without her clothes on." Larter announced.

"Oh! When have you seen her without clothes then Bruce, or are you keeping that to yourself?" John teased his friend.

"She planked her deck-chair next to mine by the pool from day one and likes to splash about in her bright red swimsuit. We got talking and shared a few drinks, before she, and her name is Alice by the way, had to leave and do some daily experiments or other. She can experiment on me any time, John." Larter said, moving his hands in a curving manner to help describe the woman's figure.

"Now now Bruce, you're already spoken for, even though she may be some thousands of miles away." John laughed, at the eagerness his friend was showing.

"She is back there in good company, I'm all alone. Present company excepted, but Alice can certainly take my mind of such things for a while." Larter said with a nod and a wink.

"What does she do? Are they all scientists? What about the men folk?" John asked in quick succession.

"There you go again John. Always rattling off questions like the machine guns we had in the desert a while back." Larter laughed, and told John what the scientists did and who did what. *

"You always were a ladies man, and that goes for Andy too. What am I going to do with you two?"

"It's all right for you, you've got a stunner stashed away that you are keeping all to yourself. If you're not careful, you'll arrive home one day and find her sitting on your doorstep with a baby suckling at her breast."

"Now that I wouldn't mind Bruce. But the thing is, Helena is a traveller just like me and doesn't seem to have the time to plan a family or whatever, certainly not for a long while yet. She and I are lovers yes, but we are free spirits and let each other enjoy life without the baggage of jealousy or possessiveness. It works for us, that's all I can tell you Bruce."

"Then you are indeed a very lucky man John. And glad you told us, because Andy and me had been wondering about you two. Still, maybe this Alice could be just like your Helena, and I'm all for giving it a go, if you see what I mean."

"Well, I wish you luck Bruce. Must go now, so see you later in the saloon." John concluded, leaving to report to Blayden.

"Rounds correct, and my daily report handed to the chief!" John stated, but found that he was speaking to Blayden's back, as he was busy with his charts.

"Thank you 3rd." Blayden replied, writing down yet another calculation on his chart.

"But there's one thing I need you to sort out, and that is our fresh water. The passengers are complaining about the water tasting foul, and because most of them are scientists, they have analysed it and state that it needs purifying by a different process, or at least alter the compound. Go and see the chief, no doubt, he'll put you in the picture better than I can." Blayden stated, then dismissed John with a wave of his arm.

John went down to Jones' cabin and found him doing his paperwork.

"The captain has told me about the fresh water problem chief, and I was told to report to you."

Jones stopped what he was doing, threw his pen onto the large pile of papers, and spoke to John in a thinly disguised voice full of venom and disdain.

"You and your bloody fancy water purifying system is poisoning everybody on board. It's your invention so you had better get down the engine room and get it sorted out. Get going Grey, and report to me when you've solved the problem." he demanded.

John stood still, shook his head slowly and said in a calm and even voice.

"On the contrary chief. I distinctly heard you tell the ship owners that you had invented a new filter system by using the exact compound that I had recommended to you earlier. It was you that they praised not me and it was you who took all the glory, not me. In plain terms chief, you took all the credit, and even patented in your own name. Therefore chief, it is your pigeon not mine. You sort it out not me, as I'm not allowed to meddle in other peoples inventions."

Jones went bright red in the face, stood up and bellowed at the top of his voice.

"You dare tell me my job? You dare disobey an order? You will do as you're told or I will see that you will be stranded in the next port of call. You are the one that gave me the concoction, therefore you are the one that will, and I mean it, will sort it out before we all get poisoned."

"You look here chief." John said in deadly earnest, leaning right over the desk to thrust his face into Jones'.

"It appears to me chief, it's your undoing not mine. And the current rule of this shipping line states that 'what I invent or adapt for use on board gets taken off me by the likes of you'. With the proceeds shared only between you and the skipper. You did that with my drawings of the cargo hold adaptations, the ventilation system, and as you did with the fresh water purification." John snarled as Jones interrupted him, going even redder in the face.

"I'm a fully qualified chief engineer, whereas you are only a jumped up 3rd and will never to get beyond that as long as your arse looks downwards. Now get down that evap room and sort out that system." He ordered.

John shook his head slowly and telling him to get stuffed, and repeated Jones words in parrot fashion as what he had said to the ship owners.

Then as he left Jones' cabin, he managed to get the final coup de gras on the chief, who looked as if he was about to have an apoplectic fit.

"I know the exact mix for that formula you stole off me. I know exactly what went wrong and how to fix it. But then, I'm only a jumped up 3rd engineer on board this vessel after all, whereas you are the CHIEF Engineer. It's your invention not mine, don't forget."

John left the cabin humming to himself, but purposefully left the door wide open, then counted to five. He was not disappointed in the result.

The roar of rage from Jones could be heard right down the entire cabin aisle-way, and loud enough for other officers to poke their heads out of their cabins to see what the commotion was.

John passed Lees open cabin door and saw him writing at his desk, so he knocked and asked politely if he could have a word.

"Yes John, what can I do for you, as if I haven't already heard." Lee said with an 'ear to ear' grin, and indicated a chair for John to sit on.

"You really must not go around upsetting chief engineers, for the fall-out will come back on the rest of us. And before you say anything John, I agree with all what you said to him, and its entirely his own fault. But for all our sakes, please reconsider your judgement. I mean, how long would it take for you to re-filter entire the fresh water system. Two maybe three hours?"

"Yes if I have to do all three evaps at the same time. Otherwise, make it about half an hour and one at a time. But then it all depends on what state 'Spanners' had left it in. I mean, as to what compound mix he used."

"Well there you are John, what's half an hour between friends against about four weeks of sheer misery? You could do it in such a way that nobody would find out your own, shall we say, special mix. That way only you will have the right formula and not him. What do you say John?"

John was still adamant in not helping Jones out, but realised that the rest of the officers and especially the men would suffer the consequences, and felt in a catch 22 situation. He was damned if he did, and damned if he didn't. Lee was still persuading him to change his mind when John finally made his decision.

"Okay Tansey. I'll do this for the sake of the men and not me, but I want you to log this incident down and in company of Radio Officer Larter. He has a legal brain, and will advise us on what can be said or not. I want to teach Jones and his ilk a good lesson and in such a way that they will not do it again. That's the deal Tansey?"

Lee thought for a moment before he spoke.

"Okay then, it's a deal. If you get the fresh water problem sorted out by say, lunchtime, I'll meet you in the wireless office at about 14.00hours. Deal?" Lee asked, and held out his hand to shake on it. Both men shook hands and agreed that it would be done as promised.

"Hello Paul, Bruce. I've come to ask you both a favour if you would." John asked, then told them what it was.

"Certainly John. We'll just add it to the pile we've already got to send off for you. Paul will keep the radio schedule whilst I see to it." Larter agreed just as Lee came into the compartment.

"All sorted and sweet as champagne, Tansey, and glad you could make it." John said in greeting Lee.

"Yes, so I hear John. The passengers and certainly the men are grateful for your intervention. Now let's get down to business." Lee replied, for them to sit down and record the entire story of Jones' deceptions, the recent near poisoning of the lives on board, and of John's involvement in each case.

Larter wrote everything down, and spoke from time to time about the words used, or the legal terms that were needed. It took them over two hours to put everything down and have it signed, by each of them in the compartment.

"That is yet another feather in John's cap 2nd, and if you don't look out, he'll be doing your job next." Larter said with a grin and a gentle friendly slap on John's back.

"I'll gladly swap with John anytime of the day on this tub, but it would mean total war in the engine-room each time 'Spanners' came into it. John will do well as a 2nd, but he'd probably have to change shipping lines, as his card has been well and truly marked, and John should have guessed that by now."

"So that's what you meant by keeping out of 'Spanners' way and my head down. But why should I? I'm only doing the job to my best ability, so I don't understand why the powers that be are always on my back. I mean, I'm being robbed of any credit and cash for my ideas or suggestions, let alone stealing my inventions and patenting them in their own names." John said glumly

Larter soon cheered him up by telling a few well-remembered anecdotes that were of their own making, which held Lee and Southgate in amusement.

The meeting finished in time for Lee to go on watch, and John to do his rounds early enough to be able to watch the star attraction for the day, the evening film show in the saloon

He finished his rounds and reported to Blayden.

"I am pleased with your work on the water system, and so are the passengers. They know who fixed it and have asked me to convey their thanks. So well done 3rd, you've done a good job today. No doubt the chief will echo those words of mine." Blayden replied, and gave John a rare smile before he was dismissed in the usual manner.

'Some hopes for that captain, but at least it was worth finding out that you do crack your face with the odd smile.' John whispered to himself, arriving back into his cabin for a short rest.

Chapter XX
Brothers and Sisters

It was sun, sea, cocktails on the deck for all and a general laze around on the *Inverlaggan* for the past 10 days when came to the end of her first 4,000mile leg of her new voyage. The ocean had been kind to them all the way so far, maybe due to King Neptune's visit. But the prospect of arriving at a piece of land in the middle of it all was a happy one for everybody, especially for the ship that was in need of a good drink of fuel before setting off again.

The ship arrived during mid-morning and docked alongside the jetty at the naval base in the Ascension islands, with many a helping hand.

As the passengers were seen to, and streamed ashore to feel Terra Firma under their feet again and stretch their now very sun-tanned legs once more; so the ship had her needs attended to.

The British have occupied the islands, since the early 16th century, as a vital Trans-Atlantic crossing point for any vessel. It had a combined armed force providing a military presence, which is maintained at all times.

The administrative centre for all the middle Atlantic chain of islands are done from St Helena and stretches way down to as far as Trisdan da Cunha (TdC) therefore any British ship travelling between them always carries a certain amount of troops to relieve those on the islands.

The *Inverlaggan* would be no exception when she embarked the extra 'passengers' just as she did for her downward voyage to Georgetown.

"We've got plenty of space now 3rd mate. So we can rig up another temporary accommodation for the soldiers and in the same place, and put their equipment, stores etc into No 4 hold alongside the extra oil barrels we'll be taking." John said, when observing the loading of the ship.

"That looks the way of it, but they could really have been put into the spare cabins." Gibson said, continuing with his hand signals to the dockyard crane operator who was lowering the cargo into the ships holds.

John chuckled and told him otherwise, due to relief government staff being transferred to St Helena, their next stop. Which strictly speaking was over the maritime safety limits.

Once John was satisfied the ship was being loaded to a proper 'trim' he went to his cabin to change for a hasty run ashore with his 2 friends.

"Right Bruce, where is the best place to visit. The NAAFI or some hotel?" John asked, looking around the small collection of buildings that constituted the principal town on the island

"We'll go to the Brighton because that's where our shipping agent is. Not only that, but have you not spotted the abundance of our new 'Triple Crown' ships that are now in harbour? We've got the *Forestlea* outboard of the old *Orchardlea* astern of us. The *Inverawe* is two berths ahead of us, and the *Hudson Bay* alongside the old *Cardigan Bay* over at the oil terminal beyond that. She is due for scrap and this is her last paying voyage, so we could expect to meet some crew from all four of them as they come ashore. Anyway, I've got to get this mail and your special parcel to send off at the post office just across the road." Larter said breezily, as they strode purposefully along the busy road to the town centre.

"I called here a few years ago but not for a run ashore, but have you been ashore here too Andy?"

"Aye. Many moons ago on the *Cloverlea*, the voyage just before we met you in Belfast."

"That seems a life time away now Andy." John replied, for all three to lapse into silence for a while before they arrived at the Post Office with its British Union flag flying in the breeze.

Once Larter conducted his ship's business as the ship's postman, all three left the large brick building and crossed the road to enter the Brighton Hotel that was just as opulent inside as it declared it to the world on the outside.

They made their way into the bar and found an empty table by one of the bay windows, with seats for them to sit.

No sooner had they sat down, when a waiter came over and took their drinks order, returning shortly with it for them to enjoy.

"This is the life to enjoy. Pity we've got to cross some very lumpy water to get here though!" Sinclair stated, taking a large swig from his flagon of ale.

"Yes Andy, given the chance, we could just about get used to all of this. Mind you, providing Belverley and his company pays for it." John replied with a smile, with the other three nodding their heads in agreement.

Larter looked out the window and saw a group of men approaching the hotel.

"Here we go! Stand by for an afternoon of swinging the lamps and dodging the muck and bullets. Here comes the Triple Crown Line's press gang. Between the three of us we can recognise at least most of them. So stand by to repel boarders." Larter announced, quickly finishing off his drink.

"Har Har! Shiver me timbers, and splice the main-brace!" Sinclair said in pirate fashion.

"Pieces of eight, pieces of eight, Jim me lad!" John added in the spirit of the moment.

Soon the men from the other ships filed in and ordered their drinks before deciding to look for an empty table to settle down upon.

"Over here you varlets and landlubbers dressed up in sailors uniforms!" Sinclair shouted and beckoned the men to join them.

When the men descended en masse onto the small table, so did several of the waiters who had the presence of mind to grab a few tables and join them into one big one. Thus a memorable reunion was born.

The three friends stood up and greeted them all, as each encounter was remembered with much handshaking and back slapping, which also included the new faces in the crowd.

It is a special time when several ships meet at the same place and time, far from home, and where most of the individual ship's crews know each other through their own rights of passage and experiences on mutual voyages.

This is one time where old acquaintances and friendships are rekindled once more, and when each person has the chance to catch up since they were last on board together. For there is nothing like it in any other walk of life other than ex-servicemen or mariners that have sailed the seven seas, or have shared such hard lives, to compare with such a get together.

The impromptu re-union went so well and was so infectious that it eventually encompassed the other smaller groups of hotel guests who were there at the time. Even to the extent that, as soon as the word got round, everybody of consequence on the island wanted to attend and enjoy the occasion.

It came to a point that as the wine, liquor, booze and champagne flowed freely, with the hotel staff struggling to keep up with the demand, they had to enlist other hostelry staff to help out.

The management decided that an impromptu barbeque be provided out in the hotel gardens which was a wise decision as the party goers almost ate the hotel out of house and home. Such was the appetite and thirst of the participants. And by the end of the evening, everybody in the lounge was almost 'next of kin' or 'long lost brothers and sisters' as the mixture of drinks started to affect the partygoers.

It was at this point, and when everybody had had the same idea, for everyone to go and have some shut-eye, get some rest, or whatever else they had in mind. So the party wound down in a peaceful manner, as everybody went their separate ways. John and his friends as the instigators once more of such a good party, walked back to the ship alone, but together arm-in-arm and singing shanty songs as they went along.

9 "We are due to sail in thirty minutes 3rd. You'd better get organised and see to your duties." the steward whispered, shaking John roughly from his alcohol-induced sleep.

"All right steward, there's no need to rip my shoulder off me." John said, sitting bolt upright and gripping his painful shoulder.

"You must have had one hell of a good run ashore yesterday 3rd, for you to not to stir on my first wake up call." the steward said almost apologetically

"What time is it steward. Have I time for breakfast, cause I'm ruddy starving." John replied, swinging his legs over the side of his bunk and leaping down onto the carpeted deck.

"It's 06.30 hours. You've missed the crew's breakfast slot, but here's a breakfast roll and a cuppa for you."

"Thanks steward, you're a good sort. Leave my cabin until you've had time for your own breakfast, providing the new passengers will let you that is."

"Well, from you that means a lot 3rd. Enjoy!" the steward said airily, slipping out of the cabin shutting the door behind him.

John ate his meagre breakfast and managed a quick shower before he donned his boiler suit and collected his round's equipment.

'That was a good evening worth remembering, especially some of the officers I had met.' He whispered to himself, stepping out of his darkened cabin to get himself on deck and ready for leaving harbour.

John stood on the poop deck to watch the island disappear behind a veil of smoke that was bellowing from the squat funnel, until he decided it was time for his first rounds of the day.

He worked his way forward, checking everything thoroughly before he was satisfied he was able to make his report to Blayden.

"Very good 3rd. Now tell me how you managed to charm virtually the whole of the Ascension Islands to a party, that I heard you were partly responsible for last night?" Blayden asked with a raised eyebrow and leaned forward to hear the reply.

"Party last night captain? Oh that. It was just a get together with old shipmates from the other Triple Crown ships that were in harbour. Nothing more, I can assure you."

"Well it seems that it must have been a good one, for it was reported to Lord Belverley and company. Not by me you understand, even though I don't take kindly to the evil drink and fornication. Anyway, lets hope for your sake we have a better second leg of our voyage than the last one, and I'm not talking about the weather either, if you get my drift. Your chief had told me of your altercation with him, but let's also hope that it will die a natural death." Blayden said at length taking his usual adopted position over the chart.

"Amen to that captain."

"So be it 3rd, you may leave now." Blayden replied with a nod, returning to his sea chart.

Danvers arrived on the bridge and asked John to provide more water for the pools again, before he finished for the day. That order was acknowledged, but John went over and nudged Sinclair gently.

"After lifeboat drill, switch 'STAN' (Steering and Navigation) on. But make sure you're alone for a while, as I've got a few minor adjustments to make with the flip-flop mechanism and other alignments, Andy. When I give you a shout up the voice pipe, I'll ask you if Stan is there. No he isn't meaning you've got problems, or yes, meaning all is working." he whispered.

Sinclair nodded as his acknowledgement before he reported his course and speed to Blayden.

"Steering 169. Speed 17knots!" he said in a loud voice.

"Very well bosun, set passage watches. 3rd engineer! Clear the bridge. First mate! In accordance with Lloyds shipping insurance policies, and in conjunction with the Ministry for shipping, lifeboat drills are to be conducted on each occasion any ship that leaves port. Therefore you will conduct our next lifeboat drill at 09.00 hours. See to it." Blayden commanded sternly.

"See you later Andy!" John whispered to Sinclair and left as ordered.

* * *

"Bridge! Is Stan there?" John asked, shouting up a voice pipe from where he was working. This type of communication used on board is just as effective as using a sound powered telephone. The voice tubes have direct access to certain important areas in the ship, such as the engine room, emergency steerage position, the captain's cabin, and the like.

"Aye, he's here. I'm on watch for the next half hour so I'll switch it off then, John." Sinclair called back as loud as he could so as not to be heard by the messenger or Blayden who was at his chart table again.

"That's okay Andy, cheers and see you later." John replied, clearing his tools and drawings away, before going on deck for a quiet smoke.

"3rd, can I have a word? Maybe you can help me in a certain matter." Menzies asked, meeting John on deck.

"Hello 4th! How can I help?"

Menzies explained his problem in detail, which was interspersed with questions or amplifications from John.

"It seems that you have forgotten the basics and the calorific value formula between oil and diesel. The latter being of a much higher value." John replied, before he wrote down the basic formula for Mitchell to read and learn.

"Thanks 3rd. I knew it was something like that, but couldn't find my crib notes to check it. Cheers, that helps me no end." Menzies stated with delight before he left John with a nod and another word of thanks.

'*It's just as well I was reading through some of my old notes, or I'd be hard pressed to answer him. Must ask Tansey how Menzies is getting on.*' John muttered to himself but was startled as Larter spoke into his ear.

"Still sorting out your engineering manual in your head again John?"

"Something like that Bruce. While we're at it, how's your A.C.U ?" John asked in reply.

"Going like a good 'un. An air-conditioned office is just great. Maybe you could fix it so that we could have air-conditioned streets in some of the places we visit."

"How about setting up in the Arctic Circle somewhere Bruce, that should do you. I'm quite happy sweating my proverbials off, instead of having them frozen like the brass monkey."

The little moment of banter between two firm friends continued until they arrived at their respective cabins.

"Oh, by the way Bruce. The steward couldn't get me Senior Service fags this time round, but got Players Weights. Any chance of swapping some of them for some of your Senior Services, or have you got the same as me?" John asked, suddenly remembering a little inconvenience with his cigarette supply.

"Certainly, but you should have asked one of the lads off the *Cardigan Bay*, they've got an Aladdin's cave of duty free stuff to take off when they dock in Blighty. I managed to get a few bottles of Dimple and a dozen Havana's. Would 100 be enough to get you to St Helena's?"

"That should be about right. I'll go get them." John replied, then went and collected some of his store of cigarettes for exchange.

John sat in his cabin drawing deeply on and savouring each draw of the cigarette from his new supply of smokes, before he started to tackle his latest mound of paperwork.

This was one of his mundane chore whilst on voyage when all is well on board, and the passengers behaving themselves to make life on board seem like a cruise liner instead of a cargo vessel with a few cabins to spare.

Chapter XXI
Umbrellas

The leg between the Ascensions and St Helena was a short one in comparison with the others before it, and it only took the *Inverlaggan* three balmy days to reach St Helena.

An island set away from the shipping lanes and some 1,500 miles off the west coast of Africa.

It was founded and settled by the British India Company in the 16th century, and of volcanic origin due to the nearness to the Mid Atlantic Ridge.

Due to its location in military terms, there is still a British military presence there, not only for themselves but also for the others under its jurisdiction.

The capital is Jamestown and has a small population but is the administrative capital of all the British Islands stretching from the Ascensions right down to Tristan da Cunha and Gough Island, and all with less than 6,000 inhabitants. Fishing and agriculture provides their living, but relies heavily on regular visits by passing ships that makes up for the rest of their comforts.

St Helena was made famous for keeping Napoleon prisoner there and ensuring that he never escaped again. He eventually died of lead poisoning on the island during 1821, but alas not from a musket ball.

This was the next brief stop for the wandering sailors and their ship, where they had just enough time to unload their much needed cargo of supplies for the islanders, and to load some fresh provisions and fuel before they were to tramp on their weary way again.

"Looks like the changing of the guard, 3rd. We still need the accommodation space in No3 hold. Mind you, we could get some of the deck timber stowed down there now." Walters commented, as John inspected the latest convolution of decking required for the cargo still remaining.

"We've got extra equipment for the scientists coming on board, and a few more hundred tons of oil to stow. Take out all the cargo from No4 hold, then reload it with the sandbags and all the oil barrels on top for easy access. Put all the Scientists stuff along with the soldiers and their gear in No3 hold, then re-stow No2 with farming equipment and other cargo. The cement and other building materials will be re-stowed in No 1 hold. In short Walters, like a see-saw and evenly balanced."

"More or less what I had in mind, but it's good as done, 3rd!" Walters replied, with John leaving to complete more of his allotted tasks, but was intercepted by Danvers, who enquired about the scientific cargo being loaded.

"All in No 3 hold, first mate. Unless that is, you want some of it on deck for easy access by the scientific team."

"Yes, but you'll need to check with one of them to see what."

"Better if you talked to your 2nd, he's the one in charge of the loading. I only see that the loading or unloading keeps the ship in trim." John replied, and received a scowl from Danvers for his trouble.

John finally reached the next item on his list, which was on the boat deck. By the time he was finished with his repairs and maintenance, the ship was getting ready for leaving.

This was his cue to stop what he was doing and get himself ready for the departure, with just enough time to have a quick smoke and a chat with his friends in the radio shack.

"Hello you two. Manage a quick run ashore?" John asked.

"Hello John, come in. We had a lot of mail to collect for the next two ports of call, including our own. Here's a little bundle for you, mostly from your Helena by the look of it. That should keep your thoughts going, to while away a few hours." Larter stated and smiled, handing John a small pile of letters.

"Looks as if the mail finally caught up with us then." John replied, sorting them out by sender, then smelt one that had a faint perfume coming from it.

"Keep them for me until I come back Bruce. We're about to sail and I'm on deck as usual. See you both later." John requested, and left the radio shack.

"Ah there you are 3rd." It was Gibson with junior deck officer Crabbe.

"Whatever it is, it will have to wait until I come back from my foc'sle duty." John replied quickly and hurried down the companionway ladder and onto the foc'sle.

He stood in his usual place, and watched the ship peel away from the jetty and turn itself around to face the open waters again.

His gaze was directed to a very large tanker that had the Triple Crown logo on its funnel coming towards them, and guessed correctly that it was one of the *Bay* tankers. It took several minutes for the two ships to pass and enable for him to read its name *Lyme Bay*. He was impressed by the size of the vessel that dwarfed his own, and decided to ask a few details about it from Larter when he had the time.

'I wouldn't mind having a few voyages on one of those beauties. Must be full of pipes, valves, pumps and lord knows what else.' John said quietly, watching the two ships finally pass each other and went their own separate ways.

Once the ship was out into open waters again, John assumed his routine of rounds, reports, and paperwork, before he could relax and read his handsome little pile of letters.

Everybody, including the new passengers soon settled down to enjoy their sleepy cruise, for each person finding things to do with their abundance of free time.

He read each one slowly and carefully starting with the ones from his family, then ones from friends, including a long one from McPhee. But he kept the ones from Helena to read last so that he could enjoy them when he had a quiet moment later on in the voyage to TdC.

On the second day out John had Sinclair test his much improved steerage system.

"Hello Andy, is Stan there!" John called up from the ship's gyro compass compartment.

"No John, but you'd better come up to the bridge immediately." Sinclair replied with concern.

John arrived onto the bridge to see Sinclair and find out what was wrong, and found Blayden taking his mid-day sun-sight, so that he could check his position on the chart.

"What is your present course and speed bosun?" Blayden asked .

"170, speed 17knots captain."

"How long have you been on this course?"

"Since we left Jamestown."

Blayden scratched his head, muttered to himself then came over to check the ships 'head' and speed for himself.

He went out onto a bridge wing and looked over the side to look at his wake before he came back and finally spotted John standing by Sinclair.

"Glad you're here 3rd. According to my mid-day plot I should be at least 150 miles to the west of here." Blayden stated, showing John the marks on the chart of where the ship was and should in fact be.

"Now unless there is a fault with the bosun's steering which I doubt, there's something wrong with the steering mechanism or, and heaven forbid, the magnetic compass. It should be a self-compensating one but go down and fix, whatever it is. Keep me informed."

"I'm on my way captain." John replied quietly.

"Don't take all day about it as each hour off course means two to get back, with not enough fuel to do so." Blayden shouted as John left the bridge.

He went down to the steering gear and emergency gear compartments and examined it all, even his new addition to it very carefully. After an hour of searching and checking he found nothing untoward and went to check out the other side of the equation.

The compass is made with de-magnetised parts, and kept in a similar compartment so that nothing can affect the critical state of the compass needle. For John to inspect it he was not to take any metal inside the compartment, so he divested himself of all metal objects and left them outside before he entered, only taking his specially made brass or rubber-coated tools with him.

His inspection discovered that the metal brackets holding up a cable appeared to be new, didn't have a special stamp to state they was de-magnetised for use in the compartment, so he could not decide if the rivets to secure the bracket, that should have had the same treatment. He measured the distance from the brackets to the compass face and removed them to take with him.

He held the metal in his hand, to decide to see how much movement there was on the needle by varying the length between it and the metal. He saw that it only needed a few inches for the metal to give a slight tremor on the needle, which, to him, meant that it could mean the difference between a true course and a false one. The brackets in fact were held only three feet away, thus giving a small but definite swing to the needle. Now it was John's turn to scratch his head.

'The helmsman only has a repeater unit to go by for him to steer his course, therefore if the main gyro is wrong so is the repeater. So who would have installed this cable and bracket?' he said to himself, trying to think who would have installed this cable. It took him less than two minutes to realise that it must have been the electrical officer, normally a 4th engineer on board if used in the engine room. So he decided to go down to the engine room and speak to him, to verify his theory.

"Yes I did that repair just as we arrived in St Helena. Nothing wrong with it surely, 3rd?"

"Nothing wrong in your actual repairs and what you did.

But! and the but is, that you forgot to use demagnetised brackets and rivets or screws. Therefore the compass over compensated itself because of those items."

The 4th engineer looked at John as if he didn't believe him, and said so in no uncertain terms.

John sighed and stated that he, the 4th engineer, was in for the high jump when, not only Jones found out, but especially Blayden. And that would be about five seconds after he made his report.

"He did what? Get the chief engineer for me bosun, ask him to come to the bridge." Blayden roared angrily, then turned back to John and beckoned him to look at the chart on the table.

"It took you over two hours to report back to me, but at least we have the problem solved. That means that we're about another 20 miles further off course and heading towards the African coast instead of downwards and TdC. The fuel is my main concern, and without enough fuel we won't make the special fuel depot on Gough island to take on more." he stated civilly, showing John the mark where Blayden estimated they were.

"Maybe if we stay on this course until sunset, you could get another sighting or even a star-sight to confirm your calculations, captain. Besides if we do overshoot, so to speak, we can always make Gough Island first. Refuel there and then go onto TdC."

Blayden looked at John, and stroked his nose thoughtfully.

"Yes that will hold!" Blayden started to say as Jones sauntered onto the bridge and asked Blayden what the problem was for him to be summoned.

Blayden explained to Jones exactly what John had told him, and showed the evidence of what was found, before it was Jones' turn to show his anger. John just stood there listening to the two senior officers discussing their options and what to do with the 4th engineer, when Larter came onto the bridge.

"Captain, I have intercepted an S.O.S. from an *S.S. Chantral.* She is a British registered cargo passenger ship like us. Says she has caught fire in a hold and needs assistance. Here is her position, which according to me, is approx Red 10 on my D.F."

"Let me see." Blayden asked gruffly, grabbing the signal off Larter and went over to the chart table.

"That makes him here, and we're about here." Blayden calculated, as he made his mark on his chart that was seemingly right the middle of a blank piece of paper.

"How good is its signal Larter, only we seem to be right on top of him."

"Loud and clear, captain." Larter replied.

"Engines! You go down and give that so-called electrical officer several lace holes of your boot so that he won't be able to sit down for a week. Bosun, get two men onto the bridge and start looking for any signs of this poor ship. Grey, get some pumps and fire-fighting equipment on deck as soon as you can. Larter, keep monitoring him until we locate him. I'll tell you when to reply." Blayden said coolly, but rattled out his orders to those around him.

John realised that nobody had had a look around the horizon for any telltale signs, and before any proper lookouts were posted he went out onto the port bridge wing with a pair of borrowed binoculars and scanned the horizon. It took him only a couple of minutes to report.

"I can see flares coming up over the horizon about 10 degrees on our port bow captain." He announced, as Blayden grabbed his own binoculars and scanned ahead of the ship.

"Good! At least now we get to know where we are, Grey. Now let's go and find where she is, and render aid to her. Bosun, port 10. Steer 150. Tell the engine room to make speed for 20knots. Grey, before you go, call and tell the 2nd radio officer to answer that ship now. He'll know what to do next." Blayden said, rushing to his chart table.

"Fire fighting equipment and a working party mustered fore and aft, captain." John reported when he arrived back onto the bridge.

"First mate, get all off watch crew on deck, and get those soldiers out too, and have all the starboard lifeboats ready in case we have to launch them.

Then instruct all passengers of what we are about to do, but for all of them to clear the weather decks, and either go to their cabins or stay in the saloon out of the way." Blayden ordered calmly yet busy despatching officers and men everywhere.

John was forced to repeat his report several times before Blayden responded to it, with his own order.

"Very well 3rd. Get yourself on the fore deck and see the 2nd mate. You will provide 3 teams of fire-fighters on both main cargo decks, and be ready to engage as soon as we close the other ship."

John thought of the previous occasions when he had to fight a ship fire and remembered what was needed that even Trewarthy agreed with.

"Captain, if we're going almost alongside that ship, then we would need an extra team to provide an umbrella of water over us to prevent us from combusting too. I already have a hand picked team standing by in case."

Blayden looked surprised and seemed speechless for a moment before he replied.

"You've obviously been doing some practice on other ships then Grey. Yes, you have my permission. Now get on deck, you have about 30 minutes before we engage."

John nodded and left the bridge, and taking a brief look at the rapidly nearing stricken ship, but dared not think of any outcome to the smoke shrouded ship dead ahead of him.

"Captain told me to see you 2nd."

"Ah 3rd engineer! I need water hoses connected up to our deck-hydrants, and long enough to stretch over to the other ship. I have several teams of 4 men in each ready to be lifted over to it by cargo derrick that will help the other ship's crew. In the meantime I need your men positioned port side to engage as we approach."

"I won't be able to give you any hoses as I've already got every last one connected up and ready, but I shall be providing a water umbrella to protect us as we come alongside. I've been in a similar predicament before and I would advise you to provide crash fenders on the port bow and scramble nets, starboard side." John replied slowly, observing the stricken ship starting to almost glow from bow to bridge.

The smoke from the fire was getting thick, and began to envelop the *Inverlaggan,* and the crew started to choke and retch from it.

"Walters, it smells like rubber. Get your men to wear their Sou'westers and gloves, but not woollen ones." John shouted over the noise coming from the other ship.

Walters nodded and ordered a junior deck officer to get it done in double quick time.

The fire-fighters were locked in battle with large tongues of fire that were trying to lick the *Inverlaggan,* as she gave the other ship a gentle nudge when she made contact before swinging herself almost right alongside, but aft of the bridge.

Whilst the *Inverlaggan's* bows were rubbing the other ship, the two cargo derricks held a gangway each, over the small gap for the passengers to cross over into safety. There was yet another derrick swinging back and forth, plucking cargo-nets full of people who seemed to be stranded up on their own boat deck.

John went around each fire crew, leading or directing them like a prize-fighter trainer. He made sure that his water umbrella crew concentrated on the critical boundary cooling and even grabbed a hose to shower the rescued passengers as they were arriving. But got a couple of the soldiers who were helping, to take over whilst he dashed to yet another crises.

He came across Gibson on the after cargo deck, helping people climb up the scramble nets.

"Are you taking count, Gibson? Get two of your men to escort these people to the saloon. If you can't see any more coming aboard, then I suggest you get port side and arm yourself with a hose and follow me." John shouted over the noise of the fire.

Gibson merely nodded and signalled two more of his helpers to take over.

Both officers stood side by side with their water hoses as they sprayed their cargo deck to keep the oil drums under it from joining the rest of the fire some feet away. The hoses were rigid with the pressure of the water being pumped through them, as they crackled and snaked over the now very watery deck.

Over the noise, John heard the ship's horn being sounded, but it was Gibson who told him that they were about to disengage, as there was nothing else they could do for the *Chantral*.

To John this meant that all the people who were on board were now rescued and that the ship was far too gone to be helped any more.

The *Inverlaggan* backed away slowly from the *Chantral* that was now glowing from stem to stern. The smoke seemed to be its shroud as the ship suddenly lurched onto its side and started to turn turtle. The sheets of flame got fewer and smaller as the water around the ship was steaming almost to boiling point.

Everybody stopped their fighting and stood to watch the ship as it gave one big blast as the engines blew up before it sunk within seconds below the waves.

Only a few pieces of flotsam were left at the scene before Blayden was satisfied no more souls were to be recovered, and he could continue his own voyage.

John thanked his men for their work as they stowed away all their equipment. Not only did they provide valuable time in getting the passengers off, but they had prevented their own ship from catching fire. Such are the valiant deeds of a fire fighter be they on land or at sea.

He finally arrived into the saloon after a cool shower and a change of clothes, and saw that there was almost double the amount of passengers than what they started off with.

"Hello Bruce. Where did that ship come from and how many did we get off?" John asked, sitting down on a rare item, a vacant stool.

"It was one of the Cathay line ships from Penang bound for Boston via Durban, Lagos and the Azores. We managed to get most of the 40 passengers, mostly children. But just 10 crew out of 35." Larter said grimly

"We did our best Bruce. They probably perished in the fire. But why was it carrying all those passengers when the ship was stuffed full of rubber?"

"It was one of those old ships just like this one, tramping around the place. Probably carrying rubber from Malaya, changing passengers as it went along, and again just like us, John."

"Judging by the amount of children there are, I should imagine that we will be forced to alter course once more and head for the nearest port. Somehow I don't think they will be too pleased to be landing in the middle of nowhere and especially on a volcanic island that might erupt at any time. Out of the frying pan and into the fire, so to speak."

"Yes, you're right there John. So what was the altercation on the bridge when I arrived earlier?" Larter enquired, trying to change the subject.

"Oh that. The stupid electrical officer forgot to use de-magnetised metal when he did a job in the gyro compass compartment. That sent us off course by a good 250 miles, which means that we didn't have enough fuel to get back onto track and make Gough Island, let alone T d C. Mind you, the irony of it all is that it took an S.O.S. to help Blayden sort out

167

where we were when you gave him its position."

"Is that right! I'll bet Blayden will have the 4th's guts for garters for that, then take the full credit for saving all these people by telling everybody he took an alternative course instead of the normal one."

"Not if your log and the bridge narrative says otherwise Bruce."

"Still, think of all the insurance money we'll get when we arrive home again. Could do with a few more guineas in my pocket again. What do you say John?"

"Sounds good to me. Anyway, I must go and get my head down now, as I'm knackered. I'll call by and see you in the morning." John stated, excusing himself to go back to his cabin.

He was too tired even to read his letters from Helena, instead he put them under his pillow and after having a quick drink of water he climbed onto his bunk and slept.

Chapter XXII
A Turn To Port

The following morning saw the crew and the volunteer soldiers cleaning the ship from its sooty appearance and giving it a lick of fresh paint where it had been blistered off by the heat of the fire. The original passengers were helping the survivors by giving clothes and other small luxuries to them so that they could cope better. The children seemed almost unaffected by the trauma they had gone through, as they played amongst themselves and generally noise making as children do. It was also time for changes in the sleeping and dining arrangements.

Fortunately for Blayden, most of his original passengers were scientists and used to roughing it out in the open, so he asked them if they would share their cabins between them to help out the survivors. All agreed that it was only fair, and created the much-needed space. As Blayden gave up his day cabin so did his officers and men in their turn.

The officers had to pair up in the cabins, so John shared with Larter, with Southgate sleeping at the back of the radio shack and so on. The crew had to 'hot bunk' their sleeping quarters, because it turned out to be three bunks to five men. Thus as one man went on watch, the man coming off watch would sleep in his bunk, the men would rotate their watch duties and their sleeping times.

The chefs in the galley had to cook for three sets of diners, with the officers and crew last, but the chefs made sure the crew did not get the scraps or leftovers. Everybody on board had accepted all this hardship, as they knew it was only for a few days. But they didn't reckon on the fresh water restrictions, as even that was in limited supply. That was when Walters and John re-rigged the open- air splash pools on both decks for swimming during the day, and for bathing during the evening. The children loved it as did their parents, as it meant that the children were kept in one place and not found roaming around the ship like lost sheep.

"Morning Bruce, didn't hear you leave this morning, and I thought I was up early enough." John stated, when he strolled into the radio office.

"Yes, Paul had a long night and asked me to take over for a while." Larter whispered, pointing to Southgate who was sleeping on a camp bed between the two wardrobe sized radio transmitters.

"So where are we heading, Capetown maybe?"

"Yes, it should take us about four more days providing Blayden keeps us in the main shipping lane.

According to the telegram from his nibs Belverley and co, it looks as if we'll have a good run ashore there instead of Td C. Our scientific friends will be pleased, I don't think."

"Not another change of route, surely! Where will we go unless it's back to Belfast or on our way to Timbuktu ?" John asked with sarcasm.

"I don't care what he decides on, just as long as we get our back pay and our insurance money before we leave Capetown. Which incidentally and according to Paul and my calculations are concerned, is approx £100 per person saved for each crewmember on board, skipper excluded. He'll probably get double." Larter replied, rubbing his hands with delight, and amusement from John.

"Hmmm spending it already Bruce. Don't forget to keep some for our next r/v in Belfast." John smiled, patting his friend on his shoulder.

"What's the weather doing for us this time Bruce?"

"Don't know yet, as the weather station on Gough Island hasn't broadcast it yet. Ask me in about 4 hours. When we meet another ship, I expect Paul will flash them up on his aldis and ask. It's just like speaking to a passing neighbour, only less of the gossip. But then you should know John, you've been down in these waters before now, with the Falklands springing to mind."

"Ah yes, never mind whistle while you shirk, it was hassle all the way, if I remember." John replied, remembering his voyage on the SFD's.

They talked about their previous voyages together for a little while before John had to excuse himself and Larter stated that he had a 'radio schedule' to attend to.

Shortly after John had his lunch and decided to go back to his shared cabin to re-read his letters from Helena, when Danvers came into him and told him about problems with the sanitary system.

"Its quite easy first mate, the pumps are not coping with the demand. In order to rectify this matter, all you have to do is shut the toilets and bathrooms down during so many hours a day. Say two hours on and four hours off. Maybe for longer and during the first and middle watches, with access limited to the crew only."

"I'm afraid that isn't possible 3rd. We need the sanitary system operational at all times else we might start an epidemic of lord knows what diseases on this self contained coffin of ours."
John looked at the deeply concerned man and thought for a moment, before explaining to him what happened on one of his previous ships and the measures taken.

Danvers shook his head and told John that it would not happen on this ship and for John to fix the system a.s.a.p. This last statement given to John and especially from a senior deck officer, provoked him to turn on his heel and walk away from the protesting man.

John walked swiftly down to the engine room to find that Lee was on watch and explained the problem Danvers had given him. He also told Lee what he had said and the alternatives that he had given Danvers, to no avail.

Lee offered a different solution but stated that as 'Spanners' was the chief, it was his decision and not theirs. Thus the decision obtained had to involve John speaking to Jones face to face, without any more bad blood being caused between them.

"Chief, can I have a word?" John asked politely as he saw Jones sitting in his favourite chair and smoking his favourite pipe.

"You may. Come in 3rd!" Jones invited, almost civilly in comparison with other times

"What can I do for the 3rd engineer?"

John told him of the sanitary system and offered a couple of solutions based on personal experiences. This was received in complete silence, with the odd nod of Jones's head, as if to indicate that he was listening.

"This time 3rd, I'll make it your call. I'll back your decision providing you tell the captain exactly what you intend to do. Perhaps the passengers will be accommodating and put up with it for the few days left on this unforeseen leg of our voyage. Any problems come and see me, and shut the door on your way out if you please." Jones replied, dismissing John with his customary wave of his pipe wielding hand.

'*What! No I've got my beady eye on you? The man must be getting senile in his old age. Thankful for an easy meeting for once at least.*' John muttered, making his way up onto the bridge to see Blayden

"Stan here today Andy?" John whispered.

"Aye he's here and working a dream. Nearly got caught this morning though. Just as well the relief helmsman was one of the seamen survivors."

"Good, keep it that way until we reach Capetown."

"Capetown? I thought I recognised the course and position on the chart. Should be there in about four days then John. We'll be able to have a good run ashore as I know quite a few places there and so does Bruce."

"Well must go Andy. I've got bad news for the skipper, so wait for the fall out in about three minutes. See you later." John concluded, making his way to and knocking on Blaydens bridge cabin door.

John told Blayden what the problem was as reported by Danvers, and what remedies were on offer. But he explained that he had the permission of Jones to conduct whatever measures were needed to rectify the matter.

Blayden blew his top as this latest setback, which seemed to be yet another curse for him and his ship. He gave John the permission to shut down the sanitary system on an agreed timetable rather than go down the road the *Brooklea* had done.

"You have been a good 3rd engineer Grey, and have saved me or my ship on a couple of occasions, you have my blessings too. I shall get the first mate to explain to the passengers before you commence. We are making for Capetown and I have the notion of making full speed to shorten the voyage. You will be mentioned to the board of governors when we get there, you mark my words." Blayden said gratefully, ushering John out of his cabin.

"Was I correct Andy, three minutes?" John whispered aside.

"Right on. He'll be getting me to increase the speed from 17knots to a full 22 before long. Capetown here we come."

"Aye, see you later." John said, and left the bridge, and hearing exactly what Sinclair had anticipated.

"Bosun, tell the engine-room to make revs for 22 knots."

The latest problem was taken well by the passengers, especially as they were told that the ship was now on its way to Capetown, and due to the increase of speed, they would be there in less than three days.

John was sitting on a deck locker on the boat deck enjoying the cool of the early morning, before the heat of the oncoming day overtook them.

"Morning John. Counting the ships passing us?" Southgate asked pleasantly, joining him to have his own early morning smoke.

"Hello Paul. Yes, but I can't make out what that ship is flashing his signal torch at us for. Maybe you could read it for me."

Southgate read the flashing light and told John what it said and that he needed to reply to it quickly. So he flicked his cigarette over the side and with John following behind, rushed into the bridge, grabbed his aldis lamp and started to reply.

"Quick John, grab a piece of paper and a pencil from the chart table and come back. I need you to write down what I say. Please hurry." Southgate said urgently, sending John quickly away.

"Right Paul. I'm ready." John replied arriving next to Southgate who was flashing his lamp.

"The ship is the *SS Blackwater*. From Capetown bound for Southampton. Says there are naval warships doing manoeuvres 50 miles south of here. Told to keep clear to starboard."

Southgate acknowledged the signal and thanked his opposite number on the ship before he finished and stowed his aldis again.

"Right John. I'll show it to the captain, who might want to take a detour around it. Although chances are he'll just plough straight through them." Southgate stated, taking the signal and disturbed Blayden from his sleep to show him.

John waited for Southgate to come back and did so with Blayden behind him saying that he needed to verify his chart and his course.

"Thank you signalman. We'll go straight through them, so stand by to speak to them as we pass. Make sure you fly our callsign and the appropriate flag signals telling them that we're in a hurry to get to port. On top of that, ask 2nd officer Larter to get a radio patch through to the chart table and I'll speak to them as and when."

"Aye captain." Southgate replied and left the bridge for the radio shack to tell Larter.

"If it's one thing I know about the Navy, they will not let any ship near their waters. Speaking of which, where would they be on the chart Paul?"

Southgate pointed the approx position of them and compared it with their own.

"That is to the east by some 100 miles. That must be an offshore manoeuvre, probably playing marines and an assault on some poor innocent strip of land somewhere. But if he wants a radio link, he shall have it." Larter concluded as he collected the equipment needed for Blayden.

"Do us a favour John, can you look at our emergency generator. It packed up on us last night, and we need it from time to time when the silly buggers in the motor room start their own silly games."

John nodded and got onto the task right away and before long, he was able to tell his friends all was well again.

Having nothing else better to do, John decided to stay with his radio friends to find out more about the intriguing message passed on to them, and borrowed a spare pair of binoculars to have a look at other ships that passed them. He noticed one ship coming towards them from further out to sea flashing its signal lamp, seemingly furious at them. Before he had chance to call to Southgate telling him about it, he saw Southgate flashing back at him.

'I must have picked the wrong vocation. Paul is enjoying a private conversation to passers by in view of everybody else, yet only he or at least those in the know, knows what he is saying' John said under his breath, drawing yet another puff from his cigarette.

This went on for a little while as ship after ship they passed warned them of the danger ahead. Blayden was having none of it and from John's advantage point and much to his delight, he knew his latest contraption worked well, as the ship made a straight white line through the blue ocean.

The warships appeared over the horizon, and John could make out several smaller ones behind them. They were all in a line abreast of one another almost like fishing boats out on a day's fishing.

The *Inverlaggan* was rapidly approached by a sleek warship from astern of her and came almost alongside with somebody from it shouting at them through a loud hailer.

"Ahoy! What ship and where bound? Speak to your captain!" came the demanding and insistent voice.

There was a short silence before John heard Blayden reply.

"This is the *SS Inverlaggan*, Captain Blayden speaking. I'm carrying survivors off the *SS Chantral* that caught fire and sank two days ago. I am making for Capetown at best possible speed. My supplies are low as is my fuel. Kindly let me pass unhindered."

"Sorry captain, we cannot allow you to go through our lines. You will turn to port now and steer 090 for 50 nautical miles before you tack onto 195 for a further 200 miles. Or of you like, keep 100 miles off land. Then after you have made at least 180 miles down that track you are at liberty to return to your original track if you so desire."

There was a long pause before Blayden yielded to the commands given.

"I've looked at your courses given captain, and see no problem. Just as long as I don't get held up with that strong continental current I'm heading into, that's running up off the coast. I'm burning fuel faster than I'm getting there."

"Very well captain. We have escorts some 60 miles astern of us should you need them. Good luck and thank you." the voice shouted before the warship raced ahead leaving the *Inverlaggan* like the proverbial hare and the tortoise.

John watched the destroyer depart through his binoculars then see it race first towards another merchantman that was miles astern of him, then at a line of little ships coming slowly towards them.

"A busy day at the office for Paul, if we get too close to those ducklings. Maybe we would be better close to land, at least we could find a small port somewhere to dock instead of going all that way to Capetown." John muttered, but got a surprise when he heard somebody asking him to repeat what he said. He turned round to find Gibson standing almost next to him, who asked him for the lend of his binoculars for a spell.

Gibson looked at the oncoming ships and at the disappearing warship that was approaching the ship behind them.

"It seems that the Royals are out in force today. Wonder what's up for us to change course?" John asked, as he saw the white curve of foam being made as the ship leaned over to port. Gibson looked at the change of course then ahead of the ship.

"We've got clear water ahead of us, but I don't like the look of those little ones now on our starboard side. We would have to turn to starboard to maintain our course for Capetown or we'll end up docking on some beach in the middle of nowhere." Gibson replied as he handed back the binoculars.

"The navy knows what they're doing and we've been given our new courses to steer. At least we won't bump into any more ships on the way." John said philosophically.

"Hope you're right. Anyway, I must continue my rounds 3rd. By the way, our supper time slot will be late tonight due to the water shortage in the galley. See you again." Gibson replied and left John to himself, who stayed a while longer before he too left to do his own rounds.

"Evening rounds completed and all deck machinery available. Sanitary system cleared, and fresh water system running." John reported for his last duty of the day.

"Very good 3rd. See you tomorrow. Bosun starboard 10 then steer 170." Blayden commanded.

"Stan is not here John!" Sinclair whispered loudly to attract John's attention, but John never heard him and carried on down to his cabin.

"Hello Bruce, here's your spare binoculars I borrowed. You can see for miles with them.."

"Oh thanks John. They are my old ones, but as I've got a brand new and more powerful pair, you may as well as keep them. You might even be recruited as a top class lookout." Larter chuckled, showing John his new possession.

They both got changed and made their way up to the dining room to take their evening meal before having a couple of drinks.

"We've been living on ruddy chicken ever since we left Georgetown. Any more and we'll all be wearing feathers." Larter moaned, as he flapped his arms and made clucking noises.

"You should be so lucky. All we get is an offal lot of pork what the passengers don't eat." the steward sniffed, before he placed their supper in front of them.

"Actually steward, how about a little swap tonight. Our chicken for your offal lot of pork!" John suggested cheerfully, which made the steward stop in his tracks.

"Oh go on! You must be pulling my plonker. Chance would be a fine thing, I'm sure!" he replied..

Larter grabbed his chicken portion, and wrapped it in his napkin and gave it to the steward, stating that he would like a ham bone or even a few sausages in exchange.

The steward pouted and then gave a little whoop of delight as he concealed the chicken before taking it away, saying that he would see them afterwards.

"It looks as if bribery would get you absolutely everywhere, Bruce." John laughed and offered some of his own chicken to him so he would not get too hungry.

The evening went slowly but genially as other officer friends came and went, also a few of the passengers who were in the know about John's efforts with the fresh water and sanitary systems.

"It looks as if Blayden kept his word by letting them know who was responsible, John. Thankfully you have yet another success story to tell your grandchildren." Larter smiled as they drank the last of their quota of alcoholic beverages for the day.

"Well Bruce, is it your place or mine?" John smiled and nodded towards the general direction of the upper deck.

Both men arrived back into their cabin and had a few more drinks with the food the steward had left for them, before they decided that tomorrow would be yet another humdrum day and they should get some shut-eye.

"Last one turned in shuts off the light, Bruce. And don't forget mine is the top one this time." John chuckled, snuggling into his bunk, leaving Larter still undressing.

Chapter XXIII
Bang!

Yet another early morning greeted the *Inverlaggan,* with the passengers safely tucked up in their cabins. Meanwhile, the deck hands were sluicing the decks down and going about their daily tasks to maintain the ship at sea. The sky was overcast with squally showers dashing itself against the marble grey ocean.

John was on the bridge talking to Sinclair and generally scanning the horizon with a borrowed pair of binoculars in idle curiosity to see if he could find any more ships.

"Hmmm! It looks as if somebody has lost a load of oil drums that are scattered across our path. Look!" John opined and handed over the binoculars for Sinclair or see.

"Yes, you're right. What do you think Bruce?" Sinclair asked for another opinion from Larter who had just arrived onto the bridge.

"What do I think about what?" He asked taking the binoculars and looked over to where Sinclair was pointing.

"They look very suspicious to me. Wait a minute! I've seen these before, and they're definitely not oil drums. In fact I will go as far to say that we're just about to enter a rogue minefield. Some of those mines are acoustic, some contact, but the deadliest of all are the magnetic type. They can sniff a ship a good 5 cables away, and move like hell to attach onto whatever ship that was passing.

"These are probably what the Navy were looking for earlier, and it's just our luck that we've just happened to find them." John said tersely.

Sinclair grabbed the telegraphs and rung emergency astern, whilst John rang down to the engine room and ordered them to shut all watertight doors. Larter went over to the chart table and took the ships position and told them that he will send out a MAYDAY' call.

"John go below and get as much of our gear together and see if you can rustle up some grub for us as it might be a long day, or perhaps end up manning the lifeboats within minutes.

Blayden rushed onto the bridge and demanded why the ship was obviously going astern by the amount of shaking and shuddering.

Sinclair almost threw the binoculars to Blayden and told him to take a bloody good look at what the ship was heading towards. Danbury and Walters arrived almost simultaneously onto the bridge and looked anxiously at Blayden.

"1st Mate! Get some men onto the foc'sle with wicker baskets and dangle them over both bows to ward off these drums coming our way. 2nd Mate! Get yourself the same and have them over both sides from the superstructure aft to the poop deck! As quick as you can, as we've just entered a very dangerous area! And tell the 3rd Mate to get himself onto the boat deck and remain there to take charge should we have to use the lifeboats." Blayden ordered then turned to Sinclair.

"Well done Bosun, that was good thinking! Get Larter for me, I need to start sending a MAYDAY. Where's the Navy when you need them? Let's hope the Navy is still around to hear our 'Mayday'!" Blayden ordered.

"He's already been on the bridge to see what has happened and is already sending out the distress call. The 3rd has ordered all watertight doors be shut down as is organising a damage control team with the 4th mate." he informed.

Crabbe made an appearance on the bridge to find that there was a flurry of activity on the main deck and offered his assistance.

"5th Mate. If the passengers have not already been woken up by the sudden reverse of the engines, then get them up, and have the galley to feed them, before they are to muster on the boat deck. Any arguments, just tell them that it is a 'Lifeboat Drill' in an awkward time as a real one can happen at an even more inconvenient time for them. You have about 1 hour to have everybody mustered.

Sinclair had his relief on the wheel arrive, but told him to act as a messenger until things are sorted out ahead of them.

"What's the panic Bosun?" the man asked with surprise as he looked down onto the foc'sle to see several men tending to the crash fenders.

"See those drums around us? They're not the usual run of the mill oil-drums, but bloody wartime mines! So go and get yourself a lifebelt and report back here on the double. " Sinclair ordered quietly.

"But I haven't had my brekkers yet!"

"The galley is being flashed up and the chef will be sending food up for us. Now get a move on!" Sinclair replied with a growl, which sent the man rushing away on his errand.

Blayden heard the order and told Sinclair that he'd make a good O.O.W. one day, but keep both eyes on the objects as the ship eased past each one.

"Don't want to wake my boss up too early and on a fool's errand! Blayden said, and gave a saintly look skyward. He went into his bridge cabin and brought out his very large bible and started to read selective verses from it in a large voice.

"Oh Lord! Have mercy upon us as those in peril on the sea! Look after thy flock, and in thy mercy take me as thy sinner and spare my poor souls upon this ship!" he ranted, and proceeded to deliver one of his famous monologue of 'Fire and Brimstone' speeches just like he did at the beginning of the voyage.

"Look Captain! There's three mines approaching, which I suspect are magnetic mines."

Blayden went out onto the starboard bridge wing and held his hand up to the rapidly approaching mines.

"Stop you Sons of Satan! Stop I say or you'll face the wrath of God!" He commanded. But just like King Canute demanding the tide to stop, the mines kept on coming.

No sooner had the messenger arrive back there was a large bang from the starboard bow, followed closely by another one just for'ard of the beam, port side. Several bits of bodies, and pieces of the ship were sent skywards before raining down onto the deck, and enough force to stop the ship completely.

"If those mines have been afloat since the war, then the explosives must have been very volatile. Just as well they seem to be the contact type captain, because if they had been magnetic then we can all look out." Sinclair stated, philosophically, as he held onto his wheel for support.

"Yes, I suppose you're…" Blayden started to say, when there was another bang that came from the starboard side, followed closely by a massive one that ripped most of the superstructure apart and send the funnel spinning upwards almost into orbit.

Sinclair managed to duck down below the bridge windows that shattered and showered the bridge with their shards, accompanied by large pieces of metal that was flying everywhere.

He got up and looked over to see that Blayden and the messenger were lying awkwardly on the deck. He had already seen the men on the foc'sle get blown away, and realised that this ship was going only one way. Downwards.

He grabbed the tannoy mike and gave the order to ABANDON SHIP, then gave a series of blasts on the ship's whistle to emphasise that the boats should be manned and away. Larter and John came running onto the bridge with a holdall each, and stood amazed at what they saw.

"I sent Paul to get us some sarnies and should be waiting for us on the boat deck." Larter said almost with a whisper, and looked at Blayden.

"It looks as if the skipper's had it. We've been holed on both sides of the bow, and the engine room has been blown apart, including the chief and some of the passengers. I gave the orders to abandon ship, but lets hope there is at least one officer that made it onto the boat deck to take charge" Sinclair said over the noise of the ships siren.

"Bloody hell Andy, whatever can happen next!" John responded with incredulity, and started to gather charts, binoculars and other items he though might be useful. Sinclair had found Blayden's gun and strapped to his waist as he grabbed the ships' log and other things and stuffed them into John's bag.

"Right, help me with the skipper, and get him into a lifeboat, in case he's still in the land of the living." Sinclair requested, dragging the man out onto the boat deck only to meet a swarm of passengers clambering into the lifeboats.

"Gibson! Where's all the deck officers?" Sinclair asked, taking a quick look around at who was organising the loading of the lifeboats.

"They've all copped it, as did the chief engineer and a lot of the stokers. Some of the passengers and most of the soldiers copped it when the engine room blasted up through the galley and accommodation area. The 2nd engineer was off watch at the time and is now on the starboard side trying to launch some of the lifeboats because there's not enough to take us all this side, especially as one of came off its traces and tipped everybody into the water. Hope they can swim. I have 5th Mate Crabbe taking charge of the passengers coming up onto the deck." Gibson stated, helping the stupefied passengers into the boats before lowering them into the rapidly approaching waves.

John climbed up the increasing slope of the boat deck to see Lee, who had some of the stokers and soldiers with him.

"Tansey, how many men have you got?" He called.

"I've got one launch full of scientists, crew and some soldiers, but the second lifeboat full of survivors slipped its traces and most are seen to have been drowned. See you on the other side." Lee shouted back with a wave.

John slid down the almost vertical slope of the deck and landed right into the last lifeboat that was ready for launching.

"For Christ sake John, where have you been?" Sinclair asked angrily.

"Tansey has managed to launch a full boat from the starboard side, and says to wait for him." John gasped, sitting down heavily onto his bulging holdall.

The quick release gear was tripped so that the lifeboat glided down its ropes and land neatly into the water. John looked around the scene and saw one capsized lifeboat, with one still dangling from its traces and two lifeboats overfull of people rowing away from the ship. The ship itself didn't seem to want to go under and stayed on its side with the funnel horizontal to the water.

Everybody stopped their rowing and looked over to the dying ship, as it finally, and almost with a sigh, slowly disappeared under the water, leaving only a large foaming bubble to where she once was.

The silence was deafening for that moment as everybody looked at each other and wondered what ever next would befall the passengers who had survived yet another sinking.

John looked at his watch and realised that it had only taken 20 minutes for the ship and its entire people on board, to go from one extreme to the other. For within that time, life was transformed from quiet and sleepy, into noisy and almost pandemonium on a crowded lifeboat in the middle of the ocean with yet more mines all around them.

There was a cheer as Lee and his boat along with another one caught up with them.

Gibson shouted over to each of the five lifeboats and asked them what officer was on board.

As he was the senior surviving deck officer, and although Lee was a 2nd engineer officer and Larter both technically senior to Gibson, it fell to Gibson to take charge of the lifeboats and the survivors.

"I, being the 3rd mate, and as senior deck officer afloat, will act as the new captain and take charge of this situation until we get rescued. Are there any dissenters, if so please state your name." Gibson challenged in an authoritative voice, but got no response.

"Fair enough, and so be it." he said, then told them to get the boats tied up the next one like a string of sausages. He then ordered each senior person to make a list of the survivors in their charge, then get their sails hoisted up and use the emergency compass to steer due east.

"We are approximately 100 miles off the coast. The emergency rations on board should last you five days, but recommend rationing for ten. With luck we should have reached land by then or even get picked up by a passing ship. But in the meantime, remember to enforce a strict rationing regardless.

Two of you have the 3 in 1 type of lifeboats, which means that you have sails, oars, and a small engine. Use your engine only in dire emergencies, as there's not enough fuel to get you ashore from here. The rest of us will simply have to row or sail our way to safety." he ordered sternly.

All five lifeboats got themselves organised and their sails hoisted as they sailed in single file through water that was getting choppier by the hour.

"Bruce, as we appear to be the lead boat, I think you'd better flash Crabbe in the last boat with Paul, and tell him there's a storm brewing and to make certain he keeps in touch with us with his torch." Sinclair advised.

"Yes, I was just thinking about that." Larter revealed, and started to flash his signal lamp to Southgate.

Once he had his little talk with Southgate, Larter shouted to Gibson on the boat behind him to get somebody that could handle a flashing torch in each boat and use them for communications between them.

Gibson agreed on that and within moments a flashing torch was winking at Larter.

"Hmm, he's a bit rusty. Lee's boat must have an army signaller on board, but they'll have to do as it's better than nothing." Larter stated to his two friends.

"If we're in an open boat, and require the sails to propel us, what about the deluge of water both fresh and sea that'll probably well inside the boat, Andy? Maybe we could use some of the sails and the rest of the canvas as a kind of shelter. We could use the oars and spread the canvas over it, like a turtle back." John asked quietly.

"Yes, John's got a point there Andy, what do you say?" Larter responded.

Sinclair looked at the extra equipment in the bottom of the boat and at the miserable looking passengers huddling together to try and keep warm.

It didn't take Sinclair long to assess the idea and he promptly stood up and told everybody to listen to him.

"Okay everybody, I'm Bosun Sinclair, with several years sea experiences and intend taking charge of this boat. I have two very able officers with me to help out. One of them has given me a suggestion, as those of you who are scientists will appreciate what I'm about to say. But for the rest of you please understand that we need total co-operation between us to survive this." Sinclair stated then went on to explain what he wanted them to do.

He concluded by telling them

"Make certain that the children keep their lifejackets on and have them sitting in the middle of the boat. Please start now, as the storm is about to hit us. If any of you need help just ask." Sinclair stated, grabbing one of the oars and showed what they had to do.

"Bruce, flash the other four and tell them to copy what we're doing, and tell them to try and keep in visual contact every hour." Sinclair requested, which Larter did without question.

"Gibson says that we're to give him more slack on our tow rope as we're going faster than him. He says that he's being pulled apart by us at one end and by the boat at the other."

"Tell him that I was expecting this, so we can give him about three more fathoms of line but that's all. Tell him also that I suggest he tells Lee's boat to let go but keep linked with Crabbe's boat."

"But what about Paul?" John asked with concern.

"That's all we can do for them, John. I'm sure Paul will understand." Sinclair said philosophically, before he changed the subject and asked everybody to settle down into their new shelter.

For two days the lifeboats were tossed around like corks whilst the terrified passengers held on for dear life for fear of being thrown out of their flimsy craft, until finally everything went calm and quiet again.

"The show is over folks, let's get out and see the sun for a change. Double rations all round." Sinclair announced cheerfully, as the passengers started to move around slowly and emerge from under their shelter.

"Just as I thought, look Bruce, John." Sinclair said as he held the end of a frayed rope.

John looked at it and grabbed his binoculars to look around.

"I can just see one boat to astern of us." John said quietly.

Sinclair took hold of the binoculars and looked to where John pointed then asked quickly.

"Bruce, can you signal them to see who they are?"

Larter looked through the binoculars himself and announced that yes he could but would be difficult as the sun was in front of them.

"Good, at least we're all going in the right direction." Sinclair said heartily, as some of the passengers gazed behind them trying to see the other boats.

Larter flashed his torch at the other lifeboat and took several minutes to piece together what had happened to them all.

"That was Paul's boat, he says that Lee is to his starboard some way off, who says that Gibson's boat was last seen way to starboard of him some hours ago, but there's no sign of him now. We are still the lead boat and it appears that the rest of them are following us." Larter said with relief.

"Right, let's find out just where we are." Sinclair stated, and the three friends commenced working their approximate course, before telling the rest of the survivors what was what.

"We should be about 30 miles off land, but where we don't know exactly. With luck we can land within the next couple of hours or so, providing we can keep our speed up above any currents that favour these parts of the world." Sinclair announced.

"Unfortunately bosun you are wrong. If as you say we're about 20 miles, even at 10 miles off the coast of Africa, then it means that we will be in the grip of the Benguela current that sweeps up the entire length of Africa, and estimated at around 6 knots.

Unless we can use our engine to power or even sail our way through that current, even in a diagonal line, and around the 8 knots mark, then we will end up off the Moroccan coast some 60 days later. By that time it would be strictly academic as we'll all die from hunger and thirst long before then." a scientist stated, and drew his finger over the chart to emphasise what he had said. Sinclair looked at his two friends then at the chart before declaring his intentions.

"Okay everybody, we have been given a suggestion by one of our scientists." he commenced then told everybody what he wanted them to do.

Soon the boat was moving through the water like a graceful racing yacht with everybody cheering themselves up at the prospect of getting back onto land again.

"We can go a little faster if we had less weight Andy. Due to the boat shipping water all the time, all we've got to do is pull the bung out of the bottom of the boat. Providing that the boat can maintain at least 8 knots, all the water in the boat will be sucked out in a syphonic action as the boat moves through the sea." John suggested.

Another scientist heard John's suggestion, and after a few mental calculations, agreed with him and told Sinclair that it was feasible.

The very thought of taking the bung out of the boat alarmed everybody, and they cursed John for even suggesting the very idea.

Never the less, Sinclair did so, and after a few minutes, sure enough, the bottom of the boat was almost dry even with the bung out. But he promised that it would be put back as soon as the boat started to slow down and enable them all to reach land.

Chapter XXIV
Skeletons

A little girl who was sitting in the bows of the boat soon spotted the sight of a couple of ships near some land ahead of them.

"Look over there! Look! I see a ship and the sea shore as well!" the child shouted, pointing excitedly to what she had seen ahead of her.

"Hurray, we're going to land at the seaside." An older boy shouted and clapped his hands with glee.

Sinclair and Larter looked through their binoculars to see two ships and the stretch of sandy beach the child had seen, and saw that there was nothing but sand dunes from horizon to horizon.

But the two ships were in fact sunken wrecks from some bygone storm, yet no sign from the survivors on shore.

"Those ships are lost but the shore line looks good to me, and by the looks of those promontories each side of it, it is crescent shaped and sheltered. Tell Paul to follow us ashore." Sinclair said quietly, pushing the tiller to steer the boat towards it.

"We've just come out of a storm so the waves onto the beach will be rather big ones. So what I need you to do, is for the women and children to get into the front end of the boat, and get covered over with the tarpaulins to protect them from the surf. The rest of you will sit aft with me and man the oars." Sinclair ordered.

As the boat neared the shore they met large rolling waves that gripped them and literally hurled them several yards onto the beach and almost onto dry land.

"Quick everybody, get out from the front, and help heave the boat up higher, away from these waves." Sinclair shouted.

Without any further prompting the boat was empty and even the children were tugging at the boats towrope to get it out of harms way.

"Right that's far enough everybody! Somebody get some food

ready, but don't forget we're still on rations for the moment."

Sinclair announced, and asked Larter and John to accompany him to explore the top dunes.

They got to the top of the beach and discovered that there was still a stretch of water between them and the main beach several yards away.

The three friends were staring in disbelief at the sight of this unexpected barrier, when they were joined by one of the scientists.

"We are on a large sandbank that was created by the tide and the strong currents as it washes away the dunes. This is the sand of the Namib, the oldest desert in the world. The sands get blown upwards from South Africa and westwards towards the sea and has taken about 1,000 years to get here, a distance of some 1500 miles. You will appreciate that it's not just a lorry load that arrives, but dunes bigger and higher than what we're standing on."

"Don't tell me that we've landed on what I've been told as the 'Graveyard Coast?" John asked as if in denial.

"This is one coastal area that even the desperate wouldn't dream of landing on. This place lives up to its name, known as, and as you say the 'Grave yard Coast' or even the 'Skeleton Coast'. This is due to all the ships that founder on these sandbars and any survivors always end up as skeletons due to lack of fresh water." Larter answered, pointing to the recent addition to the collection of wrecks that were strewn along the coastline for as far as the eye could see, and for the men to walk down to the strip of water separating them from the real shore. There was some driftwood lying near them, so Sinclair grabbed a large piece and hurled it into the water, only to see it float swiftly away from them.

"The water seems shallow enough, but that is one nasty rip tide to cross. But cross it we must." Sinclair announced, throwing yet another piece of driftwood into the water, only for it to go the same way as the first one.

"What if we wait until the others get here before we send one boat across with a line to haul the others over. Either that or we simply row across as fast as we can and hopefully make the other end of this bay before we're swept out to sea again." John suggested.

"Yes, we've got to wait for Paul's boat to arrive and with hope the others will see us to come here too." Sinclair agreed, for the men to walk slowly back over the sandbank and join the others.

Sinclair told everybody what had been discovered, and what he planned to do, but for them all to have a rest and wait until the others arrived so they could all go together.

"Andy, Bruce! Here comes Paul's boat, and by the looks of it there's one of the others following a way behind." John shouted from his vantage-point, which was used by the lookout.

Sinclair got the men to stand by to assist the people to get off and get the boat hauled out of the water.

With baited breath everybody watched as the second lifeboat got caught by the big rolling waves, that came crashing down onto the sandbar, and as if by design, left the boat almost next to their own. There was a mad scramble to get everybody out and the boat out of the way before yet another roller came smashing down to where the boat was, only seconds ago.

There were tears of joy and much hugging between the two sets of survivors, wih everybody was quickly telling each other of their own little dramas.

"Hello Crabbe, hello Paul!" Sinclair greeted, as did the other two friends and with much mutual hugging and backslapping

"Glad you managed to follow us. Better have some food and wait for the others to arrive." he added, but Crabbe sensed something was wrong, and asked what it was.

Sinclair took Crabbe over the sandbar and showed him the problem before they came back to the rest of the people.

"I know you're the 5th mate Crabbe, but for now you'd better let me handle all this. You're good at looking after passengers, besides we have 3rd engineer Grey and Radio officer Larter to fall back on if needs be." Sinclair suggested quietly.

"That's okay with me bosun, I'll get the people and a camp organised for the night." Crabbe replied with a smile and ceded to the obvious point

"Better check with our boffins to see if we can stay on this sandbar otherwise we'll have to spend another night on our boats. Look at the tide." Larter stated, pointing to the tide creeping nearer to them.

"Well, we can have a fire for a little while at least, that should cheer everybody up especially when we have our first hot brew for days." Crabbe replied cheerfully.

The friends went over to the group of scientists and conferred with them about the possibility of moving off due to the tides. They were told that although the sandbar was a temporary one, they would be safe until the next high tide or storm, so all was safe for another two days or so.

"Meantime, we had better keep a lookout for the other boats. A scientist used one of his magnifying glasses to start up a nice fire, so let's they see it." Larter concluded as the friends went and dug themselves a little hollow in the sand to shelter in.

The sun rose up from its bed behind the land to shine on the sea, which was calm and seemingly placid. Only the roaring sound of the Atlantic rollers that dashed themselves onto the sandbar and left with a hushed whisper that was heard, as a bank of sea mist started to cloak the survivors and their camp.

"We had better think of moving off the sandbar and onto mainland today, as our water supply is down to about half a pint per person." Crabbe announced, approaching John and his friends.

"We will give the other boat a chance to arrive before we start moving off, once this sea fog has lifted. Leave the camp fires burning, but start getting the boats ready for hauling over to the other side of the bank." Sinclair agreed.

"Listen, do you hear that?" John asked with a whisper, as he interrupted Sinclair.

"Yes, I can! There's somebody out there, I can hear them shouting." Larter whispered, and ran down to the waters edge.

"Sounds like Tansey," John whispered as he listened carefully to the shouting.

"Yes that's Tansey," John confirmed as he started to shout back.

They saw the lifeboat as if it was a ghost with the mist trying to mask it, and shouted their warnings about the surfing waves.

The boat was seen, first high up on the crest of a wave, then with a sickening crunch it was smashed to pieces as the boat was dashed onto the sandbar with its occupants flung onto the sand like rag dolls.

The four men raced over and grabbed as many people as they could before they were taken back to sea again by the receding water. Some of the people were bowled like a ball up the beach before coming to a stop in front of the surprised group of survivors.

Nobody said a word, but they too ran down to the water and helped the injured and drowning people out of water and to safety. Some of them grabbed whatever they could salvage from the smashed lifeboat and dragged or carried it up to the camp.

Lee was carrying a briefcase as he waded ashore and greeted John and the others.

"It's nice of you to drop in, Tansey." John joked, shaking Lee's hand in welcoming him ashore.

"Hello John. I've even brought my sandwiches with me." Lee responded, showing John his briefcase.

Sinclair, Larter and Southgate gathered around him and greeted him warmly as they strolled up the beach behind everybody.

"That makes us three out of five, as Gibson's boat and the other is still missing, Tansey." John stated.

"That's your lot. Gibson told us the other boat hit another mine and everybody got blown to pieces. His own boat was affected so much that his boat was sinking so we tried to go back to get them. But by the time we got there, all that was left was his briefcase lashed to his lifejacket as everybody had been drowned.

It's got the list of all the survivors off the ship, some personal letters that each one must have written on the boat, along with personal things from each person to accompany the letters." Lee said sombrely, holding out the briefcase for them to see.

"Better have a hot cuppa and a rest whilst this sea fog clears. See you later Tansey." Sinclair advised gently as Lee was given a hot cup of tea.

Sinclair had all the survivors gathered together and told them what had to be done to get onto the main land and what he needed them to do.

Within minutes the men had the first boat hauled over the top and down the other side of the sandbar, whilst the women and children carried all the equipment and other things over. Soon both lifeboats were facing the water's edge again, before the second phase of the move was started.

"John, give the engines a look over, as we might have to use them to cross this riptide." Lee suggested.

"It looks like we've got to things the hard way. Both lifeboat props have been broken off, so the engines are useless. I'll drain off the fuel to use for lighting our fires." John stated when he completed his inspection.

"I was afraid of something like that, so it looks like plan 'B. John, you go over with most of men and make an anchor or holdfast, and secure one end of the dragline rope to it. When you've done that go down the beach and make a second one, as that will be the snag-line in case one boat gets loose. Have four of your strongest men on each line, and one to hold the boats bow rope to haul us in. Your first boat will be the lightest, as it will have the women and children. Good luck!" Sinclair directed, patting John gently on his shoulder.

"Yes Andy, see you later!" John responded, before climbing into the first lifeboat to take command.

"Right men, we've got about 100 yards of water to cross, but you will pull on your oars as hard as you can. I shall give you a fast time so try to keep up. On my order! Ready!"

"Oars in, and pull! Oars out! Oars in and pull!" John ordered, as the men rowed the boat through the racing current.

John gripped the tiller and tried to steer in a straight line with one man letting out the two guide ropes. It took them several minutes, but they eventually arrived safely on the other side although some yards further down the beach.

As there were only two useable boats out of the three to work with, the first one was sent back over to ferry everybody off, so as one boat was being off-loaded, another one would be sent back again for more. The whole operation worked well, and by the end of the afternoon, they even managed to bring the salvaged pieces of the 3rd one across with them.

"There is plenty of flotsam and beach debris around to light a fire, but what are we going to do for shelter. In fact what are we going to do for water, let alone food." Crabbe asked anxiously.
Sinclair thought for a moment before responding, and spoke to each friend.

"Crabbe! Drag the boats up off the beach and turn them on their sides, then use the sails like a tent, for cover. Judging by the remains of sea life scattered on the beach there must be an abundance of shellfish and the like. So get some of the boffins to show the women what they can collect for cooking. Paul, get some of the men to collect as much driftwood as possible. John if you remember our trip to the Sahara, perhaps you can come up with some ideas on how to get us some fresh water. Maybe one of the boffins or even Tansey could help with that. Bruce and I will be doing a recce of the place to see if we are safe or not." He said civilly, with each man nodding in agreement.

During the first few days of landing, and as an evening topic of conversation around the campfire, each person related their own story of how they managed survive the sinking and get into the lifeboats.

Two children told of how a strange steward called Julie managed to get them out of their blazing cabin through a little hole in the wall and told them to go up onto the boat deck. They waited for him but he couldn't get himself out.

"We heard a large bang and a scream then saw lots of flames and smoke coming from the cabin but as he didn't come out, so we ran up to the boat deck as he told us to do." They finished with hushed voices

This was a typical example of the unselfish actions by the ship's crew to help as much people survive, even though they perished themselves.

"Poor Julie! He might have been a queer man, but he seemed quite a decent chap all the same." John said quietly. All that had met and befriended him throughout the long voyage shared his sentiment.

The group of survivors from the *Chantral* kept their silence as they were suffering from not one, but two such devastating experiences within the matter of a few days.

The survivors who managed to reach the shore, numbered some 68 souls out of a total of 145, with several seriously injured among them, including the 'near to death' body of captain Blayden.

After five days since the *Inverlaggan* sunk and the survivors made landfall, all the emergency food rations had now been eaten and the fresh water was down to half a cup each for the women and children and virtually none for the men, as the survivors almost waited for their deliverance from the harsh heat and the unbearable thirst. The prospect of the inevitable demise of such a large number of survivors on such a hostile place was staring them all in the face.

They had buried their captain and four others in a makeshift graveyard, and people wondered who would be next, as the scorpions and snakes crept around them during the night.

Tempers were getting frayed, and a lot of discontent was felt due to the 'unfair' distribution of the food let alone the fresh water. Two men had died through dehydration, and one woman died during the night due to the intense cold, and others were starting to suffer from heat exhaustion.

A sailor was reported missing, but was discovered from the revelation by an oppo of his that the sailor had a guilty conscience over the theft of the emergency rations, and had left the camp during the night. After a lengthy search, the sailor was not to be found, and that his body would probably end up with the countless other skeletons on the deserted beach.

With the salt water of the Atlantic Ocean behind them and an ocean of dry sand of the Namib Desert in front of them, where would they find their life saving **FRESH WATER?**

Chapter XXV
Groups

"Andy, Bruce, Tansey, wake up! I need the tarpaulins, the canvas and as many containers we have." John whispered, shaking his friends roughly to waken them up.

"Its 0500 hours, and the sun is due up soon. We have about 30 minutes before the sea mist starts coming ashore. Hurry and I'll explain as we go along." John urged.

John had his friends carry his requirements up to the top of the highest dune and then follow his instructions.

"Yesterday, when the sea mist came rolling over us, I noticed the dew forming on the side of the lifeboat. Not only that, I had noticed there were several patches of scrubland along the brow of the sand-dunes to the north of us that faced the open sea. So if we go up there and put these tarpaulins out at a steep angle, and fold the ends up so they form a gully, then all we've got to do is collect the water from the sea mist into the canvas buckets and other containers. Hey presto, well have our fresh water for another day." John explained, as the men arranged the tarpaulins and canvas sheets with John's instructions.

The sea mist came rolling in over the higher dunes to where they were waiting, and within minutes the water was running down the sheets and collecting into the containers they had. Soon all the canvas buckets and anything else that could hold anything including all the drinking cups were full by the time the mist had evaporated in the rising sun.

The men drank the cups of water to slake their own thirst, but carefully carried the buckets and other containers down to the camp to start the rationing once more. This time it was a more generous amount, with half a pint a day for the men, one pint for the women and the injured but nearly two for the children.

When everybody found out that they had fresh water again, the natural resilience of human nature took over and everybody was feeling great again.

The early morning sea mist kept the survivors with drinking water as the foragers and harvesters went out to bring back more fuel for the fire and food to eat. This was proving more difficult to find, as they had to go further away to collect it. This was the main concern of the survivors and it was decided that a campfire meeting should be held to decide what they would do next.

"It would be advisable to find out just who amongst us can do what, apart from us officers and the soldiers, Andy." Lee suggested.

"Yes, we might need certain skills to help us, such as a doctor or a nurse." Larter added.

Sinclair nodded and told them it was a good idea, as he had thought the same thing and called a mass meeting of them all.

The survivors had already split into three groups almost since they landed ashore, with the *Chantrals* in one group, the *Inverlaggan* scientists and the other passengers in another group, leaving the soldiers with the remaining six officers in the 3rd group. This suited Sinclair because he was able to address each group as *Chantrals, Inverlaggans,* or *Military*, accordingly.

"Myself and another officer have already engaged in finding a route out of here, and it's one that we all can use, not just the fittest. If we go, we all go together, as I will not be leaving anybody behind. And that goes for my fellow officers and the rest of my group. Before we leave the relative safety of this place, we need to know who has a profession such as a doctor, or a nurse, or even someone who can play magic tricks and get us out of here." Sinclair announced with a cheerful tone to his voice, then went into detail as to what their options were, before taking a democratic vote on the joint decisions made by all the groups.

"The sands are too hot for people to walk on so I have devised a simple thing that we can strap to our feet to keep us off the hot sand." A *Chantral* offered, and showed everybody a short piece of wood that was tied onto her feet.

"As long as you keep your feet about 1 inch above the surface of the sand, you will stay cool and not only that, it will keep you from being stung by any bugs or the deadly sand scorpions." she added.

Everybody that had no footwear was fitted with this invention, and everyone was given something to carry that was deemed useful. The boats were dragged right up off the beach and abandoned, but with writing scraped onto them to let anybody finding the boats know about them and where they headed.

"I think we'd better make a few wooden sleights for those young or older members to ride on. We can use some of the heaving lines to use as tow ropes. " One of the scientists suggested, which was agreed upon as a help to improve the progress of the group.

The group started off slowly, and almost in single file they walked along the seemingly never-ending beach. On occasions when they were not able to walk around a promontory due to the tides, instead they had to climb up and over several sand dunes but kept close to the shore-line, before they came to another beach that the tide had carved out of the encroaching sand.

They had walked for almost four hours before Sinclair had the word passed along the file for everybody to stop for a while.

"We might as well stay in this little sheltered cove and have a rest and something to eat before we move again. Maybe by our next stop it will be much cooler by then." John suggested.

"What about our water supply Grey?" the soldier officer asked, holding his water bottle upside down to indicate it was empty.

"There is plenty of fish in the water to catch, and by the look of all these whale bones scattered around the place, we can always use the larger bones to make tents with the canvas we've got." Southgate suggested diverting the nasty question away from John. Sinclair, listening to each person's persuasive suggestions decided against his own wish to carry on, to make camp.

Soon everybody got into the routine of camp life, making themselves as comfortable as possible.

Everyone no matter which group they were in, had a vital part to perform for the good of them all.

A fire was soon blazing away with some of the women cooking the fish and other seafood that some of the men had caught. The soldiers were as always posted the guardians of the camp, even though only four out of the seven that survived still had their weapons with them.

The children were a little more subdued as they tried to understand why all this was happening and not the usual fun of the fair at the seaside. The older ones were more or less acting as babysitters for the mothers to be able to help out with the camp chores, whereas the fathers were too busy fetching and carrying or on the scrounge for food and fuel.

A rhythmic pattern emerged for the survivors, as each day passed. Gathering up, walking for hours, making camp for the night, collecting their fresh water from the sea mist, before starting all over again the following day. Thanks to the sleighs they managing to cover an average of 15miles a day in their quest to find civilisation, or at least a permanent fresh water river instead of the dry ones they kept coming across. Each day was taking its toll on them all, as leg weariness started to creep in, especially for the older survivors. That and the temperature difference between the day and night, which in turn proved intolerable, even for the fittest of them. Because every time they decamped, they nearly always seemed to leave a dead body behind.

During their long trek, they kept coming across the pitiful skeleton remains of those would be survivors from way back when. They even found an old lifeboat that was upside down and almost buried in the sand. When it was decided to have a look at it, it was dug out and turned over for them to discover the skeletons of what was deduced as three males, two females, five children and one baby that was still in the skeletal remains of one of the females. But it was that very large leather bound book with brass hinges that drew their attentions.

It was the 'Ship's log' from the sailing vessel the *Tamar Queen*. Within its pages, they told them that the human remains found would be that of Captain Treweek and some of his passengers who were the only survivors off their ship that got wrecked in a big storm in the September of 1875. That the ship had 200 emigrants on board destined for Australia from Falmouth in England, and listed each soul on board and what had become of them. It was decided to take this very unique piece of maritime history, with the hope that it will find some authority or other who will tell the world about the demise of those poor souls. The golden rule otherwise, was that any valuables found and any remains not already buried by the shifting sands, would be done so by them, in their own little way of providing a decent burial for those lost souls, and also of the consensus that anything taken would be considered as 'Grave Robbing' and totally abhorred by all.

Due to the hard 'wear and tear' to what clothing that was worn by the survivors, and even then only during the cold nights, most of the women went bare breasted and wore a kind of a skirt around their middle, the older children wore loin cloths to hide their modesty, whereas the young children were naked during the day apart from some protection draped across their shoulders but got wrapped up during the extremely cold nights. The men had to do with shorts and makeshift footwear This state of almost nakedness was too much for one of the soldiers, who had been found some distance away with a young pubescent girl and was in the process of pleasuring himself within her body. He was seized upon by several of the men who roughed him up and kept him bound up until there was something sorted out that would normally take a judge and jury to decide on the man's fate.

A meeting was held to discuss this problem, with the unanimous decision made that the soldier was to be escorted several miles into the burning desert and left there without food and water. It was at that point when the escort returned that everybody realised that they had all acted as a democratic and lawful group of people. It also served as a timely reminder that a semblance of common law and behaviour was to be observed despite them being on a deserted beach, several hundred miles away from civilisation.

Chapter XXVI
Stay Calm

It was on day ten of the landing when the leading group stopped as they arrived on top of yet another sand dune that overlooked yet another sandy bay.

"It seems as if we've come across some abandoned fishing village." John announced, looking down across the bay in front of them.

"Judging by that shape there must have been some sort of harbour too. Maybe that cluster of ruined buildings will have some sort of clue as to where we are, Andy." He added, pointing to the scenery below them.

Sinclair, Larter and all the other officers took turns to look through the binoculars before they all agreed it would be an ideal place to stop a little while longer.

"I've spotted the remains of an aerial, maybe we will find some sort of radio." Larter said to Southgate, who enthused at the thought of putting his radio theory into practice and helping Larter build another transceiver out of their discoveries.

As the *Chantral* group arrived and were shown what had been discovered, three of them started to moan and scream, causing everybody to demand what was wrong for them to act this way.

"We mustn't go there. We'll all die there. Please don't take us there, we beg of you." an elderly man pleaded, with his wife sobbing bitterly into his shoulder

"But why? It's only an abandoned fishing village." Lee said gently, holding the sobbing pair to comfort them.

"No it's not. It was a secret German naval base with a nazi labour camp and full of death. Several ships were captured and brought here to provide the supplies they needed. Most of the crews were pressed into service but any captured passengers such as we Polish, were treated as slave labour workers. Several hundred perished either at the hands of the Gestapo or got eaten by the deadly crabs that crept around just under the sand.

Nobody managed to escape until we were rescued by the Allies that finally found the place and destroyed it in 1943."[4]

Sinclair listened to further accounts of the place, then weighed up their chances of going across open desert as their only other options, before he asked for a vote from all the others.

It was unanimously carried despite the realisation that they could be walking into more peril as described in detail by the ex-prisoners.

They arrived at the rusty barbed wire fence that marked the perimeter of the place and saw that the sand had started to cover the smaller buildings or drift against the taller ones. But discovered that a veritable warren of caves that were carved out of the sandstone rock which must have represented the main dwellings of the previous owners. And so the decision was made upon to re occupying them as the best option.

The ex-prisoners were crying bitterly as the survivors filed through the fence and into a sort of courtyard surrounded by tumbledown or destroyed group of buildings.

Sinclair picked a building that was almost intact, apart from shell holes in the walls and walked over to it. He asked everybody to gather round then asked the ex-prisoners to explain what each building was, and why there were a series of duckboards still showing in the sand. They had to explain for the sake of everyone else.

They described each building, the series of mounds, the harbour and how it was made. How the people were treated, what happened to those who tried to escape and how most of them died.

Everybody was in awe and listening intently to these poor people until they heard of why the duckboards were there.

If ever there was panic amongst the survivors, then this was it, as they all tried to get off the sand as quickly as possible.

One of the *Inverlaggan* group explained to the ex-prisoners that they were not in danger any more, as the species of crab had been declared extinct as of 1949.

---

[4] See *The Black Rose.*

Because this person was known to be a scientist, his words had an immediate effect, and everybody eventually starting to calm down and climb down from their perches.

"Let's all stay calm. If the boffins say all is well, then so it is. Start looking around for any recent signs of life, but we'll use this building. This is where we'll camp for now, so we all know what to do." Sinclair announced, signalling to them to follow him into the building.

John was busy looking around some of the buildings with Lee, when they discovered a separate entrance to one that seemed to be some sort of tunnel, which on entering it, took them deep inside the sand stone rock face.

"Smells of oil, maybe diesel Tansey. Look at the marks on the floor of the place." John said quietly, but his voice echoed loudly in the tunnel.

"Yes, perhaps some sort of underground fuel bunker, maybe some sort of garage." Lee agreed.

They advanced slowly as they went deeper into the tunnel, until they found a wall blocking them.

"Funny place to build a wall John. But judging by the broken timbers and the pile of sandstone it looks as if part of the tunnel roof has collapsed. There can't be any fuel behind it otherwise it would have leaked through it by now. Lets see what's on the other side shall we. Here grab that piece of timber, lying on the floor." Lee said, grabbing a piece for himself and started to dig away the sandstone.

"Wait a minute Tansey, I've seen these kind of tracks before. This must be some sort of garage or storage depot." John said quickly, and started to dig the rubble away.

Before long, they managed to make a large enough hole for them to climb through.

There was a large puff of stale air and the heavy smell of oil that escaped from the hole, which made both of them retch and gasp for air.

It took them several minutes to recover and for the smell to ventilate away out of the tunnel.

"Hello is anybody there?" a voice called which echoed loudly in the tunnel, and startled them as they looked at each other.

"Who said that Tansey?" John whispered, looking at the hole in the wall.

"Ah there you are!" a voice said from behind them and a hand that tapped John's shoulder.

"Bloody hell Bruce! You nearly scared the day lights out of us two" John said with relief.

"Do that once more and I'll shove this bloody lump of wood up your arse." Lee said roughly, struggling to get hold of himself again.

"We all heard these voices coming from absolutely nowhere, then we heard the whistle of the bad air and saw where it was coming from. We didn't think it was one of you nosey lot." Larter chuckled.

"Yes, well you can't be too certain with these things Bruce. I've been trapped in a mine before now. " Lee said grimly, and stuck his head through the hole.

"Better if we make it bigger so that we can all go through it." John said cautiously, which prompted the three of them to start knocking the wall away completely.

They entered into what was a large cavern, and John was able to confirm what made the strange track marks in the sandstone.

"Ah yes, I remember." Larter said, as they approached a strange looking vehicle.

"By the look of it, it's as if it was made only yesterday and it's still got a full tank of fuel. If we can get this working properly, we have finally got transport to get us off the beach and inland." Lee announced.

"Not unless we find a couple of those sleighs." John said absentmindedly, exploring other dark corners of the large cave.

"It looks as one of the previous occupiers got lost." Lee said, when he came across a skeleton.

"According to his dog tag the sailors used to wear in the war, his name was Becks. Come and look, John!"

John came over to see the remains whilst Lee was examining a smart pair of pearl handled Luger pistols, still in its luxuriously adorned leather holster.

"Finders keepers, so I'll have this as my souvenir John. Whatever this is you can have it, bag and all." Lee said, buckling the gun and holster around his waist then tossing a small hessian sack over to John.

John caught the bag, opened it and tipped its contents onto the sandy floor of the cave. It was a large ball of clay that landed at his feet with a dull thud.

"What would he want with a useless piece of clay if he was trying to escape in this vehicle?" Lee asked, looking at what had caught John's attention.

John bent down and picked the large ball up but accidentally dropped it, which broke open almost in two halves to reveal a pink coloured stone the size of an orange.

"It looks more like Humpty Dumpty now John." Lee chuckled.

"Maybe it's one of his good luck charms he wanted to keep but disguised it in case he was captured." John replied, tossing the stone in his hand to guess its weight.

"Whatever it is its pretty light, but I think I'll keep it for him in case he wants it again." John added with a grin, tucking the stone into his tattered trouser pocket, then started to explore the cave again.

"Here we are. I've found two of them but they would need repairing to be of use." John said after a little while.

"Look what I've found. A small cache of arms;, A radio complete with its crystals, and its matching receiver. You two have your fun with those machines, Paul and I will have fun with these, and see if we can contact somebody." Larter said with glee, patting his treasure trove lovingly.

"We'll leave it for now Tansey, as we've still got the problem with getting fresh water around here somewhere." John suggested to Lee, who was still busy examining the vehicle.

"I'll stay here and see if I can get it started John. You go on and look for the water supply."

"Fair enough, but you'll need some fresh air and some light to work with."

"Don't mind me John, just go and get our fresh water." Lee said, waving John away.

John went back to the allocated building as the base for the survivors, and sought out Sinclair who was organising and detailing little work parties.

"If our *Chantal* friends are right, in amongst all that heap of sand over by the outer harbour wall, there appears to be a couple of ships. There's one almost on its side with a big hole in it's hull, we'd better take a look and see what we can find. We might just find water making equipment and maybe if we're lucky other handy material we could all use." John greeted, as Sinclair finished despatching the last small team of people.

"Let's hope so John. Mind you, we've already found a galley that was wrecked, and even a small sick bay with a few surviving instruments the 'Doc' would find useful. Best of all, come and see what I found." Sinclair said and led the way to his discovery.

"Here it is. It must have been the officer in charge of this place. It's battered up somewhat, but at least somebody forgot to look closer to find this. And guess what John? If my eyes prove me correct and whether it's in German or not but Von Meir is mentioned." Sinclair said with pride, holding up a map of the area, and another detailed one for the base.

"Bloody hell! Not him again. I thought they got rid of him way back!" John groaned, as they looked at the maps for a while before Sinclair rolled them up and stuffed them under his arm.

"Yes, this must have been one of Meir's hideouts that was mentioned by that commodore, whatever his name was in Barbados. If so, then we should find at least something to keep us alive, providing the allied troops didn't go overboard in their destruction of the place. Anyway let's have a camp meeting after supper about this, John. Now what were you saying about the drinking water?" he asked as if to remind himself.

John explained that he needed help to locate drinkable water, or at least get some sort of evaporator be made to do so, otherwise they would be thirsty by nightfall. He suggested that the stokers were to be taken off camp duty to form his working party in getting this and any other machinery working. He also told Sinclair the good news of finding transport that Lee was working on for them to use. And the radio that Larter had found which they would try and get going.

"Seems perfectly clear to me John. The stokers will be pleased to get back to their normal functions again. Now we all have something to cheer about." Sinclair concluded, arriving back into the large room that he would use as his 'captain's day cabin' and general meeting place'.

"Right then, I'll round up the stokers and be off. See you later." John said, leaving to gather his men together.

"About ruddy time too 3rd! We was all thinking that there might have been more to camping out than just fishing and picking up lumps of wood." a stoker said cheerfully, for the stokers to sit around John and listened to what he wanted them to do.

"Okay then, if we can't find any water stored away, we'll get the parts needed to make our own evaps. Lots of copper tubing, old bunker oil for fuel and oil drums cleaned out as our condensers and the like. Lets go men!" John recapped, before he led the men down to the abandoned hulk of what was a magnificent tanker in its day.

The call for supper rang out, and groups of people came from all over the place and settled down in the makeshift dining room. It was complete with repaired tables and chairs, a set of cracked crockery and even cutlery for each person and also a few hurricane lamps glowing and hanging above them to give some light.

As each person arrived they stood in awe at this marvellous sight. Even the now standard diet of fish and crab smelled wonderful, as they sat eagerly and patiently to be served by the stewards and four comically dressed soldiers.

Everybody talked quietly among themselves until the meal was over, when Sinclair stood up and asked for a bit of hush.

"I think each one of you gathered here today has excelled themselves in creating this wonder here tonight, and we can all thank one another as nobody has done better than anybody else." Sinclair said, raising his cup of water and offered a toast, and wished that perhaps in the near future they all would be dining in the poshest of hotels and drinking champagne.

He went on to reveal some of the finds, especially the two maps, the vehicle and the radio and what it would mean to them all. Also the fact they would have to stay a little longer until the engineers sorted out the fresh water.

When he finished explaining what he was planning, or hoping to do for all their sakes, he invited anybody with other comments or items to mention.

Ever since day one on the first beach, Sinclair was given the backing by his seniors, the surviving ships' officers, including the scientists and other professional people, to assume the leadership of the entire group. This was his way and his adopted method of communicating and expressing the desires of any person who wanted to say something that could or would affect all the others. In turn that person would receive a decision from the collective response of everybody else.

It was democracy at its best.

The woman doctor from the *Inverlaggan* group stated her concern about everybody getting too much protein and no fibre or carbohydrates, and that was a very dangerous thing.

Yet another person from the *Inverlaggan* group who was a nurse and a trained midwife also stated her concern about two women who were nearly due for completion of their pregnancy. She also stated that the rest of the women had stopped menstruating, and the children were showing signs of lack certain vitamins even now and before the adults were to be affected.

One of the *Chantral's* group who was a carpenter spoke of the possibility of sailing out of the abandoned harbour once he fixed the holes in the launch found half-buried under the sand.

This went on for quite a while and collective decisions were made until no more topics arose to be discussed, when it became mutually obvious that it was time to get some sleep, let alone for the very tired children.

Chapter XXVII
Vintage '53

"**L**ooks as we've had it 3rd!" a stoker said disappointedly as John and his stokers finally arrived into the rusting and waterlogged engine room of yet another old ship.

John held his own torch higher to see better and found that most of the machinery was blackened as if by fire, and a lot of the metal was crumbling around them with corrosion.

"We might be lucky in the evap room. Two of you go over and have a look, the rest of you can start by getting these oil drums up on deck, but be careful you don't make another hole in the deck that you can't get out of." John ordered.

John went over to the evap room and assessed what could be salvaged from there before going into the motor room.

"Okay men. Strip down the water valves then see if you can open up the main casing. If you can see any copper piping, then try and get as much of it out as possible, without snapping bits off. I want as much whole tubing as possible." John ordered, and started to strip away the header tank off the top of the evaporator.

"If you find any tools lying around, use them, but keep hold of them in case we need them later " he added, picking up a discarded short handled wheel spanner.

The stokers worked hard and managed to salvage lots of useful bits as they systematically stripped the place like a plague of locusts.

John was up on the main deck when the last stoker appeared with the last piece of useful salvage.

"Okay then. I've managed to locate a hand-operated suction pump down below the deck plates just by No1 boiler. We'll use it to siphon off the oil from the bilges. So two of you go and see if you can find some deck hoses. We'll connect them up to the pump and have the oil pumped into these barrels. The rest of you start getting this lot onto the jetty. I'm off to see if I can find some wheels to cart this lot away over to the main building."

"Wheels 3rd? I saw some in a tumbledown shack just aft of the gangway." A stoker informed.

"Good spotting, go and see if they work. Anyway, we'd better get a move on as its nearly time for food, and there's virtually no water left until we make some."

Again, the men worked furiously getting all their needs ashore and up to the main building ready to start phase two of the operation, which entailed making a desalination plant by using pieces of scrap metal, containers and bags of hope for lots of luck.

"What have we got here John? Joined the scrap metal trade now have you?" Lee joked, watching John complete the final jigsaw to his latest invention.

"Hello Tansey! It's just an item that one likes to make up from time to time. This one is my latest, called the Hufty Pufty, because that's the sound it will make." John responded in a similar jovial fashion.

Lee had a good look around John's creation, and apart from advising him on one or two minor things, he declared that it would work a treat, providing they had enough wood to burn.

"Wood? The man said wood!" one of the stokers said in mock indignation.

"And here's me sweating my proverbials off slurping off this dirty black stuff into this dirty black barrel."

Lee looked over to see two stokers wheeling a rickety handcart that held a barrel that was slopping black oil everywhere.

"Ah yes. I see, You are Hufty and you must be Pufty!" Lee laughed at the sight of the two oil-stained stokers.

"Har-de-flippin-har 2nd. Now if you'll excuse us, we've got a real mans' job to do!" the other stoker smiled as they commenced to light up the makeshift boiler.

Before long, the sea water was boiled up that turned to steam that hissed along the copper pipes contained in a barrel of cold sea water that was the condenser, which turned the steam back into water, that flowed slowly out of the pipe and into a freshly cleaned oil drum. In fact it was a makeshift desalination machine that gave out the life giving drinkable water.

John waited until the barrel was almost full then got hold of a cracked jug to dunk into the water. He took the first jug full and held it up to the sun before he poured it back into the barrel again, then he slowly filled it again raised it to his mouth and tasted it slowly. As all the others watched him, their mouths moved in unison with his, mentally savouring every drop that he drank.

John looked at the sea of faces around him that were looking anxiously at him to give his verdict.

"Ladies and gentlemen. I declare this a definite vintage, Vintage '53. We, the stokers and I, that is, do hereby declare that we have now got clear water on tap. Roll up roll up, come and taste it." John announced with a flourish as he splashed the cup back into the water.

Everybody cheered and rushed to get a cup full, including the children. Each person drank deeply from their mugs before they declared it was definitely an improvement to the brackish sea mist and had another mug full just to be certain.

Sinclair and Larter were at the back of the crowd looking on, as John brought them a canvas bucket full each.

"Here you are Andy, Bruce. Shut your eyes and pretend its whiskey." John said softly.

They drank the liquid slowly and declared that it was the best drink they'd had since John rescued the fresh water supply off Jones, and congratulated John on a fine job once more.

"Any decent engineer could have done it, and besides I am only doing my duty for us all." John, replied softly in his usual modest way.

The first few days at this abandoned camp wore on, with more and more events and discoveries to cheer everybody up more and more.

Even the ex prisoners started to relax and show a bit more willingness to venture out of the main building.

For each day they were in this destroyed port, they explored anything and everything that would perhaps help them to escape their seemingly inevitable fate and all thoughts were turning to some sort of a rescue attempt or whatever. The escape fever gripped everybody and it seemed to be their driving force to give them all the impetus to make things happen sooner rather than later.

One evening after their evening meal which was a rapturous one, they all sensed that the day for them to leave was getting that much closer, and by the end of the evening everybody went to bed feeling almost whole again. Everybody that is, except for the navy officers and the one soldier officer.

"I need you all to come to the office for a conflab, gentlemen. Bruce here has something important to tell, but only us are to know for the moment." Sinclair said quietly.

"Paul and I managed to salvage enough parts from what was once a radio control room and put a decent transmitter and receiver together. We heard several radio stations and even tried to call them, but either I'm speaking double Dutch to them or they won't recognise any of the CQ callsigns I used. I've tried my own private callsign so did Paul and we even used the *Inverlaggan's* international callsign, but there's total silence from them. Either they don't believe what they are hearing or treat my transmissions as a hoax. The only thing we can do is to keep broadcasting on a couple of frequencies so as to cause a nuisance, so somebody will challenge our cq. Perhaps the navy would send a patrol aircraft or ship out to try and locate us, but at the moment it's looking bleak." Larter explained at length.

"Well, we can't stay here indefinitely, people are starting to get ill through lack of the right vitamins. I think we should call a meeting in the morning after breakfast, but if we do move out we've got a lot of planning and packing to do." Crabbe advised.

"I have got that strange tank looking vehicle almost ready but will need plenty of fuel to run it. If we get the carpenter and a couple of men to help him, we can get those sleighs fixed up and could hitch them onto the vehicle and tow them along." Lee advised.

"As far as I'm concerned we have food and shelter now and could wait to be rescued, but we really must get to some proper fresh water soon, as what we're drinking now is almost distilled water. If we drink too much of it, over a long period that is, it will add to the health problem because it causes boils and other medical problems." John advised.

"My men and I have examined the area around this place and we found some sort of trail heading north. What does it say on your charts and the map you found Sinclair?" the soldier officer asked.

Sinclair reached into the drawer of the broken desk, pulled out his charts and the maps that were found and laid them across the desk.

"As you can see, I've marked our landing site and an approximate place to where we stopped overnight. This is where we are now, some 120 miles away. According to this German map, there is a track leading north to this river where it branches off east and west. The easterly one takes you across the desert whereas the westerly one leads to what looks like a settlement on the river mouth. Presumably that's where the Germans did their trading with the local Arabs." Sinclair explained as the men looked over the maps.

"If we used that track I reckon it to be about 350 miles further up the coast, but how long would it take us with that thing 2nd?" Crabbe asked.

"If my memory serves me correct it can do around 20mph, but it would depend on the weight of the tow." John interrupted, as Lee was busy writing down some mathematics.

"The vehicle has a double engine and will guzzle diesel fuel like anything. If what John says is true then according to my calculations it will only do about 10miles per gallon per engine, but make it 8 to be on the safe side. Our load will be negligible in comparison to its pulling power, so I reckon we can do a safe 15mph until we find out exactly what the vehicle is really capable of." Lee finally answered.

"To allow for stops and other problems over 12 hours of daylight, and say a 10 hour drive each day, we will need to gather enough food, water and fuel for 3 days." Crabbe stated.

"Not quite. We're guests to the desert, and it's a pretty mean one that has a habit of producing extra large sandstorms. These can go on for days." Larter stated, recalling his earlier visit to the desert with John and Sinclair.

"The safest alternative is to stay put and wait for the cavalry to arrive. Failing that, we can always sail up the coast to it, providing we have enough boats or rafts to do so." Southgate said, pointing at the sea chart.

Sinclair and Crabbe looked at the chart for a moment before Sinclair spoke.

"Yes we could, as the current would take us along the shoreline until we meet the river. We could always beach below it in case the river egress took us out to sea again."

"Then again, what about those bloody mines we ran into that got us here in the first place." the soldier pointed out.

"It seems as if we really do need a full meeting in the morning. We'll put the alternatives we've just discussed, to them and let them decide. In the meantime the crewmen and your soldiers will start hunting for things we need like fuel and cordage." Sinclair stated and concluded the small meeting, before they all left for some much needed sleep.

The meeting was held and the decision based on health grounds was that they would leave the abandoned base and head for the river, with the prospect of meeting civilisation again and finally to be rescued from their nightmarish saga.

Everybody, including the children had a little job or task to do to help prepare themselves to move off the ruined base, and were seemingly happy in doing so, especially the ex prisoners.

They were used as interpreters on each occasion somebody found something with Germanic writing on it, which helped the finder to decide whether or not it was usable to the group.

Lee had caused a stir as the vehicle roared out of the tunnel dragging the broken sleighs behind it.

"It sounds and looks good, Tansey! Lets get the armour and the guns off it, maybe it will lighten the vehicle enough to give a better fuel consumption." John suggested, as Lee jumped down from the high standing vehicle.

"We need a few extra track plates John, as some of them have rotted away. Other than that, we need a good half ton of diesel just for safety sake, and we've only got about two thirds of it so far." Lee stated, pulling out the rags that acted as his earplugs.
John nodded and repeated what he had said for Lee to make some mental arithmetic calculations.

"Yes John, I think you're right. It will give us a good 5mpg extra if that was done. Let's do it." Lee stated.

The two engineers and the stokers started to strip down the heavy armour and gave the weapons to the soldiers to dispose of, then repaired the damaged tracks.

The carpenter and his helpers were busy with the sleighs, stripping down the heavy re-inforced metalwork, repairing the wooden parts and putting the salvaged tarpaulins over the top as shelters.

The sailors were making piles of things they found, which the scientists examined to see if the finds were useful or not.

The women were on the beach catching fish with a rough kettle net the sailors made for them. They were shown how to use the net, and were able to catch different kinds of fish from between the morning cast and the evening cast. Hence the saying, '*A different kettle of fish.*'

The older children looked after the younger ones, and occasionally they would fetch water for someone needing a drink. The cooks toiled away in the galley preparing food to pack into suitable containers for the move, whilst also cooking for their daily needs.

A couple of stokers were tending the makeshift boiler, keeping it topped up with seawater that they converted to drinking water. For the two stewards and three women, to wash clothes or clean their newly found crockery and cutlery they used the hot water drawn from the boiler.

An electrician managed to find a small dynamo and a few unbroken light bulbs that he used to light up the main building with.

An unknown person had put a sign up over the entrance door with the words 'The Sandy Bay Hotel' with yet another with a sense of humour had stuck a notice on a broken window frame next to it saying 'No vacancies'.

The various activities went on all day until it was decided that it was time to finish for the day and get ready to move out in the morning.

Chapter XXVIII
Sandwiches

Everybody woke up early the next morning with excitement and eager to complete their packing and have their breakfast before they moved off.

John was at the boiler with his stokers who were loading the barrels of water onto the back of one of the sleighs, and Sinclair was seeing to his sailors when a low whispering sound was heard.

"John, we've got a sandstorm brewing. Tell your men to get the boiler and these barrels covered with tarpaulins, and be very quick about it. Ask Tansey to move the vehicle and the sleighs back into the tunnel, then get Bruce and Paul over to the main building." Sinclair stated urgently, getting his own gang of men to shift the packed stores back into the building.

John arrived back into the main building with Larter and Southgate just in time, as the low whispering turned into a loud moan.

"We've got one of those storms we had back in Libya, Bruce." Sinclair said, meeting them coming in through the door.

"Has Tansey come back? What about the soldiers?" John asked with concern.

"You three are the last to come back John, so better shut the door and help me shore it up." Sinclair suggested, grabbing what they could to stop the battered door from opening.

"Paul, better go round the building and make sure all the windows and any holes in the main walls are shored up. Use internal doors and the like to do so." Larter suggested, placing their portable transmitter and receiver onto a nearby table.

The officer soldier heard the suggestion and volunteered his men to help out, which was accepted with thanks by Southgate.

Soon the building was barricaded up and as everybody started to settle down for a wait they didn't know for how long.

As the day wore on people were getting miserable and touchy at being locked inside instead of on the move to their new camp.

Sinclair, Larter and John were sitting in the 'office' talking quietly among themselves, when one of the cooks came in and asked if he could provide a meal for them all

"You might as well chef. We'll probably be here for a couple of days anyway, so you'll have to unpack the foodstuff again and start using it up. We've got plenty of water and even some light, so nobody will go hungry or thirsty until then. It should brighten everybody up when they smell the food cooking." Sinclair answered, which was received by a smile from the chef.

"You're right there bosun. If I had the flour I'd even bake a cake." he replied as he left the room.

Soon the aroma of cooking was in the air, which perked everybody up from their little world of doom and gloom.

"We've got fish and chips for dinner today, Andy!" John smiled, starting to tuck into his fish steaks with shrimp sauce.

"That makes a change, and after you with the salt 'n' vinegar John!"

The meal was received with mixed feelings but at least they knew that they were safer in their little haven rather than stuck under canvas out in the desert.

"What's for afters, chef?" a cheerful voice asked loudly.

"*Sand*wiches!" came another voice as it emphasised the word sand.

"In that case I'll have mine out on the veranda, with an ice cold beer." Somebody else quipped.

The little bout of banter and wisecracking went on for a little while, such was the typical spirit of people who had endured many hardships and whatever fate had dished out to them all.

"Of course, it now means that we've got to start all over again. Providing the boiler has survived, that is." Southgate stated.

"Only for food, Paul. We've got all four of the vehicle's tanks full of diesel and two full 45gallon barrel as standby. John's got four barrels of water already loaded, with a further two in the kitchen, all of which should last us for at least two weeks if it comes to it." Lee replied cheerfully.

"Anyway, think of it this way Paul. We're forced to remain here until the storm goes, which only lasts a couple of days. In that time, our rescuers could be catching up on us by the trail we left behind." Crabbe said with equal cheerfulness.

"Yes, we've left a marker at each camp site for them to follow." the soldier officer added.

The doctor who overheard the remark about the marker came over and joined the conversation.

"Yes, all they've got to do is follow the graves. We will probably have another death before we leave here, let alone the one from last night." she commented, then told who it was that died and who was her next possible victim.

"He was on Lee's boat that crashed onto the sand bar. So that makes a total of 17 dead, plus the 2 counted as missing." Sinclair stated."

"I've also got 4 others with medical problems, and further 4 children feeling rather poorly. Mind you the distilled water we're drinking doesn't help matters either.

John looked at the doctor and shook his head.

"Sorry about that Doc, but it's all I can do. At least we've got water to drink, which is the main thing. Once we get to that river all will be okay on that score, I promise you Doc." He said softly

Chapter XXIX
The Riviera Express

The storm finally blew itself away early in the following morning, which was marked by the absence of noise, and much to the delight of the survivors.

Everybody was up and breakfasted and ready to start another day gathering for their journey.

"The boiler's been half buried in sand 3rd. Do you want us to dig it out?" a stoker reported.

"Yes! Dig it out and put ready for transport, and give the tarpaulins over for recycling. The water barrel can go over to the galley." John replied, whilst he and Lee were checking the vehicle and sleighs over.

"The Germans were good engineers to produce this machine John. If we load it and the three sleighs with an equal load we should be okay. I reckon the vehicle can carry about 10 tons and still pull a 40 ton tank behind it, let alone the sleighs." Lee said appreciatively, starting up the powerful engines, that roared into life and giving off a large puff of exhaust smoke.

"You're right there Tansey, but we could still do with a fourth sleigh, judging by all the stuff we're going to lug from this place."

"As long as we've got enough rations to get us there, which we have, no doubt most everything else will be jettisoned."

"That's what I'm afraid of Tansey. We might get to that place and find we've got to fend for ourselves again. Out of the frying pan and into the fire, so to speak."

"So what's cooking John?" Sinclair asked coming into the conversation.

"We're just talking about all the stuff we're going to take with us, Andy. Food and fuel is fair comment, and maybe some tarpaulins as shelter until we get there, but what about all the rest?"

Sinclair thought for a moment before he replied.

"We will carry as much items for our survival as we can, John. Metal to make cutting instruments, canvas, tarpaulins and ropes for the tents and fishing nets, some cooking pots and pans, and firewood or extra oil fuel for any fire that we make during our transit. In fact anything the boffins deem useful to us. It will be put securely onto the last sleigh as I've a feeling we've got to look after ourselves until the cavalry arrive."

"I've got that same feeling Andy. We've got just the one chance to get it right this time, before we leave."

"Call a general meeting Andy." Lee suggested, which met with approval from Sinclair.

"Yes, we've got to sort out the seating arrangements too." Sinclair agreed and went off to get everybody together.

"On second thoughts Tansey, we'd better put most of the weight onto the vehicle so that the sleighs can travel better. Besides, our tow bars might not take the strain." John stated, pointing to the tow bar and the almost fragile state it appeared to be in.

Sinclair had everybody gather round and spoke about their essential needs for travelling. Only keep items for their own personal survival, as the rest will be stowed on the last sleigh. He explained what was needed before he got everybody into their 3 groups and allocated their places on the transport.

A couple of points and a few problems were aired and sorted before they knew what they were about to do. Bury yet two more of their dead, before leaving.

Finally, after seven days in the relative safety of the ruined camp it was time to leave.

"All aboard the Riviera Express. Make sure you have your tickets ready for inspection!" some wag shouted.

"By courtesy of the management, cocktails will be served in five minutes. First seating for lunch in the dining car in four hours!" one of the chefs responded, which drew a huge laugh from them all as they climbed eagerly into their allocated transport.

Everybody fell silent in anticipation, awaiting the move to a safer existence than otherwise experienced, and perhaps reach their ultimate goal of being rescued from this ongoing nightmare. The small convoy looking like a train, and leaving the battered camp behind, the vehicle chugged its way along the faint track that was marked on the map as a main highway.

"Just like before, Bruce. Can't trust the German map makers." Sinclair said, studying the maps they had found.

"This beauty is pulling just great over the sand, but finding it a bit hard on the 'road'. So if we keep getting our bones rattled we know we're still on it." Lee stated, steering the vehicle over yet another patch of soft sand.

"We found that the sleighs were better off road too, so maybe we could drive parallel to it." John suggested.

"We might run into quicksand if we did that. Besides, the Germans might have placed mines there to catch anybody trying to sneak up on them." Sinclair said, pointing to an area of sand to their right.

"That's a typical place to stop for a brew up, and a typical place for mines, just watch. Stop here if you please Tansey." Sinclair said, pulling out his gun for the very first time, and fired at a clump of sand some way off.

The sand erupted into the air with a dull thump, followed closely by several more thumps. Within a minute, there were little holes in the sand everywhere, before the sand refilled them up again.

"Now I'd better go and tell everybody what that was all about. Maybe the army boys would keep an eye out for more, as we go along." Sinclair sighed, climbing out of the cabin and walked back to the sleighs.

"I feel happier now he's made his point." Lee said, and waited for Sinclair to come back.

"Okay gentlemen, let's go." Sinclair said, climbing back onto the vehicle.

"What speed have we been doing Tansey?" John asked, watching the flickering needle on the speedometer.

"We've been making a steady 18 knots since we left. My watch has packed up so don't know for how long." Lee responded.

Larter looked at his watch and told them that they'd been travelling for four hours.

"According to this map, we've got about another 20 miles to go before we meet the junction and turn left. Suggest we stop there for lunch, Andy." Larter said, handing Sinclair the map.

"We've been keeping the sun on our right, so we're on course. Yes, we'll stop there for a brew up, but we've got to be at least halfway before we stop and make camp for the night." Sinclair agreed as everybody lapsed into silence once more.

The small convoy stopped as arranged, for them to get off and stretch their legs, but stayed on the track as Sinclair's lesson had taught them what to expect if they wandered off.

As everybody finished their food and enjoyed a few more minutes on their feet before climbing back onto their cramped transport again, Sinclair announced that when they stopped again it would be for the night, whilst John ensured that each transport had their share of water to drink as and when they wanted.

Crabbe was in charge of the first sleigh with Southgate on the rear sleigh, keeping in contact with Larter by signal torch. As it was Sinclair's turn to drive, Larter took the role of convoy leader, whilst Lee sat relaxing.

"According to my calculations, we have about two hours daylight left Andy. We'd better find somewhere suitable to camp for the night." Larter suggested.

"When we pull over, get everybody off and the sleighs formed into a loose circle. John, ask Crabbe to get the sleigh sides on the outside dropped down to keep the draught out from under the sleighs, then have some of the men rig the canvas over the top of us like a tent. Tansey, you'll see that the vehicle is protected from the sand. Bruce, ask the soldier officer to check our campsite for mines, then have the rest of the men to plug the hole between the sleighs with sand. No sense having strangers or beasts wandering into our camp. Someone ask Paul to start a fire going, and get the chefs to provide a meal." Sinclair commanded.

The camp was organised, and after their meal, they all settled down to a long night that turned bitterly cold as all the clothes they wore were getting quite threadbare or tattered.

Modesty was the main concern for all, but the children had extra garments over them to protect them from the extremely hot sun. But at night, everybody had to huddle together to keep warm, even under makeshift tents. The difference between the scorching heat of the day and the freezing cold of the night was extreme in itself, as the survivors battled out one more freezing night in the open desert.

"Paul, we'd better get another fire lit, so will you see to it. Get some drinking water heated up, as we're going to need it before the night is over." Sinclair suggested quietly to the drowsy Southgate.

"We'll be setting off early so we'd better have another good meal before we go. If our course and speed remain the same as before, then we should arrive there around 1700hours." Sinclair advised the rest of the officers who were restless and trying to sleep.

The warmth of the sun's rays reached out to the survivors camp, and as if by magic, everybody was up and without a word they all began their own allocated task before the camp was broken up for another bone shaking journey on their sleighs.

Their meal was eaten almost in silence, for they knew they had another arduous day in front of them. Once they cleared their things away and the sleighs hooked back up onto the vehicles once more, they were off.

With a roar of the powerful engine, the big vehicle started off with its smaller sleighs following meekly behind it, as the convoy left the sand to rejoin the 'track'.

"That was a fine decamping, Tansey." Sinclair stated, with Lee driving them along.

"Yes, we've got it off pat now, but I wonder if she knows it." Lee said with a smile.

"Let's hope we don't have to make too many more extra fires Andy, as we're now down to the bare minimum. Not only that, there's a leak in one of the water barrels which means that we'll have to economise on the water again." John advised.

"Thanks for telling us John, as it will alter the logistical plan. I'll go back and tell the others to go easy on the water buckets." Sinclair answered, shouting back to Crabbe in the first sleigh the instructions and for him to tell Southgate in the rear.

Both Southgate and Crabbe held their hands up to indicate the message was understood, and reported that all was well in their sleighs.

"How are we for course and speed now Bruce?" Sinclair asked

"On a steady westerly course, speed 18 knots. We're about half way and nearly time for a stop." Larter advised, looking at his watch.

"Well there's some sort of a ridge up ahead of us so we'll stop there." Sinclair stated, looking around the desert scenery, but only saw sand dunes by the thousands.

The convoy arrived on the ridge and stopped for their break before making the last lap of their journey.

"There is another ridge over to our right, with a scattering of vegetation. I think we must be near water of some sort. Let's hope it's that river Bruce. See what you think." John suggested offering his glasses to Larter.

Larter scanned the area and handed them over to Sinclair.

"I think John is right. Let's go over and recce the place." He suggested.

"Tansey, stay here with Paul and Crabbe, we're going over to that ridge and will be back shortly." Sinclair said pointing over to the ridge.

"I don't think our fare paying passengers would mind an extra half hour to walk around." Lee said jokingly as he waved them off.

The three friends clambered up to the top of the slope and looked at the vista before them.

They stood in awe at the magnificent sight of a wide river meandering along the valley below them, with all sorts of trees and vegetation growing almost right up to the river's edge. They looked along the valley and saw that where the river met the sea, there were flocks of birds feeding in what looked like fresh water lakes made by the silt and sand coming down the river, and had forming a small delta.

"I can't see any sign of human life down there, only the odd wild beast roaming around. Can you?" Sinclair asked, offering his glasses to Larter who, after his look, in turn gave it back to John.

"Not a soul anywhere, not even a wisp of smoke to be seen." John concluded

"Well it looks as if we've arrived into our own Eden, to maybe start another tribe on this continent. That's unless we can be rescued before then." Larter commented.

Sinclair took the glasses back off John and scanned around the terrain from the convoy to the river.

"We have one more ridge ahead to get over, before we turn right towards the river mouth. There seems to be a bit of a clearing among the wood near the waters edge, both sea and river. We'll make our camp there. It should take us about another hour or so to arrive there." Sinclair announced, walking swiftly back down to the convoy.

"Right listen up everybody. We've some good news, and some bad. The good news is that we've found a flowing river and lots of what looks like the right sort of trees for us to use. The bad news is that there's no settlement, not even a disused hut." Sinclair announced.

"It's just as well we brought the pots and pans with us then." a chef stated flatly.

"Then you'd better get them organised chef, as we'll be dining on roast duck and coconut milk tonight." John responded, which was greeted with a huge cheer from the rest of the people.

"Well then what are we waiting for, lets go!" somebody urged, which was almost like a starters gun, as everyone galvanised into action and started to prepare for the last lap.

"Once we've arrived, we must have a good look around in case our camp is lower than any tide or water marks. Don't want anybody drowning now having come all this way." Sinclair said calmly as Lee drove over the last stretch of sand before entering the lush vegetation and woods.

Everybody was looking at each tree and clump of grass when the sleighs moved slowly into the small clearing that was spotted earlier.

"Nobody is to get out yet, we've got to check the site first." Sinclair shouted over the noise of excited people, as Larter and John leapt out of the vehicle and ran to the edge of the clearing.

"Look at these tracks, Andy. They're not fresh, but somebody's been here before." John said, hunkering down and examined the marks in the gravely sand.

"Yes, Andy, they go down the beach to the sea, and there are some other marks in the sand of the river bank." Larter added. Sinclair looked around and made his own discovery.

"We had better get ourselves into that other clearing to our right, as this one is on the tide mark. Not only that, the river is low at the moment, which means that it floods this area where we are now." Sinclair said, pointing out to the driftwood and watermarks all around where they stood.

"We'll drive the vehicle up to it and set up camp right there." He added, pointing out another little clearing some several feet above their level.

The three friends came back to the anxiously waiting people and pointed to where they will be making their new home.

Within minutes the vehicle arrived with the now almost empty sleighs as the people had got out and were running alongside it up the hill.

The scenery was breath taking for each one of them, and for the very first time since leaving the sinking ship, everybody started to dance and shout with glee.

The shallow green water of the wide river was slowly bubbling its way into a series of small lagoons where a kaleidoscope of coloured birds of all sizes were feeding or nesting in the many patches of reeds.

There were palm trees lining the sea shore and several kinds of other trees grew in great clumps along the river banks, with large clumps of grasses and bamboo grew as a carpet for them.

The different noises of the birds and the sound of the river was music to everybody.

Sinclair and the other officers let everybody have a few minutes to celebrate before he announced that it was time to get a proper camp organised.

"I think we've arrived gentlemen. This place will do us very nicely, and thanks to your collective efforts in bringing us here." a scientist said with tears in his eyes as he gave each officer a hug.

"No. It's all down to the sheer determination of each and every one of you. All we did was to try and save as many of you as possible, as part of our shipping company's policy." Larter said softly.

"Don't forget the little bit of help from the Germans." Tansey added, patting the bonnet of the vehicle.

"Maybe we can now forget our *FRESH WATER* problem now that there's a whole river of it on the doorstep." John quipped as everybody was grinning from ear to ear.

"Yes, its been a close run thing." Sinclair concluded softly.

Chapter XXX
In Dire Need

The survivors had one of their special meetings to decide what they were going to do. Stay in their temporary overnight campsite, or whilst they were waiting for their rescue, try and live as comfortable as possible.

In the end, it was decided that the temporary overnight campsite be slowly replaced with a circle of large huts that were built on stilts and made from bamboo and palm leaves.

Within a week of arriving and a hectic period of work, a decent almost permanent camp was flourishing, with everybody still doing the tasks they had adopted during their long trek there.

The vehicle and the sleighs had a hut built over them, and immediately behind a hut built on stilts where John and his friends were to stay. This was adopted as the camp HQ, and for anybody to use when a problem arose.

The rest of the huts were house about 20 people. They all had a sturdy walking plank to get up to the hut, with crude beds, furniture, a veranda to sit out on to keep cool, and even shutters for the windows to keep out the wind blown sand.

There was a central stores and cooking area, where the chefs and stewards had their own little hut.

Lee and John created a bamboo water system for each hut that provided a source of fresh running water to drink or for the chefs to cook with, thus keeping from drawing water from the river each time it was required. They even built a separate system using salt water for their latrines.

The scientists managed to locate some sago palms where they started to process and make a thick paste of sago to cook so that at least everybody would get some sort of carbohydrates of which they were in dire need to remain alive.

The soldiers used their weapons to great effect and killed some very large birds for the cooking pots. The children would go out into the reed beds to collect the birds' eggs, into the woods and help collect the fallen coconuts, or climb the trees and collect the dates.

Sinclair and Crabbe had the seamen busy making and using fishing nets, ropes, lengths of string and other items that would be used around the camp, including screens and animal traps around the camp perimeter to protect them from unwanted guests or rampaging wild animals.

The carpenter was constantly making furniture, beds, and all sorts of useful items, and even found time to make a couple of rafts and even an out-rigger canoe for fishing.

The doctor had her own purpose built hut, which was used as the local clinic and sick bay, even though she had a very much-dwindled supply of medicines left. All except for a very large glass bottle of full of aspirins, which seemed to be dispensed as the panacea for all ailments and other medical problems.

The stokers were armed with crude spears, bows and arrows, and likened themselves to 'Robin Hood and his Merry men' as they went hunting wild boar, or catching an unwary wild camel from a large herd that was roaming around, and other such animals for the pot. For them it was a full days work to feed them all, even for just one day.

Ever since they left the original landing beach, due to the extreme heat of the desert, a state of almost nudity prevailed, but any clothing that survived was put on at night to keep warm as possible. So the women decided to clothe everybody again by making garments from bits of the tarpaulins and even experimented in making their own loom and use the leaves and fibres from the palm trees and grasses to make other wearable items.

Larter and Southgate used the back of the hut as a wireless station, and with the help of John and Lee, got the vehicle's battery connected up as a power supply to run the radio.

They also rigged up a rudimentary power supply to run the meagre electricity supply for the electrician when the vehicle engines were not in use.

"Just a few paddles on a wheel that is propelled by falling water, that turns the belt that spins the dynamo, and Bruce is your uncle." John chuckled, and even the electrician marvelled at the power source.

"I'll be able to get the rest of the electrical cables and light bulbs rigged up now but I've only got four left now. So it's one for the HQ, and one for the Sickbay for now, with the others kept as spares. But we can use tallow candles and bundles to light up the huts at night." the man said.

"Maybe John and I can get that boiler going again to provide hot water and the like. We have already converted most of the drums for the chefs to use and some of the metal parts off the machine for the axes and other cutting tools etc." Lee suggested.

"Now that would be a good idea. We'll start tomorrow, Tansey." John said, nodding his approval at the suggestion.

The river was showing signs of flowing much slower, and getting much shallower over the short stretch of sand and pebbles that marked the separation between the river and the shoreline. This didn't go unnoticed by the children, who started to gather up the bigger stones and pebbles to make themselves a nice little swimming pool just up above the campsite. The water merely flowed gently over their little dam to keep an almost good level of water deep enough for them to play in.

It also turned out to be the favourite place and a focal point for the rest of the campers who found themselves lounging around under the palm trees lining the river, and taking it easy sipping coconut milk from their shells.

It was a few idyllic days whereby everything was peaceful in the camp that somehow was conducive to the well being of the two heavily pregnant women. For within that time, one produced a pair of 5lb identical twin girls, and the other a massive 12lb baby boy.

The baby girls were given the names of Chantel and Chantelle, to keep alive the memory of their little settlement where they were born. The boy was given the name of Matthew, after Matthews, being the surname of the female doctor who helped to bring him into the world.

John found time to make himself some fishing tackle and went up river to see if he can catch some of the bigger fresh water fish, and would be away for hours. One of the scientists who was curious about the geological array that mother nature had created, came along with John if only for safety reasons.

It was during one of these little walks up stream that they came to a shallow pool that looked inviting enough for them to sit down in and cool off, whilst having a short breather.

"This river may be a permanent one but will get reduced to a trickle soon, so it's just as well as the children made their little pool or we'd be without water again." the scientist opined.

"How long do you suppose it is? I mean, does it source itself from those mountains you can only see through binoculars?" John asked, as he took a handful of sand and gravel from the riverbed and looked at it pouring from his fingers back into the water.

"Yes, it probably does. It also looks as if the desert sands have come across a natural obstruction for it not to be able to cross. That's why we've got lush vegetation on our side of the river and not the poor grasses and scrubs on the other.

"If that is so, how deep must the river be to be able to do that? I mean, we're sitting in about one foot of water, yet there's pools some fathoms deep where I catch my fish."

"I've only surveyed about five miles up river from our camp, but judging by the river mouth, I should imagine a good torrent of water some twenty feet deep would flow out to sea during the wet season. You can see the water mark from the top of the embankment to show you what I mean, but for now the river has almost reached its dry season, and for me to make my earlier statement."

"Then that would account for the small lagoons of fresh water just beyond the river mouth. I should imagine that any major storm coming in from the sea would destroy those lakes and the natural habitat it's created. A sort of fluvial marriage between salt and sea water I presume" John guessed.

Their conversation went slowly and gently for a while before they rose up and went further up stream until John found his favourite deep-water pool to fish from.

He was reeling in his second large fish when he saw the scientist come running towards him and heard him shout.

"Quick, get out of the water! There's several large crocodiles basking on the riverbank some 200 yards away, and one or two of them are following me down here.

John picked up his catch, his fishing tackle and his drinks container and dashed the short distance to the riverbank and climbed up the steep incline to safety. He realised he went to the wrong side and decided it was best to cross over to the proper side before the beasts arrived rather than let them pass and for him not knowing where they might be hiding to pounce on him when he did eventually cross the river.

'A case of preferring the crocodile that you do know is there, rather than the one you don't.' he thought, and dashed over to the other side and arriving alongside the scientist who was gasping for breath.

Within seconds two very long tree-trunk proportioned crocodiles came floating past them, intent on getting a nice meal, as the two of them held their breath and crept away backwards from the river bank so they would not be seen by the beasts.

"Bloody hell! That was a close one. I think we'd better keep track of them in case they find their way down to the pool." John suggested.

"We'd better get a move on then, as they can swim faster than the both of us, and no offence intended." Came the reply.

"None taken, so let's leg it. If we can get a decent way in front of them then we can cut our time down by getting back into the river as it's the quickest way back."

They ran as fast as they could for several minutes, before they came to a bend in the river, and a perfect place to re-enter the river again.

"Quick, down here. The camp is about another half mile from here, so you get there and warn everybody. Once' I've stopped them for a moment, with these fish that I caught, I'll be right behind you. Now get going, and get the soldiers ready with their rifles." John ordered whilst gasping for breath.

"I'm on my way, but I'll send the soldiers up to rescue you." The scientist gasped back and splashed his way down the river towards the camp.

A few minutes later the first of the crocodiles came floating around the bend and for John to throw his biggest fish at it. The other one behind must have seen the fish as well, which created a wrestling match between them to see who would get that tasty meal.

John stood ankle deep in a patch of gravel on the river bank and watched them for a while until he judged it was time to throw the second one at them, which caused yet another fight, and all designed to give the scientist enough time to reach the camp.

Once the show was over, the two beasts must have seen there was nothing else to attract their attention, they turned round and floated slowly back up stream again.

John waited for several minutes before he decided it was safe to re enter the water and make his way down river as quietly as possible.

His well-worn shoes were full of gravel and sand but he didn't care as long as he got away and back into the safety of the camp.

He arrived to find that the pool area was clear of the people and that the soldier officer and two of his men were crouched down with their rifles pointed towards him. Once they were satisfied John was alone and safe, they lowered their rifles and stood up to cheer him back.

"Well done Grey! I think we'd better get a sluice gate put across the river to prevent those beasts entering our area." The officer stated as he saluted John, military style.

"Thanks! But it looks like sardines are back on the menu tonight." John quipped with the feeling of relief as the soldiers came around him, patting him on his back, and congratulating him for his effort in saving the camp from a very nasty event.

He trudged back to the HQ and threw off his pebble-laden shoes so he could dry his feet by the warmth of the sunshine.

It wasn't until a little while later for him to retrieve and don his shoes again when he discovered several coloured stones fell out of them onto his camp bed. One was the size of a conker (horse chestnut), several the size of acorns, some the size of peas and the rest that was almost a hand full, the size of a grain of rice. The different pale pinks, lemons, greens, and milky white coloured stones made a nice little kaleidoscope of colour when the rays of the sun shone onto them.

On closer inspection, he had an idea as to what they were, if given what he had learned from his new girlfriend Helena's Father in Amsterdam. So he ripped a pocket from his shorts and carefully scooped all of it into the pocket and used a piece of string to tie it all together, then stowed his findings away where nobody else would find them.

Sinclair arrived into the hut and helped himself to a drink of water, unaware of the high drama up at the pool only an hour ago

The soldier officer also arrived and told them of what had happened up at the pool and the part to which John had played to avert such a disaster. They all heard the story being related and stood amazed at what they heard then started to cheer and congratulate John.

"We always knew there was something special about you John Grey, even way back in Belfast at the time when you joined the *Brooklea*." Sinclair said quietly as he shook John's hand, closely by Larter, who echoed the sentiment, who was followed close behind in succession by the sincere congratulations from Lee and Southgate who didn't know John so well as the other two.

"Let's put it this way. I had the fish, and certainly glad nobody had their chips." John joked in his attempt to make slight of his role in the affair.

After a little while when the glow of the moment had passed,

Sinclair stood up and addressed his fellow group members.

"Now we've got a settlement, that should have been here in the first place." he said, slowly finishing off his drink.

"Settlement is too strong a word I think Andy. Maybe a holiday location would be kinder. The stokers have already named the small bay after the *Inverlaggan*, and the others are starting to call the place *The Chantrals*, to remember their ship the *Chantral* by. And why not, it sounds a very nice place to stay in." John said, looking at the sturdy and well-planned construction of the camp.

"Yes John, you're right. We'll call for a general meeting tomorrow to discuss the next step. But it's all down to Bruce and Paul now." Sinclair nodded.

"Hope springs eternal, Andy." Larter replied, as he looked up from his radio.

"Friends, this is the meeting that we've all been waiting for." Sinclair announced, when they all gathered around in the central area of the camp.

He spoke of the rapid improvement of health by everybody, and how everyone had worked very hard to provide a good and comfortable campsite to live in. He left nobody unmentioned and praised them all for their indomitable spirit and their relentless effort of trying to be rescued

But the main question was as to how they would proceed from there.

Several suggestions were thrown open to debate before a plan of action was finally thrashed out and everybody went back to their almost 'Swiss Family Robinson' way of life.

"It looks as if some of the survivors have resigned themselves to their lot and want to stay here and don't care to be rescued anymore. But when the rest of us do go, what would they do?

There would be nobody to support them nor help them in times of crises." John said quietly to his friends, as the meeting broke up and everybody got busy with what they were doing prior to it.

"The ex-prisoners and some of their *Chantral* friends are the ones that think that way. Maybe its because they've given up hope as each day passes as we've still got no radio contact." Larter suggested.

"Speaking of which, and don't get me wrong on this Bruce. Is all your gear working properly, only I can't see any results from all your magnificent efforts?" Sinclair enquired.

"I'll agree with you on that Andy. Maybe we need to see if there's some sort of weak link or dysfunctional part in our set up. But let's face it, we're using war-time equipment that has definitely seen its day, and only belongs to some museum somewhere. But never fear, we'll get on it straight away. Mean time we still need the flashing light shining skywards at night, in case there's some ship passing by. We shine it skyward so that ships just beyond the horizon could still see it, and take our bearing from it." Larter stated.

"We have the smoke signals made four times a day and we've even got the S.O.S. markings on the ridge behind us." Southgate remarked, defensively.

"Yes Paul, we appreciate that, and please don't think that we're getting on to you, as we're not. It's just that nobody in the crows nest has seen a ship nor an aircraft since we've arrived, and the only way we can get noticed is by your box of magic tricks." Lee said softly, calming Southgate down.

"Bruce, you mentioned something back at that base, about DF'ing. What is that?" John asked politely.

"Oh that! Well what Paul and I did, was to fix up a crude transmitter and have it jammed to transmit on a well-known frequency. The idea is that when the frequency cannot be used because of some idiot, somebody will be forced to investigate it and track down the culprit. The constant transmission will be tracked by direction finding to pinpoint that culprit who will get a visit by the Broadcasting authority, and certainly by the special investigators of the military. Our gamble is that they will come looking for it sooner rather than later. So when they actually knock the radio shack door down they'll find a map and details as to who it was, and why it was made. Mind you we cannot guarantee if the transmitter is still working because of battery failure, and at the same time, we cannot guarantee if our transmissions are powerful enough to be heard especially as we're some several hundreds of miles away from anybody. That does not include any shipping that passes by because they may not be on that frequency or be switched on to listen out. Besides, all they'd do is report the transmission as and when they get into the next port of call, be it Capetown, Lagos or wherever that ship was bound." Larter explained at length.

"We left there nearly three weeks now, so how long do you think the power supply lasted?" Lee asked.

"We only found a few of the several batteries that were useable and rigged up, but had it fixed so that when one battery failed, it would switch over to the next one. If they were brand new, then I'd say about three days or so on each battery. But don't forget they have been lying dormant for years and would only give about two days output, at the most." Southgate responded.

"But what about the ones you've got from the vehicle, you're using now? Maybe your receiver is faulty or something? I mean, isn't there somebody out there to hear you by asking or challenging you by now?"

"Yes John we can hear several powerful radio stations, but they're too far away for us to speak to them. And that gentlemen is the reason why we operators don't respond to an S.O.S. until we find exactly where the distressed ship is actually found and located." Larter declared.

John and Sinclair merely nodded to the obvious explanation, but Crabbe was still unconvinced.

"Why don't you tell them to come and see for themselves." he said in exasperation.

"It's not the case of just jumping onto a No 9 bus and get off at the Strand or the Piccadilly. As I've just told you, we're probably the best part of 8,000 miles away from, the loudest one at Portishead, or the other one a good thousand miles at Capetown Wireless, although depending on the atmospheric conditions. But I won't bore on that subject. Sufficient to say, we'd be lucky on a passing ship picking us up at the time. Just think of all the bus fare you'd have to fork out, let alone having to tell the missus where've you been for the past few weeks." Larter joked.

"Well in that case, lets hope they bring a decent ship with them as I don't think some of our friends are too keen on getting on another one unless it's the *Queen Mary* or whatever." Crabbe conceded, finally grasping onto what Lee had said.

"We have every faith in you two Bruce, but I feel it's the passengers that are starting to panic and need convincing, as each day passes without a sign of our would be rescuers." John said calmly and without patronising the two radio operators.

"Indeed John, that's what we're trying to circumvent." Larter concluded.

"I'm not sure what this river is called, and it looks like a permanent one as opposed to the dried up ones we came across, but we can't be too far some major settlement or town. Maybe if the army boys got together a search patrol they might come across someone that would be able to help us." Sinclair suggested.

"Crabbe, would you go and fetch the army officer for me please. We'll put together a plan for them and see what they say." he added.

Crabbe nodded and left to find the officer.

"We could always send a patrol up-river as well." John suggested.

"The only thing I've got reservations about is, if we get rescued before the army boys find anybody or they get lost or killed in the process." Lee said glumly.

The officers lapsed into their own thoughts for a moment before the soldier officer came stamping into the hut.

"Morning all! What can I do for you?" the soldier asked cheerfully.

Sinclair explained why he was required and went through other alternatives to see if he could come up with a proper military solution.

"We would attempt the patrol in an instance if we had the fuel to use for the transport. But in this case we haven't, and anyway, the distances would be too great for legging it across the open country let alone the logistical element of it. In my opinion gentlemen, we should just remain here and be rescued all together rather than in dribs and drabs."

Larter summed the conversation up by declaring.

"That is the end of the story then gentlemen. Stay put for as long as it takes." which was met with agreement from the rest of the officers.

Chapter XXXI
Rescued

"**W**e've got somebody talking to us now! It must have been the aerial after all. I've definitely got hold of someone." Southgate shouted excitedly.

"Who is it Paul? Let's listen!" Larter asked, ambling over to the table that had the radio equipment on it.

He picked up the earphones and listened for a moment then grabbed a spare chair and sat down next to Southgate.

"He's right enough." Larter said with equal excitement, seizing the morse key and replied to the incoming morse code signal that was now audible to the rest of them.

The friends gathered round and watched the two radio officers writing quickly onto a small scrap of paper.

"He's one of your lot Tansey. He's a Royal South African Navy Telegraphist at that, and he sounds close too." Larter announced.

There was a murmur of excitement from the officers as they realised that the efforts of their two friends were finally bearing fruit.

Larter and Southgate listened and reacted to the morse signals for a little while before they read out what had been said.

"'We stated that, yes it was us transmitting and that we were the survivors of two ships, the *Inverlaggan* and *Chantral*, now numbering only 48 of us.

They said that a special rescue team is on their way to us by sea and will arrive tomorrow morning.

But in the mean time a special helicopter will fly over us and confirm our exact location for the landing. Says to be ready for embarking by 0800 hours.' Larter said calmly but with a tinge of excitement in his voice.

The officers embraced each other and cheered loud enough for some of the others to come over and ask what the commotion was.

Sinclair announced the good news in a calm and collected manner, which was met with instant euphoria from everybody.

"We have all evening to prepare ourselves and to decamp. In the meantime, we shall have one final beach party to celebrate." Sinclair shouted over the laughing and singing people.

A small group of people, with the ex prisoners in the lead, came up to Sinclair and his friends, explaining that they wished to stay on, in case some other people got stranded just like they did.

"We cannot allow that. It is our duty to have absolutely everybody off the camp. Besides what are you going to do in a crisis, such as a flood, or marauding Arabs or even wild beasts attacking you. What about if somebody is ill and the doctor is no longer around. How are you going to eat when you cannot get or harvest your own?" Sinclair asked trying to point out the practicality to them.

"We survived the Nazi concentration camp and two sinkings. Don't you think that if our maker wanted us to perish we would have done long before now?" asked one ex-prisoner.

"I'm a doctor and a good crackshot with a rifle. All you've got to do is leave us with medicine and enough ammo and supplies for us to get on with. The navy or the army come to that, could always visit us very so often, and perhaps use the camp as a base of some sort." Another person said.

"I'm an ornithologist and would take great delight in recording the wild bird life here. Maybe a few scientists could come and visit us and use the place as a living laboratory." Another said.

Sinclair and his friends listened to their reasons for staying and whilst he agreed with the logic of what they were saying, he still stood by his decision by stating that everybody had to leave the camp with the rescuers.

"If you won't listen, then we'll ask the navy when they arrive." one of the ex-prisoners said as they walked away from Sinclair and his friends.

"It appears that some people doesn't want to be helped no matter what." Sinclair sighed, shaking his head slowly.

"Never mind Andy, the final decision will be made by the navy when they arrive." John said sympathetically, patting Sinclair's large shoulder.

Some 45 days after the sinking of the *Inverlaggan*, the survivors were happy that in a few short hours they would be on their way back to civilisation. But the happiness was tinged with regret that some of them were determined to stay behind no matter what may lie ahead of them.

This issue was discussed and even got quite quarrelsome at times as the patience of those who were leaving was lost on the ten who wanted to stay.

It was one of the scientists that had the final word to conclude the bitter debate.

"My fellow colleagues and I have discovered why there is the ridge of vegetation that we came over and through to arrive at this camp. It represents the true coastline or at least an ancient one, which can only mean one thing.

This area is subjected to tidal wave activity caused by the Mid Atlantic rift, and the occasional eruptions of volcanoes such as the one on Trisdan da Cunha.

This is the El Nino year and the season for it to start, which means that this stretch of coastline and especially this river mouth will be subjected to fierce storms from the sea that will most definitely happen, at the same time massive fluvial flooding will occur.

In other-words, this entire area around us that we're camped on, most of the valley to our right, and the entire bay will be destroyed from any one of the three we've mentioned. We can only imagine what would happen if they all occurred at once. But if it did, then the best place is at least 200 feet up a mountain and several miles away from the river because the river would suffer a tidal bore measuring at least 30 feet high. It would travel right up to and probably reach its source some distance away, unless there was some even higher cataract in its way to stop it.

The rock and shingle beach on the other side of the river mouth was caused more than likely, by the last El Nino, as was the shingle and gravel that can still be.seen just under the shallow water along this stretch of it. Therefore, to remain here in this exact location is dangerous and suicidal, and that is putting it mildly, to say the least."

From the looks on the faces of the group that wanted to stay, it was clear to everybody else, the scientist was wasting his breath, and said so, which echoed all the others sentiments.

The meeting finally broke up, as people were now preparing to get their last evening meal before getting some sleep.

"I think we'd better advise and show these idiots what is what, for when they take over the camp, Andy." John suggested.

"They don't deserve it, but I suppose you're right." Sinclair sighed.

Sinclair advised the remaining group that apart from the breakfast in the morning, they could take over the stores and cook house and how to keep the food fresh.

Larter showed two of them how to operate the radio and explained what they needed to do to keep the power on it.

John and Lee showed them how to run the engine and the small generator, but advised them that there was only enough fuel for about another week or so. They were shown how to operate the water system and other technical things.

Crabbe advised them on the best areas for them to catch their food and which nets they would use on different prey or for fishing.

The soldier officer advised them on the camp security system and how best to use the rifles they were going to need, even though there were only a handful of bullets left.

The officers knew it was a waste of time by the lack of interest that was shown during each instruction. But they made sure that when they left, these people would have some sort of rudimentary knowledge to help them survive.

It was an overcast morning that greeted the increasingly excited survivors, but for them it was the sunniest day of the year.

The breakfast was eaten with much cheer and happiness and afterwards everybody washed their plates up and left them in a neat pile. The chefs even washed every pot and pan clean and left them ready for the next meal.

The camp was cleaned up, and the huts that were going to be left empty had their windows and doors shut to the outside elements. All the dry laundry was taken off the lines and left in a neat pile, and any spare footwear was dumped next to it.

John and Lee took one last look at the vehicle's engine and the other mechanical contraptions they had invented to use for the benefit of the camp.

Larter and Southgate were doing their job of communicating with the rapidly approaching rescuers, when two large helicopters came over the ridge and hovered over the camp, shattering the peace and tranquillity of the morning.

Southgate grabbed his torch and went out onto the veranda to speak to them by flashing light, whilst Larter spoke to the other contact with his morse key.

An object was thrown from one of the helicopters and landed at Sinclair's feet as he waved to them along with all the survivors who were craning their necks skyward.

Some of the children were cowering by their mothers, as they were frightened by the strange things above them that blew sand all over the place, the others were dancing and waving just as hard as the rest.

Crabbe picked the object up and unravelled a sack that contained a letter, which he read then gave to Sinclair.

'*There will be a warship and a troopship arriving. The warship will be sending two landing craft to take you off. But an officer will come to your camp and meet you first. You will then be taken to the troopship where you will be transported to its next port of call for your onward journey to your original destination. As this is a danger area, nobody is to be left behind. Please ensure all people are assembled and ready to move off. Good luck! Signed, Wing Commander O'Brien RSAF '*

Sinclair waved the paper at the helicopters and told Southgate to let them know the instructions would be carried out.

The helicopter pilot waved before he spun his aircraft around and the two left in a cloud of swirling sand.

The silence of the morning was restored in the camp again as Crabbe got everyone together and explained what was about to happen, holding out the message for anybody else to read.

Sinclair asked everybody to sit down and wait for the officer, and went back into the hut to get his packed briefcase and all the other bundles that he made up.

"C'mon Paul we've got visitors coming, so let's go. Bruce, as soon as you've finished join us." Sinclair said happily, carrying his baggage away.

"Paul, take our log books and stuff. I'll be right behind you once I've completed this transmission." Larter prompted, which made Southgate grab another parcel to take with him.

The officers were standing in a semicircle in front of the rest of the survivors who were all sitting quietly with baited breath when they heard some voices come from the beach.

A smartly dressed naval officer with neatly trimmed ginger beard that was enhanced by the crisp white uniform that he wore came into the camp compound.

Everybody stood up, cheered and clapped as the officer arrived and flanked by two others.

"My name is Lt De Bloetze, who is in charge here?" the officer asked in an Afrikaan accent.

Crabbe looked at Sinclair as did the other officers, and nodded to him to step forward.

Sinclair looked at each of his friends' faces, and felt humbled by the fact that these officers were giving him his moment of glory.

"I am. Chief Bosun Sinclair off the *Inverlaggan*. Pleased to see you Lt." Sinclair said proudly.

De Bloetze shook hands with Sinclair and introduced the other two that were with him, Dr Pauls, and a person from the press who had his usual array of cameras.

The pressman filmed and noted each name as Sinclair introduced the other officers, then the rest of the survivors.

Pauls smiled at each person as he gave them a cursory inspection, before declaring that everybody was healthy enough to travel again.

Whilst Pauls was examining the babies, Sinclair called his friends over to have a word with the Lt.

Sinclair told De Bloetze about the ten who wanted to remain and offered most of the explanation as to why they wanted to do so.

De Bloetze listened intently and shook his head.

"All people will be taken off this rescue site. If those ten wish to come back at a later date then they are free to do so. But I am under strict instructions to clear this area as I have been doing for these past six months or so. This is the top end of my operational area, which is some 500miles long and 50 miles deep.

You will be happy to know that over the past year or so, we've managed to rescue those stranded people who managed to reach this place. The rest are but piles of bones scattered along some 1000 miles of this particular coastline. As survivors, you will be treated just the same as they were, in that you will be taken from here to a place of safety and for you to continue your journey. All of which will be paid for by the taxpayers of South Africa and the Commonwealth". He announced sternly.

Some of the ten dissenters heard what De Bloetze said, and started to run away or tried to hide, but De Bloetze took a small radio out of his top pocket and spoke into it.

Within minutes, a platoon of marines came running into the camp and started to drag these protesting ten survivors away to the beach.

"You see gentlemen, we mean business. When I say all, I meant all." De Bloetze stated as the rest of the survivors started to get uneasy and unsettled.

"Mind you, it's the best run survivors camp I will ever come across. Pity about that as I'm instructed to have it destroyed by demolition. The reason is because we can't have the recent wave of insurgents and troublemakers making a hideout here, can we." he added looking around the huts and the organised way that the survivors had lived.

"So we've been camped in a disputed area and you've put a danger zone around the place so that no ships would come near enough to see or hear or distress signals?" Larter asked

"Yes, we placed a 50mile exclusion zone along this part of the coast and normally anybody found within it would have been arrested let alone blown to bits by naval bombardment. "

"In that case, can we have a little time to get a few souvenirs to take back with us, before it is destroyed?" Lee asked

"Okay, I'll give you five minutes, but that's all."

Sinclair told De Bloetze of the records that they had been keeping and briefly what happened for them all to get this far.

De Bloetze listened with awe, and stated that they were lucky to survive that wartime base camp.

"It's thanks to your radio officers pulling that stunt of theirs, that we finally found out where the outbreak of sea mines were coming from. When we arrived and found evidence of recent occupation in one of the buildings, and the fresh graves, we searched everywhere for you. There must have been a recent sandstorm that blew away enough sand to reveal a couple of old ships that seemed to form part of a harbour. In one of these ships we found a large hole in its hold probably from sheer rusting away. Every time a high tide occurred and got into the ship, it washed another load of mines from it and out to sca. These mines were not of a regular design but they have been very effective non-the-less. Some were found to be magnetic, some were acoustic, and the others were just plain contact ones.

We've had a squadron of minesweepers patrolling this coast for months now without much success. Your ship was one of five that got blown up, but not many survived even if they did get ashore. You lot are the exception and a very lucky lot to have done so." he stated.

"I bloody well had that suspicion all along. Despite him being long since dead, that bloody man Meir sunk us with his bloody mines. Let's hope you find the remainder of them, as that man was reported to be directly responsible for the sinking of many a good ship and slaughtering everybody on board." John swore vehemently, enough for De Bloetze to step back and reach for his side arms.

De Bloetze must have realised that John's sudden outburst was not directed at him, so relaxed and changed the subject.

"As I've said, you lot must have been lucky to reach here. But having seen your camp it doesn't take a genius to recognise the different skills that were used in making it work." he explained, looking intently around at the camp.

"Yes, we all had a hand in making something, even the children had their own little ventures and chores to do." Southgate said quietly, as Larter returned carrying a bulky item wrapped up in some discarded clothing.

Lee arrived behind Larter and told John that he had made a technical drawing of the vehicle, especially the engine and its details.

John had nothing except the coloured rock he was given by Lee, and suddenly remembered that he had left it and his little bag of stones behind. So he ran over to the hut, and with two leaps he was inside it, to return shortly carrying it in his hand.

De Bloetze looked at the pink rock and asked John where he got it, which John ignored.

"You do realise that you are not allowed to take that with you. In fact I shall take it from you if you please." De Bloetze stated.

"Why should I give it to you. It's mine by right." John said defiantly.

"Let's put it this way, you are in possession of a large lump of uranium. If processed, it could make several bombs of the type dropped on Nagasaki and Hiroshima. It therefore must be handed over, and taken to the HQ of the security services. I'm only a naval officer, and even I must obey these people." De Bloetze explained, holding his hand out, fully expecting John to comply with his demand.

One of the scientists saw the rock and asked to see it more closely.

John handed it to the man as requested.

"I am a Vulcanologist and Geology is obviously part of my profession. This is a pink diamond of a good 100 carets. This area is full of diamonds that you can just pick up off the beach, but this one has come, and I can guess fairly accurately, from the Mid Atlantic Ridge. It is flawed and could shatter easily, so instead of one very large and priceless pink diamond, it could end up as many little ones no bigger than a grain of sand, and therefore totally worthless.

Maybe our Lieutenant knew exactly what it was so told you about the uranium, which does tend to colour rocks pink or red, but then that's for him to decide which is which. If I were you Grey, I'd throw it back into the deepest part of the sea you can find. That way if it was uranium nobody can get to it; or as it is just a large diamond ready shatter at any time, and to keep unscrupulous and greedy people from having it. Now that's for you to decide." the scientist revealed, handing the orange sized diamond back to John.

"Thank you for your advice, I'll do just that." John said, pocketing the rock and out of sight.

De Bloetze's face went beetroot coloured at the fact that he had been found out, but managed to bluff his way out of the situation by telling everybody to clear the camp and get onto the landing craft.

Chapter XXXII
Parting Company

The landing craft was mid-point between the beach and the troopship when explosions were heard from their former camp.

John and Sinclair looked through their binoculars to witness the event, then handed them to the others to have a look too.

"Oh well, there goes another holiday camp down the pan, as their demolition charges have blown everything up sky high." Crabbe said, taking his turn with the binoculars.

"Speaking of which, here goes another one, Lieutenant." John said aloud, taking out the large diamond, and by using the weight of the binoculars he hit it. It immediately shattered almost to dust just as the scientist had predicted, and threw the lot overboard and as far as he could away from him, and saw the total shock and dismay on the face of the Lieutenant.

"If you can remember the spot where that lot landed, then you have my permission to go get it. Finders keepers and all that. Call it payment for blowing up our little holiday home." John said calmly, as his friends patted him on the back in congratulating him on his courageous deed.

De Bloetze shook his head and told John he was an out and out idiot, as that would have kept them all in luxury for the rest of their lives.

John wasn't particularly bothered about the destruction of that ball, because he still had his secret little bag of pebbles that would probably be worth a lot more than a hand full of diamond dust.

"We will be parting company when we reach the troopship, as will several others before you reach the UK." Lee said softly, looking into the faces of his fellow officers.

"Oh, where are you going this time Tansey?" Sinclair asked with concern.

"I've had enough of this navy lark and have decided that I shall return to Capetown with the warship, and go back home."

"But what would you do without ships engines and the likes of 'Spanners' to keep his beady eye on you?" John asked with dismay.

"The drawing I made of that vehicle and its sleighs have given me an idea that will keep me on land for the rest of my natural, John. For I intend to build the same type of transport and call it something like 'The Desert Road Train'. I intend for it to ply between places like Capetown to Windhoek to Grootfontain and Gaborone where no proper road exists just like the one we took to get to the river. But to understand what I mean, I'm having to cross the Namib, the Kalahari and other deserts, all of which are frequented by the big Copper, Iron, Gold and Diamond prospectors."

"But what about your contract and back pay from Belverley and Company?" Crabbe asked.

"No such thing, as we're now classed as DBS (Distressed British Sailors), they can always send it on to me, but I really don't hold my breath for when they do. No, I've decided that now is the time to go home when the going is good. Besides, I'm almost in my own backyard now and for the first time in several years."

"He's right John. Being classed as a DBS means that as the ship has been lost/destroyed, we've got no ship to sail on. No ship to sail with means no contract, so no contract means no pay from the owners. Tansey has already made his mind up no matter what we say or do to change it for him." Larter stated.

"In that case, let me be the first one to shake your hand and wish you the best of luck Tansey. You have taught me a few things on the way, and with luck, I shall relay them onto those coming up behind us." John said sadly, shaking Lee's hand firmly but gently and hugged him warmly.

The others stated similar sentiments then shook Lee's hand in the same manner.

"We have several things in common but the biggest is that we've survived and lived to tell the tale. Any of you that wishes to talk about it, don't forget, if you mention one you must mention us all." Lee said with difficulty, brushing away the tears that were streaming down his face.

"We share your feelings Tansey, and will always remember you. This is where we bid you farewell, so live well and keep an eye out for us when we call back into your neck of the woods again." Sinclair said with sadness.

"Anytime you're in Durban, just call into any hotel and book it under Lee's Desert Road Trains. In the meantime have a good voyage home!" Lee replied manfully, as the landing craft neared the large white painted troopship.

The other survivors of the landing craft scrambled up the steep wooden ladders and whooped with joy when they arrived onto their rescue craft and salvation from their previous nightmarish existence.

Sinclair led the way up the ladder but stopped to wave to Lee as the landing craft drew away from the troopship and made its way over to the sleek warship only a few cables away from them.

"Lets see him board before we do Andy." John requested, which was unanimously accepted by the others.

They saw Lee arrive on board, and heard the whooping noise of the warship's siren before it turned and sped away.

John felt empty within himself like as if something was missing, which needed an explanation. But seeing the expression on his face Sinclair and Larter explained to him, Southgate and Crabbe, that Tansey was better off ashore but would be remembered as an absent friend and shipmate.

When they finally arrived on the main deck, the ship's captain and several of the officers were present to greet them on board.

"This time we are the passengers, gentlemen." Larter said, as a series of flickering lights greeted them, due to a whole gaggle of photographers and newspaper reporters who literally pounced on the officers when they arrived.

"Tell us your story. Who was in charge? Got any diamonds to sell? What were the Arab women like? How did you survive the infamous Skeleton coast? Why did the navy blow up your camp, was it because of the terrorists you were harbouring?

How did only 60 out of 700 survive, was it cannibalism? Did the men take turns with the little boys and girls? How did the women survive without water, man juice?" were the type of outrageous questions posed in rapid-fire order from such a belligerent, uncouth and debased bunch of men that always seem to be found in such circumstances.

The friends said nothing only to state their name, rank, and what ship they were off, before they pushed their way through the scrum to the sanctuary of the captain's day cabin.

"I offer my apologies for such an outrage gentlemen, but what can one do about the actions and downright disgusting behaviour of the press. They seem to think that they have the god given right to invade the decency and privacy of individuals, just to serve their own warped self-satisfaction and depravity." the captain said glumly, offering each officer a glass of lemonade and had a box of cigars offered around.

"I give you this for now to help you re-educate your taste-buds, but we shall have a champagne supper laid on for you all." he added.

John and his friends drank the lemonade down almost in one go then asked for a refill, which was immediately forthcoming, before they all sat down and enjoyed their cigars.

"From the answers given by all the other survivors that came on board before you, I am to believe that Bosun Sinclair was your leader. How is that when there are ships officers in your group to do so instead?" the captain asked gently but with raised eyebrows. Crabbe looked at the deadpan faces of the others before he spoke.

"I am 5th mate Crabbe off the *Inverlaggan*, and the only surviving deck officer. As such I have only dealt with passenger requirements and have had no experience with all that we went through. As Bosun Sinclair has had several years of experience at sea including the Royal Navy, in my own opinion it was only right that he took charge. Mind you, and for the record, I've managed to keep a log of each day's activity, just in case of any dispute of some sort or other." Crabbe stated, nodding to Sinclair.

This left a silence in the captain's cabin, and John felt that he had to leap to Crabbe's defence.

"I'm 3rd engineer Grey, and had a surviving superior engineer, 2nd engineer Lee who has just gone back on the destroyer. As such, our knowledge was purely engineering and we are not qualified to question the judgement of deck officers and senior ratings such as the bosun. However, as bosun Sinclair was the only non-officer amongst us, I felt it right that he would take charge, thus saving any embarrassment between executive and engineering officers."

"I am radio officer Larter and this is my 2nd officer Southgate. We felt the same as Grey. No doubt if you ask the army officer, he will lend his own voice to the same agreement as what we did. Southgate not only has our radio log book updated but just like Crabbe, an account of daily matters within the camp." Larter also stated with a nod.

The captain listened quietly, writing down the answers to his questions before he responded.

"Then it appears that bosun Sinclair has the dubious honour of making out a full but separate report that will contain all his decisions, the ensuing actions, and measures taken to ensure a group survival such as has taken place. That, plus a declaration from all the other survivors to verify his statements. That way, there will be at least three drawn up accounts to take into consideration when the loss adjusters come into the equation."
John looked at the captain and declared that what he asked for was unjust and unwarranted.

"I did not know of these separate logs and diaries that were kept, but suggest that you get a written deposition from the other survivors, as I think you will find that some of them are eminent scientists and others apparently well known in other circles. But sufficient to say, that we did things in a very democratic way and with full support from the rest of them. Without the full co-operation and support from all of the people, none of us would ever have survived, I can assure you of that."

The captain looked at John then at the rest of the officers.

"For you to say that, it must be true, as the people you spoke of said exactly the same. I am satisfied that everything that could have been done, was done, to save as many souls as you did, and now no reason to keep you from any further unpleasantness." he said civilly.

"At least we know where we stand on that score captain, because I for one am inclined to sue each scumbag and deviant newspaper man for all the money they haven't got. And before you say anything else, you can take it as read that it goes for the rest of my friends here." Larter said vehemently, as each of his friends shook their heads in agreement

"I agree with you entirely. But on a much lighter note I must advise you all on the immediate state of play, so to speak. I am on my way back to the U.K. from the Orient with a shipload of wounded troops and the families of others still out there. Each one of you survivors will be accommodated in the first class area, which on this type of ship means for officers only. I have been given special instructions that passengers will be landed at my next port of call for onward shipping to where they were supposed to be going to in the first place. That is to say, the passengers and crew off the *Inverlaggan* will be landing back at St Helena's or back to the U.K it's their choice. The *Chantral* passengers will be landed either at Lagos or the Canary Islands for onward shipping to America.

From the briefcases and other parcels that you are holding, I can safely deduce that they are documents relating to the *Inverlaggan*. I am not at liberty to inspect them, as they will be required at a later date to be examined by both your shipping line and the Ministry of shipping, let alone the Lloyds Insurance Company. As for you gentlemen, you will be glad to know, I shall be giving you special passes and suitable attire to enable you to make your special flight from St Helena's back to the U.K instead of another four weeks at sea. We are but a full days steaming from St Helena with just enough time to say your goodbyes before the parting of the ways, so to speak.

My ship's M.O. has advised that each one of you must observe a strict diet to combat your lack of the one whilst ashore. However, if I know you officers, a few bottles of brandy or rum and a large box of smokes available in each of your cabins, as a special welcome aboard to you on behalf of myself and my crew, won't go amiss. Should you have any problems or difficulty, then please address them to any of my able officers." the captain said pleasantly and without patronising the group of weary survivors.

"Your kindness and generosity will be much appreciated by each of my friends, but I do hope that as we have been offered such hospitality, you will extend it to the rest of the people. Those people are, and don't forget it captain, survivors just as we are, even more so the ex prisoners and the rest of them off the *Chantral.* They should be your first concern before us, given the fact that we were their trustees despite being DBS's, but self employed to get them safely to their chosen destination." John stated, for his friends to stand up from their seats and express their vociferous backing to what John had said.

The captain raised his eyebrows then frowned before he summoned his steward.

"Steward, you heard the challenge from these officers, please make it so." he said civilly, as the steward nodded obediently.

"Okay then gentlemen, I shall see to it that you and your fellow survivors enjoy the best that the ship can offer. But then consider this, I have a ship full of survivors rescued from a vicious war. There are some hundreds of men, women and children already on this ship, each with wounds of some kind or other, and each with a tale to tell. We have been sent home the long way round, via Singapore, Ceylon and the Cape just so that when they arrive, everybody can be fit enough for the great British public to see that their citizens are arriving back wholesome." the captain said with a sigh.

Sinclair and Larter noticed the captain's weary acceptance of what was asked of him, and asked what the problem was in accommodating their joint request.

"The thing is gentlemen, I am undermanned and my officers and crew cannot cope with the demands required from our passengers, let alone the difficulties the authorities have placed us in by coming to your rescue as well. For you to realise the magnitude of what's going on, there's a war correspondent who has been given carte blanche to interview each and everyone of us on board.

Not only has this person got the permission but he also invited several of his colleagues from other newspapers and television companies to remain on board just to and I quote ' capture the essence of human suffering and survival'.

The questions you suffered were mere 'bagatelle' compared with the out and out disgusting and outrageous questions and invasion of privacy they have conducted on the rest of the passengers.

Nobody can rest or have privacy as they insist on demanding to know about absolutely anything that would be considered a story worth recording. If you don't believe me, then just wait until you step outside my cabin doorway." the captain said apologetically.

"It appears that this ship may be infested with cockroaches. The only way to deal with it is to stamp on them, or turn the steam hoses onto them and flush them out of their hiding places and off the ship. I've had experiences of this kind before captain, so if I have your permission then it will be dealt with by the time we arrive at St Helena's." Larter said ominously.

"Do what you will, I don't want to know, but be prepared to suffer any consequences." the captain shouted back, as they left his cabin.

The friends walked along the narrow service corridor between the captain's day cabin and the passengers' accommodation and arrived at the first class saloon where the ever-invasive pressmen were waiting for them.

"Here they come!" a voice urged as the pack of reporters formed their usual scrum around the men as they went over to the bar.

Each one of them saw the distraught faces of the other survivors and the apparently resigned and pained look from the other passengers who sat around the saloon.

"Which one of you blew the bosun's whistle for him?" came one lewd question.

"Looks like we've got a daisy chain of shirt lifters." remarked another, as yet another flash of a camera flickered around the saloon.

The pressmen were getting too close for the friends to even move, provoking a spontaneous action by them all. By kicking, punching, and even pushing some of the pressmen so hard that they were bowled right over several empty tables and chairs.

One pressman who got punched in the face stated that he was an ex-boxer and would exact his revenge on the person who hit him, and proceeded to attack Sinclair.

Sinclair simply sidestepped the swinging punch, and thumped the man so hard that he dropped like a stone onto the deck, out for the count.

This should have been the end of it, but the rest of them, thinking that as they out numbered the friends, they started to swarm over them. Within three minutes, each pressman was lying on the deck, either out cold or moaning with the remains of chairs that were smashed over their heads.

The other passengers never interfered, merely cheered and clapped as each pig-ignorant pressman was put down. Every bone crunching punch or chair shattering noise was laughed at gleefully, until the captain and some of his officers arrived to see what the disturbance was.

All the friends still stood in a circle, back-to-back, and gasping for breath due to their exertions, found themselves in the middle of a sprawling mass of men and broken furniture.

"What is the meaning of all this? What are all these men sprawling across my deck? You Grey, Larter, explain yourself?" the captain asked crossly, as the cheering and jubilance of the rest of the passengers died away quickly.

"What me captain? Nothing to do with me. I'm only here for the beer." John said innocently, putting the remains of a chair onto the saloon bar.

"It appears that we have some people who can't take their drink. Your steward must have served them with 'let's all fall down' beer or the purser had issued them with rubber legs, captain." Larter said with a smile.

"Yes, funny about that. One of these pressmen walked right into my fist, and decided that he wanted a chair to wear as well." Crabbe said, rubbing a bruised fist over his cut lip.

"I've never seen such an ugly lot of men before, and I'm very choosy to who I drink with." Southgate replied, finally letting go the lapels of a pressman, who flopped down onto the deck moaning and groaning.

The captain took another look around the scene of carnage, to see a pressman who almost raised himself up off the deck when a passenger sitting nearby him knocked him out again with the leg of broken chair.

"Oops, my hand slipped. Sorry about that." he said softly to the unconscious man.

"We are the local cockroach exterminator team specially hired by your shipping company to get rid of your unwanted pests. If any passenger has any further problems with these vermin then please give us a call." Sinclair announced, smiling to the rest of the grateful passengers.

"Clap them in irons. Throw the filthy lying pigs overboard. Arrest them and make them walk the plank. Bloody well keel-haul them, the filthy ignorant pigs." were the vociferous opinions voiced by some of the angry and totally fed up passengers.

The captain held his hand up and asked for quiet before he made his observations.

"It appears that several days on a deserted beach has taken its toll on these officers. They shall be confined to their cabins for the duration of this voyage and hopefully by then, they will have recovered their senses. Anybody else who wishes to make riots on board my ship will be severely dealt with. Get these men out of here and into the sickbay." he said sternly, which was met with howls of derision and catcalls.

"You are the captain, if you can't conduct your ship properly we'll see that you won't get another rowing boat let alone a troopship, like as not." a passenger vowed, making way for some stewards to clear away the damage and render first aid to the injured pressmen.

"C'mon Andy, Bruce, lets get out of here. We're docking some time tomorrow, so lets not get too embroiled with all this." John whispered to his friends.

"Yes, let's get into our cabins and take it from there. Steward, we require five suppers, some decent fags, a couple crates of beer and the odd bottle of whiskey or brandy if you please." Sinclair ordered, as the group slowly walked through and even over some of the prostrate pressmen that were in their way.

They arrived at their allocated cabins, which were large ones to accommodate four people.

"Here we are friends. A good wash down, some nosh and a belly full of beer just to make us sociable. Crabbe as you're the 5th mate shortly to become a 4th and as befitting your rank, you will have one all to yourself. But you come and join us when you're ready." Sinclair declared, when the friends piled into their temporary sleeping quarters.

During the short voyage from where the rescue took place to St Helena, all the *Chantral* survivors wore their lifejackets at all times and never dared to take them off.

They sat sitting huddled on the boat deck with a vacant stare in their eyes during the time the ship sailed through some areas of choppy sea conditions, and were drenched from the heavy downpours of fresh water. Nobody could convince these people that they were now safe and for them to come into the saloon, at least to shelter from the rain. They even demanded that their food be brought up to them, and a special latrine provided for them, for fear that the ship would sink under them just like the other two so called safe ships.

The captain had no choice but to give in to their demands, and made certain that each one of them was treated gently and differently to all the others on board, even though the ship was specially prepared for such poor unfortunate souls as those it carried. His fly in the ointment was the so-called 'the freedom of the press is paramount' brigade that hounded everybody no matter what ailed them. At least, until John and his friends arrived on board to put them in their rightful place, at the bottom of a cesspit, as any lavatory pan would have been too good for them.

The troopship arrived at St Helena and docked in a heavy and dismal mood as sad-faced people waited to greet the erstwhile passengers, clambered off the ship.

The occasion had a mixed feeling of happiness for those relatives and friends who met those survivors, but also the sadness of others who waited in vain for those who never showed up.

The Pathe news and other TV film crews were busy at their work, with a casual and professional attitude, but at least and unlike the pressmen, they never intruded nor bothered anybody save to ask who they were.

The entire group of survivors of the two sunken ships were disembarked and taken to the local hotels or to the hospital for treatment, whilst the remainder of the passengers, those from the cruel war zone of the Orient, were kept separate and on board. Although they were mentioned so that their relatives in the U K would be prepared to meet them, as they were ear-marked and to be given their own moment of glory at a later date when the troopship finally arrived back in the U.K, especially as it was the remnants of a famous regiment that was being brought back from the war.

John and his friends were kept in the local hotel with some of the more able survivors, and had a small party to celebrate their return.

The party went well, as each survivor told their individual experiences, but everyone pointed towards John and his friends, stating that if wasn't for them nobody would have survived all they went through.

These revelations made it more difficult for John and his friends to stay out of the limelight and behind the scenes, no matter how hard they tried.

Sinclair looked at John and Larter and whispered.

"Now I know what John went through. Still, better show just how well us deck hands can speak."

"Sock it to them Andy!" John replied with a grin.

Sinclair stood up and gave a short speech on behalf of them all, and ended by stating that everybody, including the children, had played a major part in their combined effort to come through their terrible ordeal. All he and his friends did was to apply their individual skills in making sure that the shipping company honoured its commitment in getting as many people back alive as possible. He also remarked on the sad plight that befell the *Chantral* group, but hoped that one day they would realise that their life jackets must eventually be discarded if they were to forget their plight and just enjoy the rest of their lives.

This was met with rapturous applause, with the film crews recording each syllable and the facial expressions of each person gathered there.

After the last speech was given, and the party had started to wane, there was a feeling of sadness all around, as each person knew that this was the parting of the ways for them all.

This was the moment when everybody was told of their new travel arrangements, which meant that each survivor group was split up as their arrangements were finalised.

Some would continue back to the UK on the troopship, some would take another ship to Lagos for onward shipping to the U.S. some would remain on the island and the rest would be shipped back to the Ascensions.

John and his friends would be flying home by the BOAC Strato-cruiser Clipper service, except for Crabbe and Southgate who opted to remain on board the troopship as they didn't like flying.

All of which prompted a sad and tearful ceremony of bidding farewell to each and everybody whose common bond was as a survivor of the famous Skeleton Coast. The group hugged each other one more time and vowed that should anybody talk about it, everybody was to be mentioned, just as Lee had said only the day before. For they were a special group of people joining the very elite few of fellow survivors that lived to tell the tale.

"See you in Belfast Paul, and you Crabbe, mind how you go." Larter said with a little smile.

"Mind you don't swap your standard issue of Mae West for harps. As you're flying, there's no excuse for being adrift." Crabbe said cheekily, but shook hands all round.

"We're flying back, so you'd better behave yourselves on the troopship, as I'll be keeping my beady eye on you." John said softly, remembering with sadness his dead adversary Jones's favourite saying.

Chapter XXXIII
All Or None

The friends were shown their allotted seats on board the massive double-decked plane, which was revving its four equally massive propeller engines up ready for take off.

"Take off in 15 minutes, please fasten your seatbelts, and extinguish all cigarettes, cigars or pipes. Refreshments will be served as soon as we're airborne." the pretty air stewardess said pleasantly.

Soon the big lumbering plane sped across the runway and sailed majestically into the air as the forces of aerodynamics took over.

As the plane banked to one side those passengers lucky enough to look out of the tiny porthole type window, saw the last of the island disappear from view below them.

"Good afternoon ladies and gentlemen! This is your captain speaking. Welcome to BOAC flight bound for Madrid and London. We shall be cruising at a height of 15,000 feet, at a pleasant 350knots. You may unfasten your safety belts and for those of you wish to smoke please do so but only on the lower deck.

Our chief stewardess will shortly be demonstrating our in-flight safety procedures, and then will serve refreshments in the lower deck immediately afterwards. We hope you have a pleasant flight." the well educated but pleasant voice stated over the internal speaker system.

"Sound pretty good to me, but who's got the smokes?" Sinclair asked, shrugging his big shoulders.

"Never mind the smokes for now Andy, who's getting the wets?" Larter asked, just as a stewardess passed them.

"Excuse me miss! We've got no means of purchasing drinks or smokes, let alone anything else. Any chance of putting it onto some sort of tally?" John asked politely.

"If you wish to relax and enjoy a meal, a drink or a smoke, then just go down those few steps into the lower deck. I'm sure you'll find that all has been arranged for you." she replied with a slight accent that John knew was from his own part of the world.

"Fancy this airship going almost as far in one hour as it takes us to go in 24. So how long is our flight stewardess?" Sinclair asked.

"If all goes well and providing our relief crew in Madrid is on the ball, the flight time is around eight hours with two fuel stops. So you'll be arriving in Belfast in about 10 hours time." she replied and escorted them down into the lower deck.

"These gentlemen are the special guests. See that they enjoy our first class service, would you Tristram?" she asked primly, retracting her steps. The friends looked and admired her female form as she disappeared up the winding steps.

The aircraft made its scheduled landings to change the flight crew and refuelling along with a reshuffle with the change of some of the passengers. But the friends didn't care because they were just as high as the plane flew, before sheer exhaustion finally took over and they fell asleep where they sat.

"Half hour to your destination, gentlemen. If you wish to wash and brush up and have a refreshment before then, now is the time to do so." A stewardess said softly, waking them up from their slumber.

John looked out of the porthole to see the coastline of Ulster and the unmistakable outline of Belfast Lough, then pointed it out to the other two.

"Now if that was the bonnie Clyde." Sinclair said with a smile.

"Or even Liverpool Bay where we first started this bloody trip." Larter quipped.

"But at least one of us has arrived home okay." he added.

"Just as well we were given a decent suit to wear, as I don't think our tropical shorts and vest would stand up to the weather. It's pouring down out there with 'fresh water', which I suppose is an appropriate welcome home." John responded.

"We've got all that gear to hand over when we arrive, which means that we'll probably get a reception committee if I know the ship owners." Larter observed.

"Yeah! Maybe some back pay to get us home too Bruce." Sinclair said, rubbing his hands at the thought of a handsome pay packet coming his way.

"Apart from that trunk of stuff, at least we're travelling light." John stated, holding up his battered holdall

"Just as well we got organised back on the ship, or we wouldn't have that. Even the passengers didn't have much with them, some with only just the clothes they stood up in. Poor sods." Larter said grimly, for each of them remembering their last moment on board.

The conversation ebbed and flowed as they drank a cup of tea served by the stewardess.

"Fasten your seat belts. No smoking." came the polite warning over the tannoy system.

"Usual routine gentlemen, only this time one out all out. Time to stretch our legs now." John said, when the aircraft landed and finally stopped.

Before they could disembark, the pilot came into the cabin and told them that a special reception awaited them. He expressed his good wishes and hoped that they would recover from their ordeal and enjoy a nice long holiday, before the aircrew bade them farewell as they stepped off the plane.

There were a gaggle of TV and journalists waiting for them as they walked the short distance from the plane into the arrival lounge of the air terminal.

"Here we bloody well go again. Stand by to repel boarders gentlemen." Sinclair said gruffly, pushing and shoving several photographers away from them, telling them to go home and read it in the papers like everybody else.

A prissy woman came up to them and stuck a microphone right into Larter's face, which he tried to grab off her before telling her that he had just survived months on the Namib coast, and just wanted to go home. So unless she took the mike from his face it would be shoved up her where not even the desert sun shone.

"Here comes the brass hat brigade." Sinclair shouted above the noise of the press, and pointed to Belverley, Invergarron, Brooks and Lowther waiting for them at the other side of the Customs barrier.

"Anything to declare?" one customs official asked snootily, and held his hands out expecting to be given their luggage to be searched.

"Yes pal! One ton of cigarettes, several gallons of wine and spirits all in this little briefcase." Larter growled, holding his small case up for the official to see.

"In that case, you had better come in for a search to see if you've got anything else." the official replied loftily.

"Look here you stupid ass! We three are survivors of a ship that sank in the Atlantic off the African coast. We've traipsed along the Namib Desert for weeks. Where do you suppose we went, or even what shops we visited in the desert, 'Ali Babas'? What do you suppose we used for money, camel dung?" John asked vehemently, taking exception to the 'jobs worth' attitude of the man.

"Where did you get those clothes then?" the official responded, undaunted.

Sinclair was just about to grab hold of the official when somebody obviously senior to him arrived and took him away.

"My apologies gentlemen. He's new on the job and just wants to make a good impression." He stated.

"Just as well you showed up as I'll 'good impression' his face onto my knuckles if he's not careful." Sinclair said menacingly, then turned to join Larter and John.

Belverley and his entourage greeted them warmly before they were whisked away in an awaiting car to take them to the shipping line's H.Q.

"We have brought you here to debrief you and find out what really happened. We shall take note of all you tell us, as your debriefing will be used in a Ministry of Shipping board of enquiry.

When we're satisfied, we shall be recompensing you before you go on your survivors leave." Belverley announced, when the friends were served with refreshments and offered a smoke.

"We have some very valuable items that we managed to save from the *Inverlaggan*, and even some of the details of the *Chantral*. To start with, here is a briefcase that 3rd mate Gibson had kept, but was rescued by 2nd engineer Lee. Plus this very heavy logbook from some earlier disaster. But before we do so, if we tell about one person then we will mention all. It's all of us or none." Larter said calmly and started to unpack the belongings.

"Then so be it!" Invergarron said quietly, nodding to the others.

As each item was revealed an explanation was offered, with a brief outline as to how it survived.

They went through the maps, charts, and even looked at the hand-written letters of the doomed lifeboat occupants who drowned along with Gibson.

They briefly explained what had happened to the *Chantral,* and their own ship and how only 48 finally survived the infamous Skeleton coast and the Namib Desert.

John told about his side of things, as did Larter, and how Sinclair became their leader.

Larter told them that radio officer Southgate and 4th mate Crabbe kept a diary each that would pinpoint various events and details.

It took the friends a couple of hours to explain things as Belverley and his team listened or questioned certain aspects of what was narrated to them.

"It appears that each of our officers have acquitted themselves well. No doubt we'll have a good report and a handsome payment off the insurance company as a sweetener too." Invergarron stated, then wrote down some figures onto a piece of paper.

"Yes, we can be a little more generous this time in view of their ordeals. I think we've got enough evidence for the moment to make our decision." Belverley replied.

"Mr Brooks, do the honours if you would." he added, as Brooks walked towards the friends.

"We have decided that each of you will receive a special compensation that will be on top of any pay or dues owed to you since leaving St Helena and prior to the ships' sinking. You will also be sent on special leave for three weeks, but will be required to attend the Ministry for Shipping board when it takes place. That will probably be when Crabbe and Southgate finally get back to get their debriefing and compensatory package like you. You will be paid exactly the same amount despite different wage structures, contracts and the like. You will be given a small amount of cash for immediate use, but the rest will be in the form of a cheque.

Unless you have any objections, then kindly sign for your pay, leave pass and travel warrants." Brooks said pleasantly, handing out three neat envelopes to them.

As Sinclair was the junior rank out of the three, he whistled and kissed his cheque when he saw the amount stated on it.

"That will do very nicely thank you very much. Pity it wasn't a regular one as I could just about get used to earning officers pay." He said, but Larter and John just pocketed theirs.

"You will be given a special box on your way out of the building, make sure you take it with you." Lowther said with a grin, drawing on his large cigar.

"On top of that, when you come back off leave, you will be kitted out with a new uniform that is in keeping with our new shipping line. Wear it with pride when you get them." He added magnanimously.

"You may leave now, and don't forget to attend the board meeting. Thank you Grey, Larter, Sinclair." Belverley said smoothly, shaking hands with each of the friends, before leaving the room.

"I wonder what's in the box waiting for us. More to the point, why are they being so nice to us?" John whispered as they left the room and went down the stairs to the foyer.

"Maybe it's because of what that navy wallah said about us finding the source of those wartime mines. Maybe because they've lost a few officers too many." Larter suggested, for them to open the surprise box.

"They must have read our minds, how thoughtful of them. All these smokes and not a light between us, not even the famous BL lighter is working at the moment." Sinclair said, looking at their hoard of cigarettes, cigars and a magnum of champagne.

"I'm going to keep mine for when we meet up again, Bruce. What do you say Andy?"

"I'll keep the fags, if you keep the cigars Bruce." Sinclair replied.

John suddenly remembered the bag of pebbles that he secreted on himself and brought it out to show them.

"Remember our last little trip into the desert and I found a nice bar of gold stuffed with precious stones? Well just hold out a hand and I'll fill it with these." He said quietly as he placed an equal amount of different coloured stones and some of the 'sand' into them.

"What's all this John?" Sinclair asked, when John had finished sharing the stones around.

"If what I can remember what my girlfriend Helena's father told me, they look like raw diamonds. The coloured ones have the most value, but the grains are perhaps only industrial type of diamonds. Sufficient to say, what I've given you should be put into some sort of a bank vault until you're ready to retire from the sea." John smiled, as he kept onto the conker sized stone for himself.

"Bloody hell John! If that customs man had've searched you, we'd all be in the nick." Larter opined as he carefully dropped his stones into his brown envelope and stowed it away.

"No wonder you weren't upset about that big ball of diamonds being crushed to dust and thrown overboard. You crafty little devil!" Sinclair chuckled, as they stowed their booty away.

"If we keep on finding ourselves in the ruddy deserts of the world , we could end up being ruddy millionaires." Larter added with a big grin.

"Anyway its time to leave and for you both to catch your ferry. My last bus is due out shortly, so I'll see you both at the hearing. Take care both of you, and have a good leave." John said softly, shaking their hands in farewell.

"It's a deal John." The other two said, as they left the building and headed for home.

The No 23 Lisburn bus sped through the now quiet and deserted streets of Belfast, as John settled down in his seat and offered his bus fare to the conductor.

"I don't know where you've been lately but that'll be an extra 2d please." the conductor said, holding his hand out for the extra money.

John sighed and felt for some more loose change but couldn't find any, so gave the man a 10/- note. (ten shillings)

The conductor muttered that he was fed up with smart arsed travellers, looking at the red note in disgust.

"Sorry, it's all I've got, but at least its money." John replied calmly.

"I'll let you off at the bus stop before yours, that's all I can do." the conductor said nastily, handing back the note, before sauntering off to the rear of the very smoky bus.

John finally stepped off the bus with a smile and thanked the conductor as he told him that the Blacks Road stop was really his proper one after all.

The curses and blasphemous ranting and ravings from the conductor drowned the noise of the bus moving off again, and disappeared in a cloud of dust.

His faithful dog came running full pelt down the cinder path and jumped up for John to catch her, when he opened the garden gate.

He put his luggage and box down, picked her up and stroked her muzzle

"Hello Bridget, been a good girl have you? You've put on a bit of weight too." he said softly as the dog licked his face and nuzzled in his arms.

"Here, off you go now." he said, putting the dog gently back down, and picked up his belongings.

His footsteps scrunched along the cinder path once more before he walked through the open door of Rathmore Cottage.

"Ma! I'm home!"

Beach Party, the fifth book in the series,
will be published in August 2009.